Robert McCracken grew up in Belfast and Australia.

He is the author of *An Early Grave* and *The Lethal Trilogy*.

RUN

Kai
Roisin
with Thanks
and best wishes

Robert McCracken

Robert McCracken

CRUX PUBLISHING

First published in the United Kingdom in 2019
by Crux Publishing Ltd.

ISBN: 978-1-909979-86-4
Copyright @ Robert McCracken, 2019

ACKNOWLEDGEMENTS

I would like to express my sincere thanks to Christopher Lascelles at Crux Publishing for giving me the opportunity to have my novels published. Thank you also to Eden Glasman for her diligent editing of this book and to David Laird who kindly read and cast a critical eye over this story. All I did was supply the coffee.

A special thank you to Roisin McAuley for her encouragement, advice and friendship. Finally, I would have achieved nothing without the love and support of my family, my wife Suzie, daughter Sarah and son David. Proud of you all.

CONTENTS

CHAPTER 1

The taxi pulled onto the sloping drive, pressing tracks into the fresh snow. It came to a halt on a flat piece of ground in front of the stone cottage. The driver left the engine running and, gazing at the front door, sounded the horn once. It was a solid wooden door, painted dark brown but weathered, faded and peeling. The brass knocker was badly tarnished and had probably never been cleaned. He knew that nowadays the place was merely a holiday home—no one had farmed the surrounding land for years. It was only good for grazing sheep. The true Cumbrian family, who had once lived here for generations, had long since departed. Someone with a sharp eye on the property market had bought it, modernised it and made money from renting or selling to city-folk who thought it twee to have a holiday home in the Lakes.

The driver noticed a twitch of the lace curtain at the quarter-paned window to the right of the door. At least someone knew he was here. If his fare didn't get a move on they would struggle on the roads. After days of heavy rain the land was sodden and, in some areas, under water. Streams and rivers had burst their banks, and today the temperature had plummeted. Why the hell someone would care to spend time here in late November, he had no idea. He could think of better places to be for a holiday and could certainly think of better places for him to be right now than sitting at the dead end of a mountain lane waiting to pick up a fare.

The sky was a heavy grey, growing darker by the minute and bulging with the threat of snow. Great for a tourist to gaze at with a sense of wonder, but more than a hassle for him as he struggled to make a living in a land that God forgot. The slopes surrounding the cottage were already veiled in white, the dark lines of dry-stone walls and barbed wire fences resembling a charcoal sketch on virgin paper. He rubbed his hands together in front of the air vent.

'Get a bloody move on,' he mumbled, 'or we'll be stuck here all night.' He glanced again at the front door. Why did he always volunteer for the awkward runs? Right now, he could be home watching TV before dinner, snug and secure as the weather did its worst. But no, he had taken the last fare of the day, and now there was a chance he might not make it home at all.

Suddenly, his horizon disappeared. He could no longer see the line of hills, nor the bottom of the valley, and his wipers were already battling the white flakes landing on his windscreen. His taxi was an ordinary car, nothing fancy, a Ford Mondeo, not a four-wheel-drive, no winter tyres. Just a car.

He watched the front door of the cottage open with a stutter as its bottom edge rubbed on the step. Swollen in its frame from the damp, it needed rehanging. A woman in a black coat with a fur collar and black suede boots emerged, battling with a suitcase and a smaller overnight bag. She struggled to pull the door closed but, finally, it slammed into place. He jumped out of the car and opened the boot. She persisted in trailing the case, its wheels redundant, over snow and gravel until she reached the car. He took the case from her.

'Good afternoon,' he said. 'Not the kind of weather for being out. Essential journeys only, they're saying on the news.' He lifted the suitcase into the boot, then reached for the smaller bag.

'I'll keep that,' she said, her eyes locked on the black leather case.

She had a tanned face, or was perhaps wearing a bronze-coloured makeup. Her eyes were dark brown; she had a small mouth, but her full lips were coated in a purple lipstick. Her nose was cute and her hair was a deep colour of rust, curled into her face. A bob, he believed it was called. He should know this, he thought to himself; his girlfriend was a hairdresser in Penrith.

The woman climbed into the back of the car, and he closed the door behind her. He jumped into the driver's seat, clapped his hands and rubbed them together.

'Where to?'

'Penrith Station, please.'

All the while, he peered at her in his mirror. She returned his gaze only once as she answered his question, then turned her head and looked out of the window. He had to reverse out of the drive the way he'd come in, and the car slid the last foot in the snow and onto the lane. Before driving off, he couldn't help another glance at his passenger. She was about his age, he decided. Thirty-four, or perhaps forty and looking great. He was useless at guessing a woman's age. She was hot, though—of that he was a good judge. He adjusted his mirror so that it was filled by her stunning face. As the car moved slowly down the lane, he continued to steal frequent glances at her. She ignored him.

CHAPTER 2

'A weekend break, was it?' he asked.

She made no reply. Her attention was focussed upon her phone and its lack of signal. He was neither a careful driver, nor a reckless one. He believed that he drove to suit the conditions, to suit the location. He knew most of the roads in this area well. He knew the Lakes; he knew Cumbria. And he knew many of the people. But he was less familiar with the lanes that wound to a dead-end halfway up one of the fells, or stopped at the entrance to the yard of a hill farm.

'The weather is really closing in,' he said, trying again to engage the woman. She did not reply.

A voice sounded from his phone system as Jan, the taxi firm's call operator, cut in.

'Did you pick up from Dowthwaitehead?' she asked.

'Yes, I'm on my way to the station, but it's slow going.'

'The bridge is out at Dockray, so don't go that road.'

He noticed his passenger looking at him in his mirror when the bridge was mentioned. He thought he would wait for her to speak, to ask the question. When she didn't, he plugged the gap.

'Don't worry,' he said, 'we can take another road.'

'I need to make the train for London.' Her voice was soft, but her tone was blunt.

'What time?'

'Three minutes past five.'

He checked the clock on the dashboard.

'Will we make it all right?' she asked.

He sucked air through his lips.

'Hope so.' He peered at the lane ahead, which was rapidly filling with snow. His wipers were only just coping with clearing the windscreen. The tyres struggled for grip. If she wanted to make the London train, he thought, she should have left much earlier.

CHAPTER 3

She felt the back end swing out as the car slithered towards an earthen bank at the side of the lane. Then it righted itself and motored onwards but, within seconds, it was back into a slide. She kept an eye on the driver by looking in his mirror. He was watching her, his eyes switching frequently from her to the road. She didn't need his attention. She just wanted him to get her to the station on time to meet her train.

The road was treacherous. She could never have driven it in her tiny Fiat that she'd left in London, nor even in a Land Rover if she had owned one. Why had she not realised that the snow was getting so bad? This was not London. Heavy traffic was not going to sweep the snow to the side of the road. Even from her brief stay here, she knew that cars did not come along such lanes very often. But she had no desire to spend another night in this place. She wanted—she needed—to get back to London.

The engine whined, and she felt the wheels spinning as the car struggled to climb a slope in the lane. There was nothing to see ahead, nor to either side, but a blank white sheet. Surely they would not be stranded. Someone would come along to pull them out, and rush her to the station in time for her train. The driver wasn't so chatty now—not since she'd told him of her schedule. But still he watched her in the mirror.

It seemed as though they were cutting a channel through the untravelled Arctic rather than driving on an English country road. The snow swept into the windscreen in a gale of white powder that was quickly dispensed by the wipers but less efficiently by the tyres. There was a jolt as the car crabbed to the side, then a feeling of acceleration as it slid down a steep slope. She had to steady herself with her gloved hand on the door, the other gripping her seat. And the driver still had time to look at her in the mirror. She tried to appear unperturbed, but inside her heart thumped and her stomach lurched with every rise and fall and with each sideways skid as the wheels fought for grip. She prayed they would reach a proper road soon. And as her mind raced to desperate thoughts, and her fears rose, the front of the car dipped. A steep hill seemed to lie before them, although she could see nothing. How had the taxi driver ever managed to reach the cottage in the first place? There were moments when he was in control of his car, but suddenly everything ran free. The wheels had no purchase. A car, a heavy metal box, became a bobsleigh sliding down an icy track. His braking only added to her fear, as the car skidded wildly from side to side and continued to gather speed.

'Slow down, please!'

'Sorry, love, not much I can do on these hills.'

She had no memory of such a sharp turn in the lane but, with gathering speed and less control of steering, the car ploughed straight on. A violent thud tossed her from her seat as the car came to a halt in deep snow. The back end of the car now sat higher than the front. Still, he was gazing at her in his mirror.

CHAPTER 4

She released her seatbelt and fumbled for the door handle.

'No, love. Stay there.'

Ignoring his plea, she pushed at the door. It opened, and she was struck by a rush of freezing air. She stepped from the car, and immediately fell three feet before sinking into the snow. She fell backwards onto what an hour earlier had been a grass bank. The driver, in his haste to reach her, jumped from the car and stomped his way around to where the woman was trying to clamber up the slippery bank while clutching her overnight bag.

'Wait!' he shouted, but her panic fuelled her determination. By the time he reached her, she had twice attempted to climb up the earthen bank without success. She lay on the snow, copious flakes already landing on her dark clothing. He stood over her, reaching out his hand to help her get to her feet. She ignored the offer, pushing herself up to a seated position.

'We need to stay in the car, love,' he said. 'It's not a good idea to start walking in this weather. We wouldn't get far.'

'But I have a train to catch.'

'I doubt if the trains are even running in this snow. We need to stay in the car until help arrives.'

The driver examined his vehicle. He saw no easy way to get it back on the lane. It was well and truly stranded. He reached down once again to help her to her feet, but she ignored his offer for a second time and instead raised herself upwards with one hand, using her bag to keep her steady. For a moment they stood face to face. He was tall and fit-looking, she thought. His shoulders were broad. His fair hair was short, and he was clean shaven. He wore a navy blue fleece jacket with the logo of the taxi company on the left breast: *Valley Cabs* was embroidered in yellow beneath an image of a car on a mountain peak. His dark blue jeans were a slim fit, and the hems were pulled down over the top of a pair of sturdy walking boots.

She took her time deciding whether or not to heed his advice. She really needed to make that train. Surely she still had time. If she could make it to the end of the lane then maybe a passing car or a lorry would stop. She looked into the driver's eyes—they were a strong blue and deep-set. In the short time they had been together in the cab, she had seen those eyes staring at her in the mirror. Would she be safe remaining here, with him? The wind blew more snow into her face and the faux fur of her collar had turned white as if dusted with icing sugar.

'Let's get back inside,' he said, 'and I'll call for help on the mobile. Maybe they can get a farmer to come and pull us out of here.'

'I can't wait that long. I've told you I have a train to catch. If you can't drive me there then I'll walk down to the main road.'

'It's nearly two miles to the main road. You won't make it in this weather. I'm sorry about the train, but you'd be safer staying here until we get rescued. Come on, I'll call for help. Get back in the car, at least until I've done that.'

He gestured to the open door from which she'd jumped a minute earlier. Before taking a step, she studied his face. He sounded genuine—helpful—concerned even. But she couldn't help feeling unnerved by the way he'd been staring at her in his mirror. Now he had a thin smile on his face. A smile, perhaps of genuine patience, or maybe a smile of a struggle for tolerance. She glanced around her. The trail they had driven had almost disappeared into a murky whiteness. The car had breached the verge at the side of the lane and now rested with its front end in a field and its rear end grounded on the hump of earth that only a few moments ago, she had tried to conquer. Frightened of what may happen if they were stranded and terrified that the driver might turn out to be some pervert who thought he had a good opportunity to do something to her, she felt there was little choice but to climb back into the car. He closed the door behind her.

CHAPTER 5

'Hey, Jan, are you there?' said the driver into his hands-free phone.

She heard nothing and wondered how he had any signal on his mobile when she had none.

'C'mon, Jan love?' Nothing. 'I'll bet she's on another fag break.'

She watched him fiddle with the mobile, held in a cradle attached to the dashboard.

'Are you getting a signal?' she asked.

'Yeah, but it's never great in this area. We're in the shadow of two mountains, one either side of this lane. The nearest mast is closer to Penrith.'

Nevertheless, he lifted his phone from its holder on the dash and called a number. To her surprise, in a few seconds he was speaking cheerfully.

'Hi, darling. I'm stuck on the moor up beyond Dowthwaitehead... yeah. Snow's really deep and drifting. The car went over a verge... yeah, halfway into a field. Any chance of getting someone out here to pull us out? Hello? Hello? Shoot.' He turned to face her. 'I'll try again in a few minutes. Don't worry, we'll not be here all night.'

She attempted a weak smile to show a little appreciation for his efforts, but all she could think about was what would happen if she missed her train. The idea of being stranded all night sent shivers coursing through her body.

He saw her checking her watch—her Cartier La Dona watch. It read four thirty-five.

'I'm sorry, but I don't think we'll make your train,' he said. He turned around and pressed a button on the console. Radio 2 came on. *Steve Wright in the Afternoon*. She fumed and tried to look out the window, but it was beginning to mist over—besides, the light was fading fast. The sound of an old song played. It was familiar to her, although she could not recall the name of the artist. She sat with her arms folded, uncomfortable on the seat because the car sat at an awkward angle. She had to rest her feet against the front seat to prevent herself from sliding forwards.

'And that was an oldie, "Meet me on the Corner", from Lindisfarne,' said Steve Wright. 'Now let's hear some traffic news. Not a night to venture out, Bobbi?'

> 'Most people have to get home first, Steve. I've had a call from Munching Mike, he's stuck in a queue at the moment on the M56 approaching junction 9 with the M6. Heavy snow causing tailbacks there. Jimmy on the A1, close to Scotch Corner, says traffic at a complete standstill. I'm hearing reports that there are queues in both directions up there caused by heavy snow and also an accident involving a lorry that has overturned on the south-bound carriageway…'

The driver pressed another button. A male voice was reading a traffic report.

'Local radio,' said the driver. 'Should tell us what it's like around Penrith.'

> '…Drivers are advised not to make journeys this evening and tomorrow morning unless absolutely necessary. Roads should be kept clear of traffic to allow ploughs and snow-blowers to clear away snow and to treat surfaces with grit. Rail services from Scotland to the south have been severely disrupted. All local services have been suspended. The A591 is closed between Ambleside and Wythburn. The A6 is closed between Garnett Bridge and Shap. The A5091 is closed at Dockray due to a collapsed bridge, and we've just heard that the A66 between Keswick and Penrith has now been closed. Snowploughs are already in operation in that area.'

'Shit.'

'What's the matter?' she asked, her fear rising once again.

'Looks like we'll be here for a while. They've closed all roads from the west leading to Penrith.'

'We'll have to walk, at least to the nearest village. I need to catch my train.'

'Listen, love. There are no bloody trains. Didn't you hear? You're going have to content yourself until someone comes along to dig us out.'

'And when is that likely to be?'

'It won't happen tonight, that's for sure. We're too far off the main roads.'

CHAPTER 6

She was certainly a strange beast, but very appealing. Worth a few quid, he reckoned, judging by her clothes and that watch on her wrist. He didn't know squat about jewellery, but he'd certainly heard of Cartier before. And she had a shiny stone on the third finger of her right hand. That had definitely cost; no way was it a piece of glass. Beneath her heavy coat, he imagined, was a shapely figure. He had caught a glimpse of her thighs when she was fumbling about in the snow. Her suede boots reached her knees, and then there were black lace tights. Above those she wore either a black skirt or a dress, he wasn't sure which. Very fetching. There were worse passengers to be stranded with on a night like this. The only downside was that so far her good looks were not matched by a friendly disposition. Maybe it was just her concern over the weather and her eagerness to catch her train. To London, she had said, or at least it was the London-bound train. She was certainly not a northerner—not with the way she spoke. Nor was she a cockney. She was well-educated, he guessed. She was classy. Wouldn't think twice about the likes of him.

He rubbed two fingers over his rear-view mirror to clear the condensation, but the darkness did not allow him a good view of her. She hadn't said a word for over half an hour. She'd browsed on her phone for a while, but it was clear that she was getting no signal. Besides, it was hardly likely that any of her mates would come to her rescue all the way from London. In fact, he didn't believe that anyone, even from Penrith, was going to rescue them tonight. He turned around in his seat to face her. She didn't immediately look up at him which gave him time to gaze over her body, hidden beneath her heavy coat.

'Are you warm enough, love? I can run the engine for a while to get the heater going.'

She made no reply.

'No point in sitting there freezing?'

'Whatever,' she replied, grudgingly.

He turned away, switched on the ignition, and started the engine. 'It'll take a few minutes to warm up,' he said.

The blizzard intensified periodically, and after each surge another inch had settled on the car. He could no longer see anything through the windscreen. If the storm continued through the night, he thought, they would soon be buried completely. He tried to visualise exactly where he had crashed. Was there anyone nearby who could help them? Take them in for the night? It was at least two miles further along this lane before the junction with the road to Dockray. He hadn't noticed any farms or inhabited cottages on his way up to collect the woman, nor did he recall seeing any other buildings since leaving the cottage. Two miles was too far to venture out to get help—it was too far to expect his passenger to accompany him, and he did not want to leave her alone. Maybe they could walk back to her cottage? At least they would know where they were going, even in deep snow and darkness. But how far had he driven before coming to an abrupt halt in this damn field? It may have been three miles. He checked his meter. Sometimes he was remiss in setting the trip to zero when he picked up a fare. Out here, it didn't seem to matter. It was different from a city, where you might only travel a couple of miles in half an hour because of heavy traffic. None of his local passengers ever seemed to pay it much heed. Most of his customers were housewives travelling home from ASDA with their shopping. Those journeys were standard rate fares. Then there were his school runs for special needs kids. On Friday and Saturday nights he ferried people to and from the pubs. He didn't often have special fares. And the woman sitting on his back seat was definitely a special fare. He had to get her chatting—get her spirits up. If he played his cards right the two of them could spend a cosy night together. It was a long time to be stuck here, two people with nothing to say to each other. Who knows, if his luck was in, he might even get his leg over.

CHAPTER 7

'Aren't you going to try your phone again?' she asked him.

He looked at his watch, a Seiko not a Cartier.

'Everyone has probably gone home by now. Jan wasn't going to have many calls to handle on a night like this.'

She gave a loud sigh.

'I'm sorry, love. I think we're stuck for tonight.'

There was a pause between them for what seemed to her like an age.

'If you want to, we could try and make it back to your cottage?' he suggested.

She glanced at him, trying to fathom his motive. Was he simply concerned, hoping to make the best of things for her sake? Or had he something else more sinister in mind? After all, she knew nothing about him, nor he about her. He may not be trying at all to figure out how to get them out of this situation. He may be more than content to spend the night here with her. Should she be frightened? Hell, yes. Surely not every taxi driver would examine her the way he had done?

'That won't achieve much,' she replied sourly to his suggestion. 'Apart from us both getting cold and wet. And in the morning we would still need to be rescued.'

'Best make yourself comfortable then.'

She felt warm for now, but how could she ever feel comfortable when she didn't feel safe? Pulling the edge of her coat down over her knees, she sat back in a position where she hoped he couldn't see all of her. One thing to be stuck for the night with a stranger, another for him to have his eyes clapped on her the whole time. She clutched her overnight case across her stomach; it provided a peculiar degree of comfort.

'May as well introduce ourselves,' he said. 'My name's Joe.'

She didn't reply. Didn't want to engage him. The silence was awkward. She heard him fumbling about, but couldn't see what he was doing. Then he turned to her, holding aloft a small thermos flask.

'Cup of tea? Should still be hot.'

'No thanks.'

'Come on. Where's the harm? It'll warm you up for a while at least.' He turned away and, reaching upwards, flicked on the interior light. She watched him pour the tea into a plastic cup, the steam rising. He reached out and handed it to her. 'There you go. No sugar, but I'm sure you're sweet enough.' She looked deprecatingly at the man offering his tea, and for a second was touched by his gesture. Maybe she was too much on edge, too much on her guard. The guy was only trying to be friendly. She took the cup from him.

'Have a biscuit.' He grabbed an open pack of chocolate digestives and offered her one.

'Thank you,' she said, removing one of the biscuits from the pack. Sipping from the cup, she was certain that tea had never tasted so good. The warmth of the liquid coursed through her, and a shiver ran from her lower back down her legs.

'Aren't you having some?'

'Only one cup. I'll have some when you've finished.' She watched him remove two biscuits from the pack and proceed to eat them both at the same time. The radio fizzed with white noise.

He reached again for his mobile.

'Hey, Jan are you there? C'mon, anybody there?' There was no answer. 'Cleared off home, like I thought. Who wouldn't want to be home in front of the telly and a warm fire on a night like this? And you're having to slum it with me.'

He turned to watch for her reaction.

She forced a thin smile. Again, she thought, his eyes lingered for longer than was necessary. It set her on edge. She rubbed at the window with her hand, still in its leather glove. She saw little but the settled darkness and the flakes of snow swirling in the wind. Another shiver passed through her. She sipped at the tea until the cup was empty. Feeling guilty that she'd taken so long, she handed it back to the driver.

'Thank you. That was very nice.'

'No problem, love.' It didn't take him long to refresh the cup, but instead of drinking it himself he again offered it to her.

'No, it's your turn. I've had enough, thank you.'

'Another biscuit?'

'I'm fine, thank you.' For the want of some activity, something to keep her mind off her current predicament, she removed her phone from her coat pocket and began an aimless browse through old emails. Frequently, as he munched his biscuits and slurped his tea, she felt his eyes upon her.

'Any signal?' he asked.

'None at all.'

She read through an email from a long-standing client. He had put in a request for 15 December. His office Christmas party, she surmised. As was usual with him he had attached a list of finer details that he required, but she was unable to open the attachment. It would have to wait until she got back to London. Another email, three days old, had come from her accountant. A query over some recent out-goings. She had no idea what they had been. She would have to sort it out when she got home. The next email was a booking confirmation for a flight to Malaga. She had missed her train and, consequently, she would also miss the flight.

'So, what was your hurry in getting to London?' he asked.

CHAPTER 8

He dozed off. He had finished his tea and biscuits, reclined his seat, lain back and gone to sleep. Obviously, she realised, he was peeved at her refusal to answer his questions. They were such clumsy attempts to hold a conversation. But she had no interest in talking. No interest in talking with him, no matter how friendly he appeared. He meant nothing to her, and would continue to mean nothing to her. Why should she lay her life before him for the sake of chatting? She could have plenty to say. Plenty that would interest him, make his ears twitch, but she very much doubted that he could tell her anything worth hearing. He was a taxi driver, for goodness sake.

She had also tried to sleep. She had managed to rest her back in the corner between the rear seat and the door, allowing her to lay her legs across the remainder of the seat. But now, with him sleeping, the engine switched off and the tea no longer warming her, she was growing cold. Despite the long boots, her toes were nipping. Her expensive lined overcoat kept her warm except for her knees, which seemed to react to every tiny exposure to the night air.

Her thoughts drifted. A blurred vision of happy times past swirled with darker moments, with pain, sorrow and frustration. In recent years she had been happy: she had a lover to greet her each evening when she got home, someone to cook her fabulous meals, to chill the wine and to warm her bed. Her lover had satisfied her like no other had done, leaving her wanting more every time. They strolled through the park on a Sunday, drank coffee in Covent Garden, got drunk on a Friday night and held hands in the theatre on a Saturday. She had someone to love and someone to trust. The positives in her mind fought to warm her against the bitter cold of the negatives.

She heard him stir. With his seat reclined, he could see her directly. He rubbed vigorously at his face to rouse himself.

'Hi there,' he said, 'I must have nodded off.'

She didn't respond, and tried not to look at him.

'Are you all right? Get any sleep?'

'Not really,' she replied curtly. 'It's very cold. Can you put the heater on again?'

He sat up, bringing his seat up with him. He turned the key in the ignition, and the engine burst into life as lights on the dashboard flickered.

'Ten-to-eight,' he said. 'Shit, I thought it would be later.' He rubbed at his arms and blew out a long breath. He was fidgety, she reckoned. Feeling awkward, perhaps, but not as awkward as she.

'What's happening outside?'

'It's still snowing, and the wind seems to be getting stronger,' she said. Foolishly, she thought, he lowered his window, and a pile of snow toppled onto his lap.

'Bugger. That was stupid.' He quickly raised the window again. Then he switched on the radio, still tuned to a local station. 'We may as well listen to the news.'

The bulletin came on at eight o'clock, dominated by road and weather updates. It was obvious that no one in their right mind would be out on a night like this. But she had at least hoped to hear that major roads were being cleared and attempts made to reach motorists in distress. The newsreader said that the clearing of arterial routes was in progress. The minor roads in the Lake District, however, were cut off. What worried her most was that no one knew she was here. To her dismay, the driver again attempted to strike up a conversation.

'Is there anyone still at the cottage?

CHAPTER 9

The heat from the engine was coming through, but he couldn't run it all night. He didn't know, and had not checked, what damage he'd done when he crashed through the earthen bank into the field. If the snow was piling up around the car he worried that exhaust fumes might get trapped inside. He had heard stories of people suffocating in their vehicles after being stranded in a snow storm. When cars got trapped in long queues, bumper to bumper, engine fumes could pass from one vehicle to the next. Then there was the horrific incident years ago when Russian troops suffocated after their convoy was halted by an accident in the Salang Tunnel in Afghanistan. The drivers of vehicles kept their engines running to keep warm, and there was a build-up of carbon monoxide fumes in the tunnel. Hundreds of soldiers had died.

He suddenly remembered about the blanket he kept on the parcel shelf at the back of the car. He should have offered it to her much earlier.

'There's a blanket on the shelf behind you. Sorry, I forgot it was there.' He watched as she pulled it from the shelf and quickly draped it over her legs.

'Thank you,' she said with a shiver.

'You know,' he began, 'you can tell me to go to hell if you want, but when I was a kid I heard this story about a lorry driver in Canada.' He turned to see if he had her attention. So far she hadn't been interested in talking. Maybe she was simply not a friendly person. Hell's bells, she hadn't even told him her name. When she didn't protest or cut him off, he proceeded with his story. 'I think it was Alberta, or maybe that place... Saskatchewan. Anyway, this lorry driver had just passed through a town when he came across two hitch-hikers. Both were girls—late teens, he guessed. They were hardly dressed for bad weather: jeans, T-shirts and anoraks. So, he gave them a lift, and off they drove into the middle of nowhere. Then the weather closed in and the driver had to stop because of the snow and ice. Worse still, the engine failed so they didn't have any heater to keep them warm through the night. And in Canada the temperature goes a lot lower than it ever does here. The three of them grew colder and colder. The driver told the girls that he had only one sleeping bag. He explained that the best way to keep warm was for the three of them to huddle together in the sleeping bag and, better still, to do so naked. Both girls thought that the guy was a perv, and that he just wanted to have his way with them. So they both laughed it off and turned down his suggestion. But as the night went on and they grew colder, one of the girls finally agreed to get into the sleeping bag naked with the lorry driver. Her friend refused to have anything to do with the idea. When they were rescued thirty-six hours later, the pair in the sleeping bag were alive and reasonably well. The girl who refused to get naked had frozen to death.'

He smiled at her, but she blanked him. She pulled the tartan blanket up to her chin.

'If we're to survive through the night,' he said, 'we need to huddle together under the blanket.'

CHAPTER 10

They both were cold and getting colder. In truth, he couldn't even make an attempt to go for help until daylight, or at least until the snow abated. Besides, it wasn't as if he was intending to get his leg over. If she had been more forthcoming, by now they would have known each other a little better. Was she stuck up, or what? And what was it with her bloody case? She had not let go of it for a second. Even now she had it concealed under the blanket. They were both in a desperate situation. It was not his fault. She was the one who'd decided to travel on a God-awful day. Holidaying halfway up a mountain and winter setting in. Who the hell does that? He'd had plans for this evening, too. It was supposed to be his night off. Even with the bad weather he could at least be home in front of the telly. He'd only volunteered for the fare because his previous drop-off was just down the road in Troutbeck. Now look where he was. She should have called for a taxi earlier in the day and caught an earlier train. Then she would not be in such a strop for missing the damn thing. And what was so important to her that it could not wait for another day? That's what he would like to know. Now he was getting himself in a tizz. He was not going to sit here all bloody night freezing his balls off when he could at least share a blanket with the woman. Without a word, he climbed onto his knees in the driver's seat, then manoeuvred his wide frame between the front seats and ungracefully plonked himself beside her in the back. Immediately, she moved as far to the left side of the car as possible without her pushing open the door and scurrying into the storm.

'We both need to keep warm, love,' he said. 'Needs must.' He took hold of the blanket and moved closer. Without a word she relinquished her grip. Soon they were both covered by the thin blanket.

'Now, since we're all wrapped up nice and cosy we should maybe try again,' he said.

'What do you mean?'

'Well, my name's Joe, and you are?'

She hesitated, and he thought that was an end to it. They would spend the night huddled together in silence.

'Alex,' she replied at last.

'Good to meet you, Alex. I'm sorry for any inconvenience.'

She sneered in response. It was enough to stifle his latest attempt at conversation.

CHAPTER 11

She felt warmer, but she did not feel comfortable. Not with a man, a perfect stranger, sitting next to her, his body thrust against hers and the two of them sharing a flimsy piece of blanket. Her toes felt detached from her feet, and at times the cold seemed to travel up her legs, beyond her boots and up to her knees and thighs, protected only by a pair of lace tights. They were expensive, but that didn't mean they were warm. At first, when he had fumbled his way into the seat beside her, she had decided that she would stay awake. She would fight off sleep. She did not think that it would be difficult to do, not in such cramped surroundings with the car perched at such an angle where she tended to slide from her seat. Only by bracing her feet in the foot-well could she prevent herself from slipping to the floor. He, however, was soon snoring and snorting in a deep slumber. It was better for her that he had done so. She was saved from making idle chat. She had too much to think about and had no interest in befriending a taxi driver. She did not get the impression that he had any great intelligence and could not have much money because if he did, why was he driving a taxi for a living? She longed for the night to be over, for the blizzard to cease and to be on her way to London. The vision of the city in her mind was all that was keeping her going.

Suddenly, his bulk shifted in the seat. The car shook at his movement. He had dozed off with his head pointing forwards. Then it had rolled towards her, and she'd eased herself as far away from him as she could. Then he turned to his right, his back facing her. It was a blessing that she could breathe without inhaling his exhaled breath. She attempted to pull more of the blanket towards her. She could hardly believe that anyone could sleep so soundly in such a stifled space. She kept telling herself that it would soon be over. She glanced at her watch; it was only nine-twenty-five. It was going to be a long night.

Sleep did come eventually, however. He was right: two bodies huddled together made more efficient use of body heat. Consequently, she fell into a fitful doze. It was a deep enough sleep for her to dream. None of it was pleasant—not tonight, after the day she'd had. But she lost awareness of her surroundings and of the man sleeping beside her. She did not stir when his hand came to rest on her arm. She slept on.

A while later, his hand had slipped to her thigh, albeit resting on top of her coat. For a time there was no further movement. A hand, controlled by the thoughts and desires of its owner, waited for the right moment. When she moved on the seat, her feet shuffling in the cramped space of the foot-well, the hand slipped under her coat. Again, it knew to wait, to be patient and to prepare for the next opportunity.

She felt warmth on her leg, a throbbing warmth, and yet she slept on. Slowly, that warmth seemed to permeate her skin, and she felt its comfort and shifted her body on the seat. Soon the warmth spread, moving to her wider thigh. She moaned, an unconscious sigh of relaxation. Each of her tiny movements, her minuscule reactions, was encouragement to his hand, as it fondled and squeezed her flesh and moved closer to her crotch. And still she swooned. Her dreams continued, visions of her lover touching her, already knowing her so well, knowing what she liked and what she expected.

She jumped and awoke with a startled cry. He had gone too far. She had felt something push inside her—something that seemed to be in her sleep, but not in her dreams. Suddenly, she felt the hand releasing her and draw away from her body. In the darkness, she peered at a grinning, yet equally startled, face.

'What the hell do you think you're doing?' she said, angrily.

'Caught red-handed, eh?'

'Don't you dare touch me!' She tugged at her dress and coat in order to cover her legs. Tears welled in her eyes. She wanted to run, and she reached for the door handle, but he thrust his body on top of her. She fought for breath. 'Get off me!'

'Don't be like that, Alex. I'm just trying to keep us warm. You can't go running away in this weather. You'll catch your death.'

She punched at his chest, but it had little effect. Her arms were trapped below his weight.

'Get off me... or.'

'Or what, Alex? You'll scream? Go right ahead. There's only me to hear you.'

'I'll go to the police when we get out of here,' she said.

'And tell them what? That I touched you? Or that I saved you from freezing to death? That I kept you warm? That's all I was doing, you know. Just trying to make you comfortable. If you just relax for one minute, you might even enjoy yourself.'

He grinned, and she stared fearfully into his eyes. She dared hope to find safety, that he might even comfort her, now that she had foiled his plan. But he matched her stare with mischief, and for her the seconds felt like hours as he pressed his full weight on her trapped body.

Then he lowered his head and tried to kiss her.

CHAPTER 12

She turned her head away. His lips touched the white flesh of her neck. He tried again, but she flicked her head from left to right. A strong hand, stronger than she would have imagined, gripped her chin.

'Go on, Alex, play hard to get. We've got all night.'

Once more she resisted his mouth, but this time he made it to her lips. She cried out, but his mouth stifled the sound. She felt his weight shift, his body forcing its way between her legs. As panic and fear crashed through her, she was suddenly consumed by visions of her life's experiences—times when she had known real fear, when she had been the object of men's violent desires, merged with feelings of ecstasy at the hands of her lover. In an instant she blinked them away.

Repulsive though he was, and sickened by thoughts of what he intended, she realised that in this moment she would have to make the choice of whether she was to live or die. Survive, she must survive. If she continued to fight him, he might hurt her, really hurt her. He could decide that she would never see the light of day again. He could rape her and kill her, or she could acquiesce, lie back and let him have his way. Then he might let her go. In the morning they could part and, although she would have to live with the horror for the rest of her life, at least she would still be alive.

As she battled with this abhorrent logic, he became more aggressive in kissing her and continued to press his body into hers.

'Why can't we enjoy our night together, eh?' he whispered. His stubble rasped across her chin as she cried out.

'Please, Joe, don't. Not like this.'

Immediately, he stopped and peered into her watery eyes. She knew then that he had sensed the change in her attitude. She knew then that she would be safe from him. Now she had the better of him.

'What do you mean?'

She kissed him, a mere peck on his slobbering mouth.

'You're much too heavy on me. And I still have this.'

He raised himself upwards and extricated her bag that had been trapped between them.

'My God, you're still holding that bloody bag. What the hell have you got in there?'

'Nothing.'

She raised herself towards him and gave him another kiss. Then she intimidated that he should climb off her, and to encourage that she tugged at the zipper on his fleece jacket. With an expectant grin, he dropped to his back beside her. Now she knew exactly what to do. It had not taken much for him to relinquish control. She lowered then released the zipper of his jacket and pulled both sides apart to expose his polo shirt. Her hands immediately pulled at the shirt until it came away from his jeans. She ran her gloved hands over his chest. He began to open each button on her coat, and she giggled as he struggled to deal with her dress. Knowing that she still must encourage him to believe that he was about to have her, she pulled her dress upwards revealing the tops of her tights and her panties beneath. His hands, though, went to undo his own belt and she feigned her own haste, trying to help by pulling down his fly. He didn't seem to realise that he was getting naked while she remained fully dressed. She leaned over and kissed him, allowing his hands to fondle her breasts beneath her dress and bra. He hasn't a clue, she thought. Pushing herself upwards once more, her hands, still in purple leather gloves, held him down firmly. His head was pressed against the opposite door, his back on the seat and his legs outstretched beneath hers. She pulled violently at his jeans, and he helped her slide them down his thighs, all the way to his knees. This was not the first time in her life she had been forced into doing this. As his hands grasped her waist, and he tried to pull down her tights and panties, she slid his boxer shorts down his legs. Briefly, to keep him excited, she rubbed her hand over his crotch. He sighed aloud, and she laughed.

'Wow,' he said, 'I didn't really think you'd be up for it.'

She smiled, a smile of utter deceit, and glided her hands gently over his legs, until they again took hold of his jeans. She eased them down to his ankles. Unable to see clearly in the dark recesses of the car floor, she felt for his boots and, with the fingers of one hand, managed to tug on the lace of the left one. With the boot loosened, she pulled it off his foot. The right boot was not so easy. She abandoned the attempt, deciding that now was her opportunity. Moving her hands up his body, she touched him at his crotch once again and planted kisses on his flat stomach. Raising his polo shirt, she bit down on his left nipple, before gazing into his hateful face one last time. She pecked him on the lips, and smiled at his moans of ecstasy as she moved down his body. In doing so, she readied herself. She kept him sweet by rubbing her hand over his crotch. She saw his eyes closed, savouring her touch. With her right hand she pulled on the door handle and her foot kicked the door open, an icy wind sweeping inside. As she parted company with his body, she rammed her fist hard into his balls. He cried out.

Before he could do anything but grope his privates, she took hold of her bag and pushed herself backwards until she tumbled out of the car.

CHAPTER 13

He thought he would throw up. Shock waves swept through his lower back. He couldn't move. Could hardly find a breath. And she was getting away. Bitch. Freezing white powder billowed into the cab, the storm relentless. For a few minutes, he didn't care what happened to her. She wouldn't get far. More than likely, she would freeze to death or stumble into a river in flood. Fuck her. And she was a bloody strange one, too.

Maybe he should not have forced himself on her. He should have left well alone. But it was worth a try. You don't often get the chance with a woman like that, he thought. A real woman. Sophisticated, cultured, alluring—and well-off, he had no doubt. Not the type you would find on Friday nights in the pubs of Penrith, or even Carlisle.

He tried to sit up. His privates throbbed. He'd never had a put down, a brush off, quite like that before. He must have had dozens of girls in the back seat of his cab; the perks of being a taxi driver. Not one had ever been brave enough to do what she had done. In fact, when he thought about it, only two girls had ever put up a fight. Most of them had been up for it, and he always threw in a free ride home for their trouble.

Now he was freezing. He wrestled his boxers and jeans up to his waist and found his left boot on the floor. Pulling it on, he scrambled from the car, fastened his fly and belt and then crouched to tie his bootlace.

He peered into the whitened darkness. Was there no respite from this weather? He could hardly recall a snowstorm like it, and there had been plenty of bad ones in this part of the world. Standing knee-deep in snow, he noticed her trail of footprints leading away from the car. Judging by the direction they led, she'd hurried off without a thought of where she was going. She hadn't climbed onto the lane but instead was making her way across the field.

Tucking his polo shirt into his jeans and zipping up his fleece, he grabbed hold of the car's rear door and flung it closed, loose snow cascading down the window. The keys were in the ignition; he had no need for them while the car remained stranded on the bank and buried in the snow. For reasons that he could not entirely understand, he felt compelled to go after her. She'd fought with him, punched him in the frigging balls, but she didn't deserve to die for it. And that's what would happen if he didn't find her or if she didn't get help quickly. Besides, he wanted to give her a good slap for what she'd done to him. He was only trying to be friendly, only trying to keep her warm. What the hell was her problem? He pictured himself having a showdown with her and then, in the morning, helping her onto the London train.

He kept a torch in the boot of the car for emergencies. He should really keep a hell of a lot more in case he got stranded in bad weather, but this was not the time to give himself a rollicking. Scrambling in loose snow, he clambered on all fours up the bank and onto the lane. The boot of the car sat high in the air because the rear wheels rested on the apex of the verge. He had reached inside and retrieved his torch when he saw her suitcase. Shining his torch onto it, he pulled the zipper around the case and raised the lid. It was awkward trying to examine it within the boot, so he hauled it out and threw it onto the snow. Powder snow billowed around him. His adrenaline, it seemed, was keeping him warm for the time being. The case had not been neatly packed. Clothes had been bundled in; a woollen jumper was wrapped with a skirt into a ball. There were two pairs of jeans, a pair of flat brogues, a pair of white trainers and bathroom slippers. An open wash bag sat on top of the clothing. He found nothing unusual inside: shower gel, make-up, a toothbrush, toothpaste and a bottle of perfume. Chanel. A selection of underwear lay at the bottom of the case: panties, bras and tights. Two dresses had been poorly folded and lay next to the underwear. He found himself somewhat surprised—it was not that he had any real expectation of what else might be in the case other than a woman's belongings, it was just that this woman was a mystery to him. He thought he should have found something more.

He dropped the lid, ran the zipper closed, chucked the case into the boot of the car and slammed the lid shut.

He shone his torch into the night and saw nothing but the light reflected against the whiteness. He gazed up the lane in the direction he had driven from her holiday cottage. At least he had referred to it as a holiday cottage—she had never said so. It might well be her permanent residence, although he doubted it. She was definitely a city dweller. She had an air about her and an ignorance of the countryside. Why hadn't she bolted to the cottage? Perhaps she reckoned on him coming after her and breaking the door down. Or maybe, at this moment, she was doubling back towards it.

He slid down the bank into the field and set off following her footprints in the snow before they were completely obscured.

CHAPTER 14

With every awkward step she sank to her knees in the fresh snow. The ice-cold wind nipped at her face, but she kept going with a determination that somehow she would make it to the station in Penrith and onto a train for London. If she kept that objective uppermost in her mind then the vision of his hands on her body were nothing but a horrible memory. She had already convinced herself that he would not come after her. He was much too lazy. He would stay in the relative warmth of his car, sit out the storm, and by morning he would put his encounter with her down to experience. He would be right in thinking that she would not go to the police. She could never prove that he had assaulted her and had forced himself on her until she had acquiesced and pretended to be willing. She hoped at least that she had left him with a painful reminder of her.

The snow was deeper where it had drifted, and it felt like she was wading through a dense liquid. Frequently, she tumbled forward, her arms going out to save her, but instead she sank up to her shoulders. If only the blizzard would ease, she might see where she was headed. She hoped she had put some distance between herself and the taxi. Glancing behind, she could not see the car or the lane. Gradually, she became aware of the slope of the field levelling out, but her progress was no easier. In the darkness, she saw a line of trees whitened by the snow. She hoped for a road beyond them, but when she got there and stood under a thick bough, she saw that the ground dropped away in front of her. She was looking upon a dark line—not a road but a mountain stream. Until a few days ago it had been merely a stream. Now it was a torrent of rushing water, a river in flood, exceeding its banks on both sides. There was no obvious way to cross it. It would be much too deep to wade through.

She was cold, especially her legs and feet, although her heart pumping adrenaline gave her the impetus to keep going. Staying by the line of trees, some tall sycamore, others young ash and birch, she walked in the direction of the river's flow, hoping to reach a bridge or a road.

Her bag felt twice as heavy as she struggled to keep it from trailing through the deep snow. She could not leave it behind. Her entire life was inside this case. Her past and her future.

A short while later, the blizzard eased, and she began to make out shapes in the near distance: the outline of a stone wall, an old barn and the line of trees thinning out, leaving the river exposed on both sides.

She was exhausted. Her breath was laboured, and she realised that if she didn't get to help soon she would freeze to death. But she had to stop for a rest. She had to steady her breathing, wipe the snow clinging to her coat and hope to stay dry. She leaned her back against the leeside of a tree, free of any snow. Tears slipped from her eyes but quickly froze on her cheeks. Her throat ached from breathing cold air. She couldn't believe the situation she was in. When she had woken up that morning, cosy in bed, smelling toast and coffee from downstairs, she could never have imagined ending up in a life or death situation.

'Hello, Alex.'

She drew a sharp breath. Her heart pounded. She didn't dare look.

'I thought you'd be further away by now,' he said.

She was too slow in trying to run. He was upon her as quickly as she had heard him speak. They were face to face, his body pinning her to the tree. She felt his warm breath on her face and the prickling of his stubble on her cold skin.

'That wasn't very nice,' he whispered. 'I thought we were going to have a good time. Where was the harm, eh? We could be snuggled together in the car instead of staggering about in a blizzard.'

'Please. Let me go. I won't say anything. I won't tell the police. I'll catch my train to London, and you'll never hear from me again.'

He unbuttoned her coat and slipped his hands inside to clutch her waist. He pulled her even closer to his body. He pressed a kiss on her mouth, and she tried to turn her face away. Suddenly, he released her and stepped back, his hands wrenching the bag from her grasp.

'Just what the hell is in this bag that's so important?' He fumbled for the zipper.

'Please, Joe, let me go.'

'I want to see what's in here.'

He dropped the bag on the ground and knelt down beside it. While he slid the zip open, she eased her body from the tree. He lifted the lid of the case, shone his torch and gazed inside.

'What the hell?' he gasped. 'There must be thousands in here.'

He rifled through the contents, ignoring papers and jewellery, a silk nightdress, items of makeup and a bottle of perfume. He lifted a bundle of new twenty-pound notes held together in a paper band.

She watched him carefully and dared to take a step closer. She would only get one chance.

'Where did you get this? '

She swung her foot, making sure her toe pointed outwards. Her suede boot was caked with snow. It caught him on the side of the head, close to his ear. She had used every last ounce of her strength. Still clutching a wad of cash, he flopped to the side. He lay motionless on the snow, but she had no time to wonder if she had killed him or merely knocked him unconscious. She didn't care either way. Extricating the bundle of notes from his hand, she replaced it in the case, closed the zipper and hurried off.

CHAPTER 15

The going was no easier, but a fierce determination had erupted inside her. She had a strong will to survive—not only the trials of this night and a stupid man trying to seize his moment, but to continue with her life, her new life, beyond this time and place. By now she should have been in London and making preparations for her future, but the weather had scuppered that plan. She was adamant that only the weather could stop her or slow her down. A brute with sex and greed on his mind would not prevent her from getting to London. She hoped she had killed him. And what if she had? Eventually, his body would be found. He would have died from her kick to his head or from freezing in the winter night. It did not matter how. No one could connect his death with her. She did not exist. The silly man should have known better than to abandon his car in a blizzard and then wander off into the wilderness. That is what the police would say.

She tried to run, but the deep snow sapped her energy, and within seconds she was reduced to panting, bent double beside a raging stream. When she had recovered a steady breath she stomped off, staying close to the river. Hopefully, she would soon reach a road and, if she were lucky, a sign that pointed the way to Penrith.

The sky began to clear of clouds, and a partial moon afforded more light to an eerie landscape. There was nothing ahead that gave her any hope of safety. Her mind began to play tricks on her, pitching one thought against another. It was better if Joe was dead. If he came after her again it would not be just to have her body. He would take her money. Firstly, he would rape her, then kill her and steal her bag. He would not know, of course, the significance of the papers that lay within the case. He would only see the cash, yet what was printed upon a few sheets of paper was so much more valuable. He would never know that. If she were going to die at his hands she would not tell him, and a fortune would be lost for ever.

She dared a glance behind her. A dark figure moving across the snow would be easily noticed now in the clear night, but she saw no one. Then she realised that she also would be easily spotted. He could be watching her, waiting for the right moment to pounce again. He could be hunting her, stalking her. He was bound to know this countryside well, definitely better than her. She could do nothing about it if he was trailing her. Despite her fears concerning the taxi-driver, she needed to get indoors and get some warmth inside her.

It was impossible for her to know accurately how far she had walked from the stricken taxi, or how far it was to the nearest road. She could guess, but how would that help? She had never been here before. This was the only occasion she had stayed at the cottage.

A barbed wire fence prevented her from continuing to walk beside the river. She searched for a gap, a break in the wire, or a section where the wire was lower and she might be able to climb over it. A hundred yards along the fence and up the hill, she found a metal gate. Clutching her bag, her future, she climbed over the rungs and stepped into another field. Rather than return to the river, she strode across the open land. She could see a building at the far perimeter of the field, but she realised that it might only be a disused barn. There seemed to be plenty of those in this part of the world. The snow was deep, up to her waist in places, where it had drifted and accumulated within the dips of the field. She set herself the target of reaching the building. When she got there she could set another objective. That is how she had always dealt with struggles in her life, and there had been many over the years.

Reaching the broken-down pile of stone she had hoped was a cottage, she looked back across the field she had just crossed. There was no sign of him. If he lay where she had left him he would be dead by morning. She looked at her watch. It was approaching midnight. Surely, she had been walking for hours. It seemed like an age since she had been sitting in the taxi, wondering if the driver was a nice man, or if he was likely to take advantage of a woman alone in his car. And now she was running for her life.

The ruined building, fortuitously, lay at the junction of two lanes, both buried in snow. There were no tracks apparent, no indications that anyone—a farmer in a tractor perhaps—had travelled this way in the last few hours. She had to choose a direction. This was a crossroads in her life. To the right, the lane climbed a hill, beyond which lay open moor and a rounded mountain peak. She chose, instead, to walk down to the river. Going in the direction of the river's flow, she hoped that she was getting closer to safety. She prayed that soon she would find civilisation. Setting her next objective of reaching a main road, she decided to time her journey. This was England, not Siberia, for goodness sake. She must find human life somewhere close by.

CHAPTER 16

Another fifty minutes passed with her tramping through deep snow. Despite walking down a lane, the weather had not discriminated between trail and field, the snow deep in both, and the distance she had covered was not great. She glanced at her watch. It read ten-to-one. It was the moment when she first saw what she hoped would be rescue and safety. She had rounded a bend in the lane as the river, too, wound its ancient path down the valley, and up ahead, no more than fifty yards, was a stone bridge. Just to the right of the bridge was a two-storey house of dark stone, its pitched roof thick with the evening deluge of snow. She felt warm inside just to see a house in front of her. It spurred her on.

When she reached the cottage she saw that it sat close to a road. There was a small garden to the side, while the rear stretched to the bank of the river. This was the direction from which she'd come. She found a gap in a low hedge and, stepping through it, reached a driveway at the side of the house. A Range Rover, ensconced in snow, was parked at the front. Its presence suggested that at least the house was occupied. The building was in darkness, and not even security lights came on outside. There wasn't a sound from the house or from the road, but already she felt relief. It was late, she realised, but she had a reasonable excuse to come knocking on someone's door at this hour. She prayed it was a family home, a welcoming place. For now she'd decided to explain only that she had become stranded in the snow on one of the mountain lanes. She wouldn't mention a taxi or its beast of a driver who had tried to rape her.

Her knock on the varnished wooden door was not immediately answered. She tried again with a more vigorous clatter of the brass knocker. Only then did she notice the doorbell to the right of the door, and so she pressed the button. She stepped back on seeing a light come on at an upstairs window to the left of the door. She looked around nervously, hoping that Joe had not followed her. The door creaked open, and a slight figure of a man in a towelling bathrobe and slippers peered out through a crack.

'I'm so sorry to disturb you at this time of night,' she said, beginning to cry. 'But I got stuck in the snow. I'm trying to get to Penrith.'

The man looked quite old—in his seventies—although he may have been younger and not looking his best having been awakened from his night's sleep. He opened the door wide and stepped outside, looking around him. His face was ruddy, with sunken grey eyes and silver-grey stubble. His hair also was silver and neatly cut.

'Where is your car?' He asked, his voice neither friendly nor hostile.

'I got stuck in a lane up on the moors earlier in the day. I've been walking for ages.' She couldn't help her tears or the breaking of her voice. The man looked her up and down.

'You'll not get to Penrith tonight. All the roads are closed round here until the plough can get through. You look worn out. Come inside and get warmed up.' He was already walking back indoors.

She hesitated. Was he alone in this house? Could she trust him? Surely there can't be two sex fiends in such close proximity. Somewhere, there had to be ordinary people. The man appeared to sense her fears.

'It's all right, love. My wife is asleep upstairs. Come in; I'll put the kettle on.'

Feeling relieved, she entered the house, and the man closed the door behind her.

'Not the first person this has happened to,' he said, 'getting stuck on the moors. You don't look dressed for fell walking though?'

'No, I had been staying at a cottage. I was on my way to catch the London train when I got stranded.'

The house was warm. Just to be out of the snow and those fields dispelled the chill from her bones.

The entrance hall of the house had quite a modern feel. There were cream-painted walls and prints of European city-scapes, one of London at sunset, another of Marseille, she thought, and a larger framed print of Paris, the Ille de Notre Dame. She followed him into a rear kitchen, spacious, with an Aga, an island bench, and a sturdy oak table set against a wall. She decided that this was no farmhouse. It had more the feel of a home for a retired couple, or maybe a professional pair who had chosen not to live in a city. She didn't get the impression that the man was a native of the area.

He filled an electric kettle with water from the tap.

'Tea or coffee?' he asked.

'Tea would be great, thank you.' She remained standing in the middle of the kitchen, gazing around her, still holding her precious bag. When he had plugged in the kettle, the man turned to examine her again.

'Not the kind of weather to be going anywhere, if you ask me. Heading to London, you said?'

He motioned her to sit at the table.

'Yes, I live there. I was booked on the five o'clock train.'

'Please, take your coat off, it must be soaked with snow.'

She slipped off her coat and draped it over the back of a wooden chair. She pulled off her gloves and set them on the table. The man plated some chocolate biscuits and crossed the kitchen to set them on the table in front of her.

'I'm Richard,' he said. 'My wife is Sandra.'

'Alex. I'm really sorry for calling at this time of the night.' Her voice struggled with emotion once again.

'No need for that. You could have frozen to death out there. You know, usually they tell you to stay with your vehicle when you get trapped.'

'I know, but it felt so isolated up there. I had no idea if I would be rescued.'

'Fair enough.'

He brewed the tea and then left her alone in the kitchen. She munched on a biscuit. Chocolate digestive was again the fayre on offer.

Richard returned a minute later and poured the tea into three green mugs. He set one in front of her and another at the opposite end of the table. A short while later, a woman padded into the kitchen wearing a flowery pink dressing gown and a pair of fluffy slippers. She looked much younger than the man. More like his daughter, she thought, and she carried quite a large pregnant bump.

'Hello,' said the woman and then failed to stifle a yawn.

'Alex, this is my wife Sandra.'

'Pleased to meet you. I'm really sorry for the intrusion.'

Sandra swept long fair hair from her face and smiled.

'Don't worry, honestly,' she said. 'We're happy to help.'

'If I could use your phone to call for a taxi, I'll be out of your way as soon as I can.'

'There's no chance of a taxi in this weather,' said Richard. 'I don't think the main road to Penrith has re-opened yet.'

Sandra sat down at the table and sipped on her mug of tea. Her husband remained standing, leaning against the worktop by the sink.

'You can sleep here tonight,' he said, 'or what's left of it, and I can drive you into town in the morning. I have a Range Rover—a four-wheel drive. It'll be more reliable than a taxi.'

If only he knew how right he was, she thought.

'Thank you, that's very kind. I'm so sorry for disturbing you at this time of night.'

'You don't have to apologise,' said Sandra. 'You're lucky to have found us. You might have been wandering about all night out there. Where were you staying?'

She sipped her tea and tried to compose herself before answering the question. Something close to the truth, she hoped, would suffice.

'I was staying at a cottage for the weekend, near Dowthwaitehead, I think the place is called. I was supposed to catch the evening train to London, but the weather got so bad.'

'I don't know Dowthwaitehead,' said Sandra. 'We're not from the area. We moved here from Manchester two years ago. So how did you become stranded in the snow?'

She was beginning to feel threatened by the woman's questions. How could she avoid mentioning her ordeal in the taxi? Perhaps it was time for the truth. She lowered her head, sniffed, then wiped tears from her eyes. Her body trembled.

'What's wrong, Alex? What happened?' Sandra indicated to her husband to fetch a box of tissues from the workbench. He handed the box to his wife, and Sandra removed a couple and reached them to her guest. Alex grasped the tissues and dabbed at her eyes. Then she felt Sandra's warm hand upon hers. 'You don't have to tell us if you don't want to?' Sandra said, softly. 'You've had a really bad experience out there. Lucky you didn't freeze to death.'

'It's OK, really. I was in a taxi. We were going down a lane, but the car skidded into a field and got stuck in the snow.'

'Oh my, are you hurt? Maybe you're suffering from shock?'

'No, I'm fine. It was the driver...'

'Was he injured? Is he still out there?' Sandra looked to Richard in alarm. Now wearing dark-framed glasses, his eyes widened in shock.

Alex continued to sob. She was unsure of how much was down to shock and how much was actually down to her relief at having escaped from, Joe, her attacker.

'What happened to him?' asked Richard.

'I... he...' she stammered, and now tears flowed easily.

'Is he injured?' he asked.

Immediately, Sandra signalled to her husband to leave the kitchen. When he had gone, she spoke gently to Alex.

'Tell me what happened, Alex.'

'He told me that we would have to spend the night in the car and wait to be rescued. He forced himself on me...'

'Did he hurt you?' Sandra moved her chair closer to Alex and put an arm around her. 'It's OK, Alex, you're safe here; no one's going to hurt you. Try to tell me what happened.'

'He tried to rape me... I got away.'

CHAPTER 17

He came to, shivering uncontrollably. If he didn't get out of the cold soon he would die. He recognised the signs of hypothermia. His trembling hand moved to the side of his head and came away covered in blood. Could he make it to his feet? It took a moment for him to realise what had happened. She had outsmarted him twice. Damn well might have killed him. Boy, was he sorry he had ever tried it on with the likes of her. Should have left well alone.

Rolling from his back to his front, he managed to raise himself onto all fours, afflicted, like some wild animal crawling about in the snow. Tentatively, he pushed himself upwards, at first onto one knee then finally to his feet. His head throbbed, but he was too cold to care. His body continued to shake. He must get back to his car. Visibility was good now, and he saw the lane at the top of the field. Somewhere, along its edge, was his stricken car. He stumbled forwards, feeling sorry for himself, wondering what had happened to the bitch who'd ruined his night. His only aim for now, however, was to get warm.

By the time he reached the lane his teeth were chattering, he'd lost all feeling in his fingers and still his head pounded. Snow was piled high along the bank that separated the field from the lane. At first, he saw no sign of his car, but he tried to picture the spot where he'd skidded over the verge and into the field. If he didn't get to the car soon, he would drop where he stood, and that would be the end of him. He wondered what the police would make of such a situation. A taxi driver stranded with his car tries to walk to safety but perishes. And what about his passenger? They would find her suitcase in the boot of the Mondeo. Had she died also, or had she made it to safety? He imagined what she would tell the police, what she would say about him, how he'd tried to rape her and how she'd fought him off—twice. He pictured her seated on a London-bound train, still clutching that damn case of hers. Thinking about her, of how she had behaved, he decided that if she had made it to safety she might not want to tell the police anything. She had secrets, that woman. Secrets, perhaps, that she would not wish to share with the police. For instance, why the hell was she carrying so much money in that case? He had definitely stumbled upon something rare—a woman capable of defending herself—a woman able to scheme and plot to get away from him.

After struggling for another hundred yards, he spotted the raised back end of his car poking out of the drifted snow. Quickly, he scrambled to the driver's door, his fingers numb to the icy cold. He had to pull hard on the handle to free the door. It was frozen to the car's body. Once open, he fell inside and drew a deep breath. The keys were in the ignition as he had left them, and he prayed the starter would turn. Fortunately, it sprang to life straightaway. In a few minutes he could divert hot air into the cab, and he would get warm. And when he felt better and stronger, he would walk down the lane and find some place warm to spend the remainder of the night. Then in the morning he could arrange to have his car pulled from the ditch.

CHAPTER 18

Sandra insisted that Alex sleep in her spare room. Alex did not protest much. She was exhausted, frightened and unsure of how to behave with this couple. They had both been very understanding; Sandra, in particular, showed her great sympathy when she recounted her ordeal. They seemed puzzled, however, at her insistence that the police did not become involved.

'I just want to catch a train to London and get home,' she said. Richard had stepped back into the kitchen, and the couple communicated silently by facial expression of their amazement at the woman's story.

'Let's get you upstairs to bed,' said Sandra. 'Things might look clearer in the morning, after you get some sleep.'

Sandra led her through the hallway, up a narrow but newly restored staircase of brushed pine and onto an equally narrow landing. She was shown into a small bedroom at the rear of the house. It was simply yet tastefully furnished, with a single pine-framed bed, a chest of pine drawers and a small wardrobe. The ceiling sloped to the outside wall that held a quarter-paned sash window.

'I've turned up the heat,' said Sandra. 'It should warm up quickly.'

'Thank you. I'm really sorry for causing all this trouble, especially with you expecting a baby.'

Sandra patted her bump.

'Not another word of thanks or apology. I'm just glad you made it here. You're safe now. Try to get some sleep. Goodnight, Alex.'

'Goodnight.'

The door closed, and she was left wondering what might happen when morning came. Sandra had been very understanding, but her husband seemed concerned when he'd heard of the trouble she'd had involving a taxi driver. Nonetheless, she did feel lucky to have stumbled upon this place.

She unzipped and removed her wet boots and set them close to the radiator, beginning to spread its heat. Before sitting down, she peered through the window. Now, from the comfort of the room, the landscape resembled a winter wonderland of peace and purity. She shuddered at the vision of the taxi driver's hands on her body, his face rasping against her soft flesh. Now that she'd told someone of her plight, she hoped that he had survived. How could she believe that she would simply climb on board a train in the morning without facing the consequences of what she'd done to him? Then again, she thought, it would be better if he was dead. She'd told Sandra about what happened to the point when she had run off, but she'd told her nothing of her striking him in the head and knocking him unconscious. The couple knew nothing about her, not even her surname. If only she could get on the train without fuss she would be in the clear.

Pulling back the flowery-patterned duvet, blue under the yellow lamplight, she lay down, feeling instant comfort when her head touched the pillow. So many bizarre thoughts and emotions swirled in her mind as she lay staring at the ceiling, the lamplight casting a shadow over the walls. Soon, though, sleep overcame her.

It proved an unsettled doze. Her movements on the bed were enough to wake her. During one such event, her blood suddenly ran cold, and she drew the duvet close into her body. There was a knocking sound coming from downstairs.

There was someone at the door.

CHAPTER 19

She listened to the disturbance in the household. A door opened on the landing. Assuming it was Richard going to answer the door, she rose from the bed and went to listen. She opened her door a little way and peered into the landing. She heard the front door opening downstairs and a man's voice.

'Richard, sorry to wake you at this hour, but I got stuck in the snow.'

'Joe! Come in. You must be frozen out there.'

Her heart thumped, and shock waves pulsed through her body. It was Joe and, by the sounds of it, he and Richard knew each other. Her first thoughts were to run, but she wanted to hear what was being said. She placed her ear to the crack in the door.

'What happened to your head?' Richard asked. 'You have a nasty-looking gash.'

She heard the front door closing again.

'I slipped on some ice.'

Thankfully, for now, the two men remained in the hallway. She heard every word, because they didn't spare their volume.

'You need to get that seen to at the hospital,' said Richard. 'It might need stitches. Where did you get stranded?'

'Up by Dowthwaitehead. Narrow lane—I lost it at a bend—car went over a bank—front ended up in a field.'

'Did you have any passengers?'

'I did actually, a woman. I was driving her to the station. She's not here, is she?'

Richard's voice lowered. She had difficulty hearing every word now, but her mind raced with options of what to do next.

'Asleep upstairs,' she heard Richard explain. 'What the hell happened, Joe? She claims that you assaulted her.'

'A misunderstanding, Richard, honest. I suggested that we huddle together, to stay warm until we got rescued. She got the wrong idea. Went nuts, then ran off, me chasing after her. Thank God she made it here. She might have frozen to death out there.'

She could no longer make out Richard's softly spoken voice, but it sounded as though he was still asking questions of the taxi driver. How well did the two men know each other? Friends? Relations?

'She's a strange one, Richard. Truth be told, she gave me this smack on the head when I caught up with her. I was only trying to help her. She damn well near ran into the river. But there's something odd about her.'

Again she heard nothing of Richard's response, but was aware, suddenly, of him climbing the stairs. She closed her door. A few moments later, she heard Richard and Sandra whispering on the landing before descending the stairs.

'Hi, Sandra,' said Joe, 'sorry to bother you at this time of night. Did Richard tell you what happened?'

'Yes, Joe,' Sandra replied. 'The girl was very upset when she got to us. I think you need to explain. She didn't mention your name to us—just that her driver had tried to rape her.'

'Bloody hell, Sandra. You know me better than that.'

'I hope I do, Joe. But at the moment I have a very upset woman asleep in my spare room.'

'Sandra, she got the wrong idea and then bolted. She damn near tried to kill me when I caught up with her.'

'Looks like a nasty cut. It needs cleaning up.'

'But, Sandra, there's something odd about that woman. I was telling Richard.'

'Odd, what do you mean?'

'She wasn't very friendly or talkative.'

'Doesn't make her odd, Joe.'

'I know, but she had a small case with her. It's filled with cash, thousands, I'd say. There's definitely something strange about that. And she was in a hell of a hurry to catch the train.'

She'd heard enough. She had to get away. She couldn't face him again, and now they were in the same house. Sandra and Richard were more likely to believe his version of events. They knew each other. She was the stranger.

Closing the door again, she lifted her boots and put them on. Her hand, instinctively, reached for her case. How could she get away? She'd left her coat and gloves in the kitchen. Standing in the bedroom, wearing only her dress, she gazed out of the window, already feeling the ice-cold penetrating her skin.

CHAPTER 20

Sandra cleaned the wound on Joe's head with cotton wool and some disinfectant. He felt no pain from the actual cut, but his head throbbed to the point where it felt detached from the rest of his body. He felt obliged to retell his story as Sandra worked on him. Richard, once again, made tea and seemed content to listen to the conversation. He passed no comment when Sandra brought up what Alex had told her.

'She doesn't want to involve the police,' she said, placing a gauze pad over the cut and securing it to Joe's head with tape.

'I'll bet,' he replied.

'A woman feels great humiliation, Joe, having to report their experience to the police. Some women are made to believe that being raped is their fault.'

'Hold on a minute, Sandra. I didn't rape her. She's lying.'

'Did you attempt to have sex with her?'

Sandra looked sternly at him, awaiting his reply. She worked as a criminal solicitor; she knew how these matters could play out. At this hour of the morning, bags had formed beneath her eyes. She was tired and becoming fraught.

'Look, we were huddled together to keep warm that's all. I may have tried it on, but I thought she was willing. Next thing I know, she's punched me in the privates and run off.'

'Your Julie won't be happy to hear about this.'

'You're not going to tell her, are you, Sandra?'

It seemed as though a night's sleep was not going to happen for anyone in the riverside cottage. Richard and Joe had started into whiskey when Sandra left them to return to her bedroom. When she reached the landing, massaging her back with both hands, feeling her baby move uncomfortably inside her, she decided to look in on her mysterious guest. A woman who had either suffered a tortuous ordeal, or a woman who had lied and had secrets to protect.

Sandra eased the door open and peered into the room. Instantly, she felt the coldness and glanced from the empty bed to the open window. Rushing in, she peered through the window into the darkness. She saw the trail of footprints across the snow, disappearing into the night. From the landing, she called out for her husband.

Richard came to the foot of the stairs.

'She's gone,' Sandra called.

'What?'

'She's jumped from the window and run off.'

'But she's left her coat,' said Richard. 'She'll freeze to death out there.'

Joe came from the kitchen, holding his tumbler of Scotch. He tipped it to his face and emptied the glass.

'I'll go after her,' he said.

CHAPTER 21

Her right knee was slowing her down. She had bashed it on a clay flower pot when she landed. It was a risk to have jumped from the bedroom window, but she had had little option. Joe seemed to be friendly with Richard and Sandra; they were not going to dispute his version of the story. She had been more concerned about what they would try to do about her overnight bag and the money within it. Even if they were honest people, they would ask questions, maybe call the police, and she could not afford to let that happen.

So she had escaped. She had left her coat on a chair in the kitchen. There was no way she could have retrieved it without alerting her hosts. She had lifted the latch on the wooden-framed window and pushed it open, ice-cold air once more biting at her face. Peering downwards, she had seen a patio bordered with plant pots and tubs, well-covered with snow. Beyond the patio was an expanse of garden. She hadn't been able to tell if it was a lawn or was perhaps planted in vegetables. A greenhouse stood at the top of the slope in the left-hand corner.

She had heard Joe deny his attempted rape and decided that she must jump. Sandra might come to fetch her. She'd been very understanding of her plight, but confronted with another version of the story she might insist that the police were called.

She'd known that her dress would not keep her warm, and her feet had already become chilled again inside her damp boots. Quickly, she had looked inside the small wardrobe for something that she could wear, perhaps a coat or a jumper. There was nothing but a few items of new baby clothes hanging in plastic wrapping. She had decided she would have to manage without a coat, but an idea had occurred to her as she was about to climb outside. Stretching towards the bed, she had pulled the duvet from the mattress and bundled it through the open window. Next she had dropped her bag, with its precious contents, onto the snow. She had climbed through the opening and sat precariously on the ledge before slipping to the ground. As she bent her legs on landing, her right knee had hit the edge of a pot, and she had stifled her cry of pain. But there had been no time to roll around in agony. She had to get away. Shaking snow off the duvet, she had wrapped it around her shoulders and hurried into the darkness. Her footprints were clear for anyone to find, as she had stamped a trail through the garden and back through the gap in the hedge from where she'd emerged a couple of hours earlier.

Now, she realised that she was headed in the wrong direction, up the mountain rather than into the valley and towards Penrith. But she didn't dare take to the road. Not right away. Joe, and probably Richard also, would come after her. If Joe came alone, she would be in real danger. She had no doubt that he would harm her and then take her money. For now she would stay in the fields and would cut back to the road when she had walked further from the house.

The duvet kept her warm, although none of her body heat was getting to her toes. She cried with frustration, knowing that she was headed in the wrong direction. If only she could be certain that they hadn't come after her, she could head back to the bridge beside the house and be on her way. Her throat ached once again from drawing the freezing air, and her lungs struggled under the exertion. She flopped to the ground beside the raging torrent of the river. She couldn't maintain this pace, not when she was going the wrong way. Gazing at the land to her left, which rose above the river, she hoped for a lane beyond the field that would lead her to a road. Making for the edge of the field meant that, for a while, she was in open country and easily visible to anyone in pursuit. But she had no choice.

She cried with relief to find that there was indeed a lane, and the sight encouraged her to keep going. The pain in her knee was suppressed by her adrenaline, but as she hobbled along, her going was slow. Already in the clearness of the early yet still-dark morning, she saw that she was approaching a road. It was the same road on which Richard and Sandra's cottage stood, but that at least was several hundred yards away. She saw lights on in the upper floor of their house and wondered if Sandra had been able to sleep with all the commotion of the night. Maybe they had not discovered that she had fled.

It was easier to walk on the lane; there were no sudden holes where she could sink to her waist in snow. For the first time since fleeing the house, she felt that she would make it to safety, that Joe had not come after her, and that soon she would be on a train back to London. Once again, she timed herself. When the lane joined the road, she checked her watch. She had been walking for forty-seven minutes. Instinct suggested that she turn to her right and risk proceeding along the road. She could see the lie of the land now, and also that she was headed away from the higher hills and getting closer, she prayed, to Penrith. She had almost forgotten that someone might be coming after her, and she fell into a rhythm in her walking that kept her at a steady pace and no longer gasping for breath. Half an hour later, she stood at a junction in the road and looked forlornly at the sign: *Penrith, 11 miles.* She couldn't believe that she wasn't closer. Trying to stifle another bout of futile tears, she looked around her. She had reached Dockray, the village she'd heard mentioned on the radio earlier in the evening. The bridge was closed, or had been swept away, and there was no route through for vehicles. But, judging by the signpost, Penrith was indicated in the opposite direction. She was confused. She could the see damaged bridge to her right, with a *'ROAD CLOSED'* sign standing a few yards off, but the way to Penrith was indicated to her left. Had Joe deliberately misled her, telling her there was no way through to Penrith even if they had been able to rescue his car from the field? It hardly seemed to matter now.

On her left was The Royal Hotel, a whitewashed stone building, its picnic tables in the garden poking through a covering of snow. A light was on inside the entrance porch. She thought about going in and getting a room for the night, and in the morning she could order another taxi to drive her to the station. The idea of another taxi, of another driver, filled her with dread. She knew that she could trust no one. It was a harsh lesson learned. Tempting though it was to get into the warmth and security of the hotel, she continued to walk in the

direction of Penrith. Eleven miles, she told herself, was nothing. She would make it to the station in time to catch an early train.

When she reached the edge of the village, on a straight section of road, she saw a figure ahead. It was coming towards her.

CHAPTER 22

She couldn't risk waiting to see if it was him. She had to run. Immediately, she turned and ran back towards the village. The hotel—if she could just make it there—surely he wouldn't come inside after her. If he did, she would make a rumpus. Cry out for help. Let everyone see that this man, this animal, intended to do her harm. She dared to look behind her. He was running now. She would never make it. Where was Richard? Surely he had come searching for her, too? She released the duvet from around her shoulders, hoping to gain some speed, but it was useless. He was only a few yards behind her.

'Alex! Wait! It's all right, I'm not going to hurt you. Please stop!'

If only she could believe him. He had attacked her twice already. She sobbed helplessly. A few more steps and he would be upon her. Without a care, she veered to her right and straddled a low stone wall. She cried out, as she fell through branches and ferns, tumbling on a steep bank, scraping through snow and mud, finally splashing into ice-cold raging water. She had lost her grip of the bag. It was snagged on a branch six feet above the water. She stretched to reach it, but the current took control of her. The cold water sucked the air from her lungs. Her body was paralysed. It sailed like deadwood on the white foaming water. Her feet scraped over stones, her knees and hips smashed into boulders, as she was swept away.

'Alex?'

She heard his call above the noise of rushing water. Now she needed him. He was the only one who could save her. Suddenly, the breath was forced from her, as her back crashed into a huge boulder. The pain of the collision and the freezing cold was too much to bear. She felt close to passing out. But now, at least, she was no longer moving. The flowing water had pinned her against the rock. Chest deep in the bubbling cold, she would die if she didn't get out soon.

'Alex! It's OK, I'll get you out.'

She watched him scrambling down a steep bank. What little snow that lay upon it caused him to slide out of control until he, too, splashed into the river. Instantly, he was swept away in the torrent. Suddenly, he reached upwards and caught hold of an overhanging branch. She saw him battle his way out of the raging stream to the opposite bank. The land was flat on this side but had been breached by the flood. When he scrambled to his feet he ran back towards her, while searching for something he could use to get her out. She watched him drag a large piece of branch to the water's edge. He struggled to move it over the river towards her, and he again fell into the water. But somehow he kept hold of the tree, and jammed it between the bank and the rock where she was trapped.

'Take hold!' he called. 'Climb on top.'

'I can't. I can't do it.'

'Yes you can, Alex. If you don't you're going to die.'

She struggled to raise her arms from the water to grasp the branch. Once she got hold with both hands, she pushed with her legs against the boulder. It helped to raise her body from the river. She lay straddled over the branch, as Joe held it in place.

'Crawl over to the bank. That's a girl.'

She could see that he was struggling from the cold as water crashed into his back, threatening to sweep him under the branch and away downstream. Slowly, she edged along the wood. Eventually, she grappled with both her arms onto snow and solid ground. Breathless and shivering, she slid her legs off the branch until she was safe from the flowing water.

'Help me out,' he called.

For a second, she lost all awareness of what was happening. Then she saw him clinging to the tree.

'Hold the branch steady,' he shouted.

On her hands and knees, she crawled to the water's edge and reached for the log. As her hands took hold, she saw him moving through the water towards her. His legs were taken by the current: he depended entirely on the branch and on her keeping a firm hold. As he grappled with twigs and then branch, just as she had done seconds earlier, she felt the structure turn in the current. She fought, with all of her remaining strength, to hold the log in place. For a brief moment, she locked eyes with the man who had attacked her and now had rescued her. Then she let go.

'No!'

In seconds, she lost sight of him. His head dipped beneath the foaming water, and he was swept away.

Chapter 23

She realised, and not for the first time that night, that she would die if she didn't get warm soon. But she must retrieve her bag. Without it, there was no point in living. She stood, wet and shivering, on the opposite bank to where she had toppled into the river. Snow was falling again.

She felt nothing for him. In the end he had tried to save her. For what reason? So that he could rape her? Rob her of her life? He had caused all of this trouble. He deserved his fate. He had been foolish, getting stranded with his taxi in the snow, and then failing to reach safety. Richard and Sandra would go to the police with what they knew. But what did they really know about her? Nothing. Once she made it back to London, she wouldn't care. They would never find her, never trace her. From this moment on, she would think nothing more of Joe.

She could not see a convenient way to cross the river and retrieve her bag, so she walked in the direction of its flow, back towards the village. It would not be far. Not once did she peer at the water in search of him. Maybe he was trapped, as she had been, against a boulder, or he was clinging to an overhanging branch. She didn't care. If he had not tried it on with her in his car, none of this would ever have happened.

She had walked another two hundred yards before the river bank met the rear gardens of a row of cottages. At the first, she clambered over a low wall into a garden. From there she hurried across a lawn, through a trellis gate and into a driveway. Soon she was on a road leading to the centre of the village. This time she had difficulty reading either the sign at the road junction or the large board hanging above the door of the Royal Hotel. She dithered. Should she rush inside to reception and ask for help? She needed to get dry. But she must retrieve her bag. Surely, she could last until then. Hurrying along the road where she had encountered Joe and had jumped over the wall, she reached the spot where she had cast off the duvet. It was partially obscured by the fresh snow, but she picked it up and shook it free of the new flakes. Draping it around her, she retraced her steps back down to the wall and to where she had tumbled into the river.

Leaning over, she scanned the trees and bank below in search of her bag. She prayed it hadn't fallen into the river and got washed away. It was difficult to see more than a few yards in the darkness but, edging along the wall, she finally spotted the bag snagged in some branches, resting precariously six feet above the turbulent water. The bank was steep—as she already knew, to her cost—but she must reach her bag. Her entire life depended upon it. She noted the position of each small tree, mostly young ash and silver birch, clinging to the bank between the wall and the river. If she could move from one tree to the next, she might be able to get close enough to grab hold of the bag. She realised that just one slip would mean she wouldn't be able to stop herself from crashing into the river, and this time, there would be no one to save her. Casting off the duvet once again, she raised one leg over the wall, followed by the other. She sat facing the bank of trees and the river below. She reached her right hand outwards while at the same time easing her body from the wall. Her feet slipped on the muddy bank, but she caught hold of a slim tree to steady herself. Once she had a firm grip of the tree, she reached for the next one below her, crouching and sliding her feet downwards. Too soon, she released her hold and her feet continued to slide. Her legs went from beneath her, and she lost control. Frantically, she grasped at earth and branches as she fell. Her feet, once again, met the ice-cold water of the river. She screamed. Her right hand clutched at twigs which quickly snapped from her weight. She was now in the river up to her knees. She clung to a thin off-shoot of a tree. Desperately, she tried to gain a foothold on the riverbank. She raised her feet from the water, praying that her grasp of the branch above would hold. She dug her right foot into the snow, creating a step. It held long enough for her to pull herself upwards using her grip of the branch. She reached for a thin trunk of a silver birch. As she did so, her feet slipped downwards again, but with one hand she managed to grasp the tree.

Above her, cradled between branch and trunk, she saw her precious bag. She dared to pause for breath. Her body trembled with cold and fear; she had lost all feeling in her legs. But she must somehow get to her feet. With her hands and arms wrapped around the slim tree trunk, she straightened her body. She reached a hand towards the bag. One wrong move and she knew it would drop into the river. If she lost it, she thought, she may as well follow it. Fortunately, the strap of the bag was close enough for her to grab hold, and then she tugged. The bag slipped from the branch and swung downwards, striking her leg. She sighed with relief, although now she had still to figure out a route to safety.

To her left, the riverbank was sheer; a few saplings of ash had managed some purchase, but there was no way she could climb to safety by moving in that direction. The slope to her right seemed to flatten out and disappear altogether about thirty yards downstream. The river, of course, was in flood, and much of the level ground was swamped. But it was her only option. Nervously, and ensuring her feet were not in immediate danger of sending her back into the torrent, she reached for a tree to her right and slightly above her. With a few carefully placed steps she managed to grab hold of it, keeping a firm grip with one hand on the tree, her other fastened tightly around the straps of her bag. She repeated this movement for the next tree and the next, eventually reaching a point where the slope was less treacherous and she was able to scramble up the bank to where it met the road. When she had climbed over the wall, she re-traced her steps. It was no more than fifteen yards. Once again she gathered the duvet from the snow and wrapped it around her shoulders. She didn't think she would ever feel warm again.

CHAPTER 24

The blizzard had resumed, but she plodded on into the vague whiteness, praying that the miles would fall away and dreaming of a seat on a warm train to London. Her legs ached with every step, her knee still felt stiff and her toes had lost all feeling, as her feet squelched in wet boots pressing into the snow. Minutes seemed like hours. She tried not to check the time on her watch. It only made her feel worse. It was tempting to seek help at the next house she came to, but for a long time there were none to be seen. She wondered if she would have been fine staying at Sandra's cottage. Sandra would have taken her side and protected her from Joe's accusations. She no longer had to worry about him, but her survival of this night remained in doubt.

She read the sign. *Matterdale End.* Not a village, more a settlement of houses on a bend in the road. There were no lights to be seen in any of the windows. Cars parked in driveways were buried in snow. Which house should she choose? Who within this place might help her? Filled with self-doubt which was rapidly becoming regret, she passed through the hamlet and continued on the empty road. The snow had abated once again, and she saw, in the clear night, that the higher hills were now more distant. But the road seemed to stretch to oblivion. Rounding each bend, she hoped to see a sign for Penrith, another hotel or a waiting bus, but she saw only the country road, covered in deep snow.

She came to a metal gate at the side of the road and threw her arms over it to rest. Her tears resumed, and she had to hold onto the gate to stop herself from collapsing to the ground. Cradling her head in freezing hands, she heard a distant rumble, the sound of a vehicle muted by the surrounding snow. When she looked up she saw it was a lorry, yellow lights flashing on its roof. A plough was fixed to the front, and the road she had just walked was now swept clear of a night's snowfall. Without a thought, she stepped into the middle of the road and waited for the lorry to reach her. Brakes hissed and squeaked as the huge vehicle came to a stop only a few feet from where she stood. She dropped to her knees. The driver climbed down and rushed towards her.

She reached out two hands, her precious bag still by her side.

'Are you all right, love?'

Dressed in warm, water-proof gear, a high-vis anorak, heavy-duty boots and leggings, he was a stocky man with metal-rimmed glasses and looked about fifty. He wore a dark bobble hat, and his hands were warm to touch. He raised her gently to her feet.

'What are you doing way out here? What happened?'

She struggled to speak through her sobs, so grateful for human contact and the thought that now she was safe.

'I got stranded in the snow. Up in the hills.'

'You could have died out here. You're freezing. Let's get you into the cab.' Taking her by the arm and lifting her case, he led her to the nearside door and helped her climb into the cab of the lorry. He closed the door behind her. It was so warm inside, she saw steam rising from her wet dress. Rock and roll music blared from the stereo. The driver switched it off as he climbed into his seat.

'I'll turn up the heat,' he said. 'We need to get you warm, darlin'. I've some soup in a flask. It'll make you feel better. I'm supposed to go left at Troutbeck, but I think you should get to a hospital.' He poured a thick-looking broth into a plastic cup and handed it to her.

She managed a couple of mouthfuls, but she had to tell him now.

'No hospital. I'll be fine. If you can drop me at the station I have to catch a train for London.'

'No trains running at the minute, love. Are you sure you're all right?' He handed her a *Snickers* bar. 'Get that into you, it'll give you some energy. I'd be worrying that you're suffering from hypothermia.'

'I'll be fine, honestly. Thank you for stopping.'

'No problem. How long have you been walking?'

She wiped tears away with her damp sleeve.

'Why didn't you stop for help at a house or a pub?'

She couldn't answer his questions. She didn't know the answers.
How long? How far? Why? She could never tell him the whole story.
All she wanted was to get warm and then get on a train to London.

CHAPTER 25

She had merely to endure the driver's bland conversation for an hour and a half while he completed his route, clearing snow and spreading grit. He talked about the weather, the worst he had ever seen; he talked about his home, how it overlooked Lake Windermere, and he spoke of the summer deluge of tourists, the congested roads and the overcrowded pubs. When it brought him close to Penrith, he abandoned his route and drove her to the station. The time was six-fifteen. She would have to check on the time of the first train to London and hope that the trains were even running in the adverse weather.

'Well, Alex, get home safely. Don't go wandering in the snow for a while.'

'I won't, thank you so much.'

She climbed down from the lorry, her feet once again sinking into deep snow. A chill wind caught her legs, her tights were ripped and her dress not long dry from the heater in the cab of the lorry. Holding firmly to her bag, she tramped to the station entrance. She felt safer, aware that the driver had waited to see if she had got inside the station building and out of the cold. If not, she was sure he would invite her back inside his cab to wait. Fortunately, the station was open. Several people were seated inside, awaiting the first trains of the morning. She felt secure among other people, albeit perfect strangers. Her main concern was that the London train would be running.

There was little heat in the entrance hall of the station as she looked around for a noticeboard showing news that trains were operating on schedule. She realised that to the people waiting along with her, she must look an absolute sight. No coat, ripped tights, wet boots, dishevelled hair and face and, bizarrely, a flowery duvet wrapped around her shoulders. She shivered in the hallway but wasn't tempted to venture onto the platform. According to an updating departure board, she had another two hours to wait.

A girl, probably late teens, smiled at her as if she understood her plight. The girl could never imagine half of what she'd been through. Well-muffled in a padded anorak, pink scarf and bobble hat, she wore black, suede, over-the-knee boots on top of her jeans. Her face looked tiny and child-like, ensconced in hat and scarf, her nose reddened from the cold. She managed to return the girl's smile, and it prompted the girl to speak.

'Wild morning.'

'Terrible. I just hope the trains are running.'

'The train to Carlisle is half an hour late so far. Where are you going?'

'London.'

'Don't know about that one.'

'It left Glasgow on time,' said a young man in a heavy anorak and balaclava. 'The snow's not so bad up there.'

She nodded acknowledgement.

'I've never been to London,' said the girl. 'I'd love to go.'

She smiled her understanding of the girl's longing but made no reply.

'I've been to Manchester and Glasgow and Ibiza but not London.'

She was aware of the girl examining her appearance, looking her up and down.

'Did you get stranded in the snow?' the girl asked.

She nodded once. Her enthusiasm for any conversation had already waned.

'The same thing happened to me two years ago. Up on Scafell. Duke of Edinburgh's Award. We had to take shelter in our tents until we got rescued. Nobody got hurt or anything, but it was scary.'

The automatic door at the entrance slid open and a man entered. He was well-dressed for the cold and carried a briefcase. The distraction allowed her to edge away from the girl and to feign interest in the updates on the departures board. Her back was facing the door when a woman entered the station.

'Hello again, Alex.'

In horror, she turned to face the person who had just greeted her by name.

'Sandra? What are you doing here?'

The pregnant woman stood before her with a sympathetic smile. She was dressed in a long, waxed jacket and fleece-lined boots, and she held Alex's coat and a plastic carrier bag in her hands.

'You left without your coat. I thought you might need it.'

'Thank you.' She took the coat from Sandra and handed over the duvet. 'I'm sorry I had to take this.'

'No matter. I'm glad it came in useful.' Sandra reached her the plastic carrier bag. 'I put a change of clothes inside—in case you were soaking wet. And I made some sandwiches. I'm sure you must be starving.'

'Thank you, but you didn't have to do this. How did you know I'd be here?'

The young girl had moved closer, keen to hear what was being said. It unnerved Alex, but Sandra was oblivious to the girl's presence.

'You said that you needed to catch the train to London. I took the chance when the weather cleared a bit. I drove the Range Rover down. I saw you getting out of the gritting lorry.'

'But…'

'You don't have to say anything, Alex. I don't want to know your business. I'm just relieved that you made it here safely.'

'I'm so sorry for all the trouble I've caused, but I couldn't face him when he called at your house.'

'I understand. But I would never have let him come near you. Not after what you'd told me. Richard and I know Joe and his girlfriend from the bowling club. He's not exactly a close friend.'

'Did he come after me?'

'Yes, but I assume he didn't find you. He's probably at home, tucked up in bed.'

She doubted that Joe had made it home, but she was not going to tell Sandra what had happened at the river.

'Thank you so much, Sandra.'

'Take care, Alex. Get home safe.'

Sandra turned and left. Alex saw the Range Rover sitting outside, its engine still running, the headlights shining through the falling snow.

'The toilets are over there,' said the young girl.

'Thank you,' she replied.

Sandra's clothes were not a perfect fit, a little big for her, but at least they were dry and clean. She pulled on a pair of black leggings and a blue animal-print tunic. There was also a pair of trainers at the bottom of the bag. She decided not to wear them until she had boarded the train. Her coat was dry; she pulled it on and wrapped her scarf around her neck. Welcome though it was, her coat did not feel as warm as the duvet had been. She wondered what Sandra would think of her when she learned of Joe's death in the river. Would she blame her? Would she tell the police what she knew about the woman who had called at her house in the middle of the night?

At two minutes past eight o'clock, she boarded a first-class carriage on the London train.

Chapter 26
Twenty-Four Hours Earlier

The aroma of toast and coffee drifted up to the bedroom. Her lover had risen early. She smiled to herself and rolled from her side onto her back. Slowly, she opened her eyes. Her entire body tingled pleasantly from the warmth and comfort of her bed. She wallowed in the recent memory of a night spent in the arms of her lover. Rather than sliding out of bed, she longed for the woman she loved to return so they could repeat what they had shared. An evening spent by an open fire, South Australian red wine and Schumann's Third Symphony warming them inside. And this followed by the rapture of slipping into bed together, naked in the darkness of the bedroom, illuminated only by the light of a half-moon shining through the dormer window. From gentle caresses to the rigours of full passion, they had enjoyed each other until they fell into sleep. Already, she longed for the next time.

Soon though, it was clear that her lover was not intent on returning to bed. Their desires were not always in perfect synchrony. Reluctant to abandon the warmth of the duvet, she reached for her phone sitting on the bedside table. She checked her messages. It was not unusual for them to communicate by text even when in the same house. But there were no messages, no love notes or emojis. Just after eight o'clock, a grey dawn having taken hold of the landscape, an autumn scene of rusted bracken and faded greens, she rose from the bed naked and stood by the window. The room was cold; it made the day outside seem even colder. Maybe she could coax her lover back to bed. They had no plans for the day, a walk perhaps, but nothing more.

Her hand reached for the handle of the bedroom door, and she pulled it open. Then she heard the voice below in the kitchen. She paused to listen. Her lover was speaking on her phone.

'Yes. I'll see you tomorrow,' she said. 'No. No, I haven't told her yet. I'm waiting for the right time. I have the cash—and the codes. I'll have them with me when I see you. I'm catching the train to London at three minutes past five. No, she won't be with me. I'll have to go. I'll see you tomorrow in Malaga.'

She heard her lover giggle.

'I can't, she'll hear me,' she said, chuckling. 'Love you too, bye,' she whispered.

It was still loud enough for her to hear.

She could not pretend to understand any of the conversation she had just heard. Deep confusion descended upon her in the cold of the room. What should she do? Pretend that she had not heard? Carry on as if nothing was wrong? She had heard one side of a conversation, yet so much had suddenly changed. The meaning to her life had altered completely. Who had been on the other end of the phone? Still naked, she stepped into the narrow landing of the cottage and padded downstairs.

'Morning,' she chirped, as cheerfully as she could manage.

'Good morning, Sheena. Would you like some toast?'

'Great, and some coffee please. I could smell it from upstairs—wonderful.'

She climbed onto a wooden stool at the breakfast bar and couldn't help a worried stare into her lover's face. She could tell nothing from the gaze returned. It was a mask of innocence.

'I really came down to ask you back to bed,' Sheena said, trying hard to keep the confused emotion from cracking her voice.

'Sounds great, darling, but I have a lot of things to do today.'

Sheena was cold now, sitting naked in the kitchen, watching Alex pour coffee into a mug for her. She could see that her lover was naked beneath the gold silk wrap, her voluminous breasts straining the cloth, erect nipples apparent in the cold kitchen.

'What sort of things?'

Alex set the coffee and a slice of toast in front of her. She slid a butter dish across the counter and reached her a knife. Sheena noted the flicker in her lover's eyes. She seemed nervous, and she had not yet answered her question.

'What sort of things, Alex?'

'I've got to get back to London this evening.'

'What for? I thought we were staying here all week?'

'I know, we were, but something's come up.'

'What's so urgent it can't wait till next week?'

'Just business.'

'What business, Alex? I'm your partner, for goodness sake. Why aren't you telling me? I can come down to London with you.'

'No, Sheena. You stay here. It's something I have to sort out on my own.'

Distractedly, Sheena spread some butter on her toast and tried hard to think of what could be so important in their business that would cause Alex to rush away, leaving her alone in a cottage in the middle of nowhere. And to whom had Alex been speaking on the phone? Why was she going to Malaga? And to whom had she just said I love you?

CHAPTER 27

'What codes, Alex?'

'I'm sorry?' Alex ran fingers from both hands through her deeply auburn hair, pushing it backwards, then lifted her mug from the bench and drank some coffee. She was older than Sheena by four years, but the two women often passed as twin sisters, so similar were their looks, stature and style. On several occasions, merely for fun, they had dressed in identical clothes and gone out clubbing. This morning, Alex's brown eyes were full of concern, her heavy lashes at times rested on her cheeks and her mouth seemed taut. Not her best look, thought Sheena. But Alex was stalling. Sheena probed further.

'I heard you talking on the phone. Whoever you were speaking to, you told them that you had the cash and the codes. What codes?'

'Please, Sheena, don't do this. It's not what you think.'

'And what do I think, Alex? What am I supposed to think? That you're doing business behind my back? That you're intending to meet someone in Malaga tomorrow? Someone you love?'

Alex dropped her head and drew a long breath, her chest rising then falling. When she spoke her voice was reduced to a whisper.

'I'm sorry that you heard any of that. It wasn't supposed to happen this way.'

'What wasn't supposed to happen this way, Alex?' Sheena was freezing cold, the coffee doing nothing to warm her. She sat naked on the kitchen stool waiting for the person she loved more than anything in the world struggle to reveal the truth, a truth that she did not wish to hear. Alex regained some strength and finally managed to look her partner in the eyes.

'I'm sorry, Sheena, really I am. I didn't want you to find out this way. I'm dissolving the business, our partnership.'

'And what about us? You're dissolving us, too?'

'I think it's best if we make a clean break.'

Sheena leaped from the stool and squared up to her lover. Their faces were only inches apart.

'Who is she, Alex?'

'It doesn't matter. You don't know her.'

'Of course it bloody matters. You're leaving me for someone else. You're taking God knows what, closing our business, and you can't even tell me her name.'

Sheena lifted the bread knife from the bench. She didn't know, or wasn't conscious, of what she might do with it, but Alex gasped in fright.

'Sheena! Please don't do this. Calm down. I'm sorry for upsetting you, but we're over.'

'Who is she, Alex?' Sheena was yelling. 'Tell me her name!'

'Ella! Her name is Ella!' Alex screamed back. 'Are you happy now?'

Tears streaked down her lover's face, but Sheena was incensed. She lashed out. The knife swiped across Alex's chest. It cut open the silk gown and drew blood on her left breast. Alex cried out and reeled backwards.

'And what about me, Alex? What am I supposed to do now?' Sheena brandished the knife in front of her. Alex drew her arms protectively across her body.

'Please, Sheena. You'll be fine. I've put money in your account. You're free to do what you want.'

'But I want you, Alex! I only want you!' Both women sobbed, one in fear, the other in desperation.

'We're finished, Sheena. I'm so sorry.'

'Don't say that!' She swiped again with the knife. It caught Alex across her right forearm. Alex screamed in pain as the red gash expelled blood that dripped onto her gown.

But Sheena realised that she'd crossed a threshold. She couldn't stop herself. She slashed again with the knife. Alex drew back.

'Please, Sheena, don't do this! We built a business together, surely that still means something.'

'Not to you, apparently.' Sheena swiped at her lover, the blade catching her left shoulder, ripping the silk gown from her skin. Alex screamed and moved further back until she met the wall. She had nowhere to go.

'And what about you, Sheena? Don't forget where you came from. You were nothing but a hooker when I found you. I gave you a fresh start, a new life. Is this how you want to repay me?'

Sheena yelled as if she wanted to bring the roof down upon them.

'I want you to love me,' she cried.

'I can't, not anymore. I'm going to be with Ella.'

Tears, panic and loss of control drove her on. Sheena swung her arm wildly. The knife cut Alex across her face, and blood seeped from the gash on her cheek. Yet another swipe snagged her gown and tore it open. Sheena was beyond reason. Alex screamed, trying to fend her off with flailing hands.

Sheena ripped then pulled the gown from her body. The two women faced each other naked. Alex was drenched in her own blood. She tried to move around the kitchen to a spot where she might find refuge. But Sheena was the stronger of the two women. With anger and rage on her side, Sheena blindly swung the knife back and forth. Alex staggered, battling to remain on her feet, struggling to avoid the blade. Sheena howled. She saw Alex's legs buckle and, for one final time, she lunged with the knife. It sank into Alex's back, and she crumpled to the floor.

Sheena stood over her body, the knife in her hand, yelling in anguish at what she had done.

CHAPTER 28

Sheena awoke with a start, freezing cold. Seated at the breakfast bar, she had passed out, her head and shoulders slumped over the breakfast crockery. As she raised her head, she saw the knife—dull stainless steel marked with blood, and the flesh of her lover caught within the serrated edge. She winced as she straightened her back. Suddenly, the realisation of what had happened gripped her. She turned quickly on the stool, and her elbow knocked a half-full coffee mug across the bench, the cold liquid dripping to the floor. She gasped at the sight of Alex's still body lying on the floor. Her flesh was deathly pale. The tiled floor was smeared in blood, and the silk robe lay in a heap where she had ripped it from Alex's defenceless body. She lay face down. Her arms, having reached out to break her fall, had floundered on the floor, her bloodied hands now resting above her head. Her legs sat askew, and there were several gashes across her buttocks. Dark blood had spewed from the stab wound on her left shoulder blade, and a trail of blood ran to the floor where it had gathered in a small pool. Dead. She must be, Sheena thought, but she didn't dare approach the body of the woman she had loved. The woman she still loved. The woman who had broken her heart. She cried helplessly for what she had done, her tears dripping onto her own naked legs.

The kitchen still held the aroma of toasted bread, and it made her feel sick. She bounded to the back door and opened it wide. She stepped outside. The chilled air swept across her blood-stained body, sending a shiver down her back and into her legs. But instantly, she felt revived, as if a veil was lifted, as if a spotlight was now shining upon her, signalling a new beginning. It was her life now. Hers alone. She hadn't asked for it, or wished it to be this way, but the cold wind blowing across her bare flesh struck her with the realisation that she was now on her own. Self-preservation was a trait she had always known, the only virtue ever apparent in her turbulent life. She stepped back inside the cottage and closed the door. Standing in the centre of the kitchen, gazing around her, she began to make a mental list of the things to be done.

Questions came at her in quick succession, each one begging an answer. For the moment, she had none. Her life had just been hit by a wrecking ball. So far, she was conscious only of being able to stand on two feet. The silence of the house unnerved her. She had a sudden fear that someone would soon call. They would find her here. They would find her with the body of her lover sprawled on the floor. She would spend the rest of her life in prison. She must act now. She had fought Alex; she would fight to survive. Struggle was all she had ever known.

Making sure both the front and back doors were locked and the curtains were drawn, she went upstairs and stepped into the shower. The water was instantly hot. It stung like pinpricks on her skin, but it quickly washed away the bloodstains on her hands, arms, chest and legs. It flushed away the smeared tears on her face, and soon she felt warm and revived. Finally, she applied some body-wash cream, expensive stuff bought by Alex. For six years she had been so used to showering with her lover that it felt strange now to be spreading the cream over her body all by herself. She rinsed it off and stepped from the shower onto the tiled floor of the bathroom. With a soft towel, she padded herself down until she was dry. Then she cleaned the shower cubicle thoroughly and folded the towel, hanging it over a chrome rail.

By now her mind had processed all urgent objectives, but ignored the mystery of why Alex had intended to leave her. She knew exactly what she must do for the remainder of this day. There would be no going back, no getting sucked under to drown in pools of guilt.

In the bedroom, she spread the duvet across the bed and fluffed the pillows on both sides. Next she removed Alex's suitcase from the bottom of the double wardrobe. All furniture in the cottage was relatively new and made mostly of brushed pine. No real homely feel about it but more than adequate for a holiday home. Alex had surprised her when, four days earlier, she had invited her here then told her that she had bought the place for them. A quiet spot where they could escape London and all its pressures. She had been delighted though confused, since Alex had always favoured an escape to the sun, to Spain or France. She realised now that the purchase of the cottage was not the only thing Alex had kept as a surprise.

The suitcase was empty. She retrieved a smaller case from the wardrobe, a black leather overnight bag that Alex used for carrying her laptop, a few files, her washbag and sometimes a change of clothes. It was the type of bag easily carried onto a plane as hand luggage. Judging by its weight, however, this bag was far from empty. When she unzipped it she gasped at the sight before her. Inside were bundles of cash, twenties, tens and five-pound notes. Despite the fact that she was still naked and growing cold once again, she tipped the money out of the case onto the floor and began to count it. There were wrapped bundles of twenty-pound notes. Removing the paper band around one of them, she counted 200 notes, amounting to £4000. Arranging the similar bundles together, she counted another fourteen. Added together, that made £60,000. Another bundle appeared to consist only of ten-pound notes, and she estimated the total of those to be £2000. There were also loose notes of fives, tens and twenties. Added together, she counted another £800. Her final total came to £62,800. She wondered if there was any significance to this amount. She tried hard to think of her last look at the company accounts, of her personal account and of Alex's account. She couldn't think of anything relating to a value of £62,800. It didn't take her long to realise that while she had always trusted Alex, her trust had been misplaced. Alex may have had this money lodged in another account, or she may have just come into possession of it. Sheena struggled with all the questions associated with her discovery but soon decided that her thinking was merely delaying her immediate objective: to get away from this cottage. To reach safety. To go somewhere that she could not be found. Then she could deal with all of the mystery.

Also inside the bag, Sheena found a buff-coloured, loose-leaf folder. When she opened it, she found several A4 sheets stapled together at the top left-hand corner. It appeared to be a printout of an Excel file. There were columns of numbers, none of which made sense to her. Again, questions swamped her thinking. She recalled hearing Alex say on the phone—to her lover Ella, she now realised—that she had the cash and the codes. Her head pounded from the questions. She must get on. Trying her best to dismiss from her mind the overheard phone conversation, she returned the cash and the files to the bag and closed the zipper.

From a chest of drawers, she pulled out Alex's underwear and tossed it on the bed beside the suitcase. From the pile, she chose a non-padded black bra and black pants and put them on. She and Alex were almost identical in size and build, although Alex had, a few years earlier, opted for some breast enhancement. Although they looked similar in many ways, their taste in clothes was quite different. Sheena had always felt most comfortable in trousers or jeans, with T-shirts, blouses or tunics. Alex was fond of wearing skirts and dresses, and she had a penchant for expensive shoes.

Sheena went to the open wardrobe; her clothes hung on the right, Alex's on the left. She chose one of Alex's dresses, a black, mid length, long-sleeved dress. It was perhaps the plainest-looking dress that she owned, but it would be the warmest for travelling in the cold weather. From the pile of underwear on the bed she selected a pair of black lace tights. She was also intent on wearing Alex's black, suede knee-high boots, which lay in the corner of the bedroom.

When she had finished dressing in Alex's clothes, she packed the remainder of her lover's belongings into the suitcase. Everything she could find in the cottage that belonged to Alex, she would take with her. She would leave her own clothes behind.

Once the bedroom and bathroom were cleared of Alex's belongings, she stood before a full-length mirror and examined herself closely. The clothes were so obviously Alex, smart and expensive. Her height, in the three-inch, block-heeled boots, was slightly taller but not something to be concerned about. Her hair, at the moment, was of a different colour and styling to Alex. When she got back to London she could put that right. To all intents and purposes, she could pass herself off as her lover Alex Chase.

CHAPTER 29

Downstairs, in the open-plan kitchen and living room of the cottage, she avoided the naked body lying on the floor by the breakfast bar. In a determined manner, she set about cleaning the room of any traces of her own presence. She washed the dishes from breakfast and wiped down the work surfaces and the handles of pots, pans, crockery and cutlery, including the knife she had used to kill Alex. Her only concessions to wiping the place clean were to make some fresh coffee and to switch on the heating. The entire house was cold, and when she gazed out the window she saw, with some trepidation, that it was starting to snow.

She pondered on how best to leave the cottage. Alex had planned to travel by train to London. She'd overheard her telling this to Ella on the phone. She would use Alex's reservation. Alex's handbag lay on the floor beside the sofa. She emptied it by turning it upside down, and the contents bounced onto the beige carpet. Amongst the lipstick, mascara and tissues, there were a few coins, Alex's keys to the office and flat they shared, her pocket diary, her passport and her mobile phone. A small leather purse in black held some banknotes and her bank, credit and various store cards.

Sheena spent ten minutes examining the recent activity on the mobile, searching for clues as to what Alex had been planning, and for information on this other woman, Ella. There were hundreds of texts and WhatsApp messages between the pair. Some of them were intimate exchanges, but most were of a practical nature—Alex reporting on where she was and what she was doing and Ella replying in similar fashion. One text, the penultimate message to this woman, hurt Sheena deeply. She had set herself on a course where she would no longer cry for her lover, but this short passage induced tears.

'Last night with Sheena. Has to be done. Soon I'll be lying with you, my darling.'

She threw the phone to the floor. She lifted Alex's pocket diary, but a brief look through its pages told her little. Alex, it seemed, had been meticulous in hiding her secret. Trying to process the myriad of questions coming at her, she began to replace the contents in the bag. Next she gathered several personal items from her own handbag, intending to add them to Alex's bag. She quickly changed her mind, however, deciding that she must leave every one of her belongings behind. If she was to become Alex Chase then the dead Alex must become Sheena Bateman. She resisted the temptation to take her own mobile and even her own bank cards. She retrieved the phone belonging to Alex from the floor and slipped it into a pocket of the coat she intended to wear. She hoped that whoever found the body of her lover would not question that her name was Sheena Bateman. If she was lucky, it would be months before anyone came across the scene of the killing, and she would be long gone. Alex had planned on running away: the only difference now was that Sheena was taking the place of her treacherous lover.

As she was replacing the contents of Alex's handbag, she noticed a business card for a local taxi company, Valley Taxis. Using her newly acquired phone, she called the number of the firm. It soon transpired that Alex had already arranged a pick up.

'Your pick up is at four o'clock,' said the woman.

'Thank you. I'd forgotten what time I'd booked it for.' She ended the call. Everything was arranged.

Her final act in transforming into the persona of Alex Chase was to remove Alex's watch and diamond ring from her body. She had always loved the Cartier La Dona watch that Alex wore. Yellow gold, set with diamonds and a Roman numeral face. She had bought the ring for Alex as a Christmas present a year earlier. It was a round-cut diamond set in platinum. It cost more than she had ever spent on anything in her life, but she had wanted to demonstrate her love for Alex.

Awkwardly, she stooped over the body and tugged the watch from Alex's right wrist. It took more effort to remove the ring from the third finger of her left hand. She struggled to control her breathing and prayed she would not throw up. Alex's hand was cold. She could not bring herself to check if Alex was still breathing. With a trembling hand she finally pulled the ring off her finger.

When she stood clear of the body, she slipped the ring onto her own finger and the watch onto her wrist. Now her transformation was complete. For the next few days, at least, she was Alex Chase.

The taxi pulled onto the sloping drive, pressing tracks into the fresh snow.

She heard the sound of a car horn and, going to the window, she moved the curtain and peered outside. Alex's woollen overcoat hung on a peg in the hallway. She put it on and drew the fur collar around her neck. The coat was a perfect fit and would keep her warm on the journey to London. She found a pair of purple leather gloves in the pockets and pulled them on. Gathering the suitcase and overnight bag, she dared one last look at the stricken body of her lover. She told herself that Alex had merely been a chapter in her life and now it was closed. There would be no more tears and no regrets.

CHAPTER 30

The questions came at her once again. This time, as her train sped south through snow-covered hills and over fields dappled with flood waters, she allowed them in. She tried so hard to process them. Uppermost was the obvious question of why. Why had Alex been unfaithful? Why had she been intending to go away? Why give up her business? Why had she done this to her?

In her mind, too, she was making plans. What should she do when she got back to London? She might get away with playing Alex until she went back to work. Why was she even doing this? Something within her was telling her it was necessary in order to survive—in order to get away with murder. But, according to Alex, the business had gone. Maybe Alex had wound things up before going to the Lake District. It wouldn't have been difficult to do. It wasn't as if they ran a shop or a factory, and that customers would be expecting deliveries. She and Alex had been in a service industry. A service industry for rich and successful people. An escort agency, of sorts: they provided women and men to people willing to pay a lot of money for the privilege of enjoying their company. It was true that she had been little more than a hooker when she first met Alex. Not a street-walker, but a girl willing to sell her talents, her company and her body to wealthy men. She had immediately struck up a friendship with Alex that very soon progressed to an affair and a shared life, in business and in private. Then, three years into their relationship, Alex had left her in charge of the day-to-day affairs of the escort business. Without explaining the details of what she was doing, Alex told her she had found a way to make even more money from their services. They could hit these rich clients for higher sums. Sheena had thought it simply meant they were charging more for their services, but Alex told her that she was embarked on a scheme that would make them millions. Alex spared her the details, but Sheena understood that she meant blackmail. Some of their clients would not be happy to have their sexual proclivities made public and were resigned, though hardly content, to pay Alex to protect their secrets. When Sheena mentioned the word blackmail, Alex scoffed and described her actions as selling her clients insurance against being exposed. Data protection insurance, she had called it. But why had Alex suddenly decided to shut up shop? Had it merely been to accomplish the break with her, or was there something else behind it? The name Ella clawed at her. Of course, she thought: a new life with Ella, a clean slate, an idyllic retirement with more money than Alex knew what to do with. That would have been Alex's intention. And just how much money had she left behind for her? She itched for the train to pull into Euston Station. When she had left the cottage the previous afternoon, she could not have imagined the ordeal that lay before her, caused entirely by that animal taxi driver. But she had come through it and now she had to know what remained of her life. The small bag sat by her side. She could make use of the cash, but what of the numbers on the spreadsheets? Were they her ticket to freedom?

CHAPTER 31
SIX MONTHS LATER

A warm sun of early morning cast its heat on her tanned legs, outstretched on the private balcony. Eight-thirty and already people were going about their business, mostly concerned with enjoying their summer holiday. Several boats moved silently through the canals making for the open sea. Aboard were fit-looking men in shorts and glamorous women in bikinis, dance music thumping from sound systems strategically positioned above the cabins for maximum effect. Where the sunlight had displaced shadows, the colours of each building became apparent: reds, oranges, pale blues and primrose, with white-painted shutters and wrought-iron balconies set above open quays and the striped awnings of restaurants, already open and serving coffee and fresh croissants.

Sheena felt completely at ease in Port Grimaud, a place that agreed with her, a place for soothing the soul. She could happily live here forever. She had taken to smoking, not so much in order to relax but more as an accompaniment to her drinking of strong coffee. It felt appropriate. Bravely, she'd begun with Gitanes then Gauloises, switched to Royale and finally settled on Marlboro. Each morning, she sat on the balcony of her first-floor rented apartment, smoking, drinking coffee and watching the laid-back world of Port Grimaud gently slide by. An hour later she would be showered and dressed in shorts and sleeveless top, and would wander through this peculiarly modern Venice with the architecture of Provence. By mid-morning, she would be seated at her favourite café, at a table under the awning but close to the water's edge, with more coffee and cigarettes and either her laptop or a good novel before her. This was her life for now. She did miss London, the vibrancy of the city and the life she use to have there. It was a life she had shared with Alex, a blissful and exciting time. They had made a lot of money together, and they knew how to spend it well. But darling Alex had brought everything crashing down. She had ruined both their lives forever. Now her lover was dead, and she could never feel safe returning to London.

By the time she had arrived at Euston Station that freezing November morning from Penrith, she had worked out exactly what she must do. She would flee the country before anyone found Alex's body lying in the mountain cottage. She didn't think it would be long. Once the body of Joe the taxi-driver was discovered, his car was found on the lane and Richard and Sandra became involved, the police were bound to pay a visit to the cottage.

From Euston, she rode the Tube to Bayswater and walked only a few hundred yards to the flat she had shared with Alex, just off Queensway on Inverness Terrace. The flat was on the second floor of a four-storey building, a rental only because Alex had never quite got around to buying. She had always intended that, when they'd made enough money, the two of them would leave London for somewhere more exotic. She had never understood what Alex meant by enough money. In recent months there was always a hint of concern in her tone when she talked about it. Now Sheena realised why. Their escort business had been doing well, but Alex thrived on the excitement of taking some clients for a ride, whether by syphoning off their money through inflated charges or purely by blackmail. She had the cheek, of course, to call it her insurance business. Sheena recalled her saying that one day one of her clients would be brave enough to come after her. Four days earlier Sheena had been sitting at her desk in their office in Soho finalising several weekend liaisons between her clients and their escort workers, nothing too exciting: a Saturday night date for a politician with one of their best girls, Kirsty, at a flat in Kensington; a Friday drinks reception for a rich Saudi requiring eight girls; and a rather innocent appointment for one of their girls to be the companion of a rich bachelor at his niece's wedding. Alex had been out of the office all day and Sheena had no idea where she was or what she was doing. Late in the afternoon, she received a text from Alex, a clear instruction. Sheena was to leave the office immediately and take an evening train from Euston to Penrith. A second text provided an address. She was to travel by taxi from Penrith station and Alex would be at the address to meet her. She would explain all when she got there. From the moment Sheena entered the cottage, however, Alex had played down the mystery and the urgency by saying that she had simply wanted to surprise her with their new hideaway, their brand new love-nest. Until that fateful morning when Sheena overheard the phone conversation between Alex and Ella, she had believed all that Alex told her.

She slid the key into the lock and entered the flat at Inverness Terrace. The flat was furnished in contemporary style, mostly to the taste of Alex. Sheena had no real talent for design. It had two bedrooms, one of which was used as a study. There was a lounge, a kitchen and a bathroom. Most nights they worked late at the office and then dined out. They spent weekends ensconced in the flat with newspapers, books, TV, music and takeaway food. Outwardly, it seemed a gentle, uncomplicated existence, and to some of their friends it was the subject of much envy. Few, of course, knew of the secret life of their business dealings and now, as she wandered around her home, fear began to take hold. A fear of what Alex may have been running from, a fear also of what she might now have to flee.

Beyond a brief reminiscence of her years spent with Alex, she wasted no more time. In the study, she went through every document she could lay her hands upon. Bills, correspondence, lists of clients: she downloaded the entire file contents of their shared PC onto a laptop. When she came across papers with her name upon them, she discarded them, removing only those items concerning Alex Chase. She repeated the process with Alex's clothes, her extensive collection of shoes, her jewellery, her books, her CDs. It was well into the evening when she had finished packing. All traces of her lover were ready to be removed from the flat. It would seem as though only Sheena Bateman now lived there, except that Sheena was now taking on the persona of her dead lover Alex and was about to leave the country. She couldn't think of anyone who would dispute that Sheena Bateman had lived at the flat, had travelled to the Lake District and was murdered—probably by a taxi driver named Joe.

She had arranged for a storage company to collect most of Alex's belongings. Next morning two men arrived with a van and took away several cases and boxes. What remained of Alex Chase would go abroad with her. Overnight, she had decided on France, the Côte d'Azur, as her destination. It would be her hideaway, if she dared to call it that.

CHAPTER 32

Within a few days of travelling to Paris by Eurostar, and from Paris south to Nice, Sheena Bateman, living a new life as Alex Chase, was settled into her rented apartment in Port Grimaud with a pleasant view over the main canal. She knew that the cash she had brought with her would not last indefinitely: prior to leaving London, she had decided it was safer not to make any transactions from her own accounts, and that meant leaving behind all of her personal finances. At a bank in Nice she opened a new account in the name of Alex Chase and deposited her cash over a period of weeks, hopefully avoiding any suspicion. When she had checked Alex's accounts—those she knew of, anyway—most of them were already low in funds. She guessed that was where the £62,800 in cash that she had found in the overnight bag at the cottage had come from. She was well aware that Alex had operated other accounts, several of them off-shore. It was to these banks, Sheena believed, that Alex had deposited the income from her dubious 'insurance' activities. Sheena couldn't begin to guess how much money was hidden in this way. All she had was a list of supposed account numbers and access codes set out on a spreadsheet. She didn't know which banks they were associated with, and she certainly didn't know anything about how to gain control of the money.

Seated comfortably beneath the awning in Café Avellino, she spent day after day searching online for information that would lead her to discover a means of getting hold of the fortune that Alex had secretly accumulated. The laptop had belonged to Alex and held all of the files Sheena had downloaded from the computer at their flat in London. Sheena thought that she had full access to all the files within it but soon discovered that Alex had applied a level of security to some folders and files that she had not been aware of. She also discovered that this was the information she needed most. One number, however, that she read from the printed spreadsheet did appear within several files on the computer. An email she came across, over two years old, also made reference to the number. It had come from a bank in Zurich, a simple statement to confirm that the account of number 23236669 had now been opened and was available for use. Sheena's heart leapt at the information. At last she had found a lead. She sent an email to this bank, to a Josef Brunner at Banque Honziker, inquiring after her accounts and quoting two other numbers she had selected from the spreadsheet. She received an immediate reply stating that the two additional account numbers did not relate to any accounts she held at Banque Honziker. She wrote back to Brunner, apologising for her mistake and informing him that she intended to be in Zurich quite soon and would like to review her accounts, and that she hoped to open another. Brunner again replied swiftly, stating that he would, of course, be delighted to assist her in any way possible.

Two weeks later, she drove from Port Grimaud to Nice and took a flight to Zurich. She was now living her life completely as her former lover Alex Chase. Her hair was the style and shade that Alex had worn on the morning Sheena had attacked her with a bread knife. It was a rich auburn colour fashioned into a neat bob. She had the clothes, personal belongings and access to Alex's life; the only thing she didn't have were the secrets of her financial dealings. No one, she believed, was looking for her. No one, she hoped, was looking for a woman by the name of Sheena Bateman either. On first coming to France, she had scoured the daily papers and checked online news reports for information on the deaths of two people in Cumbria during the recent heavy snowstorms. She found nothing. She couldn't care less about the damned taxi driver, but she wondered if anyone had discovered Alex's body in the cottage. It continued to niggle her, always on her mind as she settled into her new life in the south of France. If Alex had been found in the cottage, would the authorities be convinced that the identity of the woman was Sheena Bateman and not Alex Chase? She could find no information that police in England were searching for a woman with either name in relation to murder.

She rode the train from the airport to Zurich Main Station, and from there she walked half a mile to a grey stone building on Bahnhofstrasse that housed Banque Honziker. Inside, the building was every bit as austere as she had imagined from looking at the outside, with black tiled floor, dark wood-panelling and heavy-set furniture. When she asked a receptionist for Josef Brunner, she was invited to sit at a leather sofa next to a coffee table, upon which sat four financial publications, two in English, one French and the other German. She was dressed in the best of Alex's clothes: a brown dress, a woollen coat, sheer tights and brown mid-heel shoes. Suddenly she was struck by the thought that although she might look like Alex, inside she was trembling as Sheena Bateman. If she failed to be convincing here then her new life would very soon unravel. She must keep her nerves in check and project the confidence of Alex Chase. Within a few minutes, a smartly dressed young man stood over her with his hand outstretched. He had short, neatly-cut brown hair, lightly gelled and combed to the left. He wore a royal blue tie and dark grey suit with well-polished black shoes. His face held a polite smile; his eyes were narrow but suited to his fine features and small mouth. She decided that he looked no more than thirty years old.

'Ms Chase, it is a pleasure to see you again. Welcome to Banque Honziker. I hope you are well.' His English, as she had expected, was excellent, and he showed every indication that he recognised her, and had no doubt that it was his client Alex Chase who was slowly getting to her feet.

'I'm very well, thank you.'

'Please, come this way. I'll arrange for some coffee and we can discuss your visit.' She followed him from the lobby through a set of heavy doors and into a silent corridor, with a deep carpet of steely blue running its length. She tried to look as though all around her was familiar, because she had no idea how many visits Alex had made to this building. Brunner showed her into an office housing a secretary, a young woman she guessed to be little more than twenty. The girl greeted her in perfect English, and Brunner proceeded through another doorway into what Sheena assumed was his private office.

'Please, make yourself comfortable, Ms Chase.'

She sat with her legs crossed in one of the two wing-backed red leather chairs opposite Brunner, who occupied an equally impressive desk chair.

'Your journey was good I hope?'

'Yes, thank you.' She tried not to appear self-conscious as images of the naked and bloodied Alex wracked her thoughts. She blinked them away.

'You came from London?'

'Em, no. I'm staying in France at present. Côte d'Azur.'

Brunner appeared to study her for a brief moment, as if surprised by her answer.

'I'm sure it is quite pleasant at this time of year.'

'It is,' she replied, feeling her cheeks warm.

The secretary entered the room carrying a tray.

'Please, have some coffee,' said Brunner. The girl poured from a silver pot into two wide cups.

'Some milk?' she asked.

'Yes please.' The girl added the milk and handed the cup and saucer to Sheena. Brunner was already reaching for his cup. When the secretary left them, Brunner wasted no further time in getting to business.

'How may I be of service to you, Ms Chase?'

'Please, call me Alex,' she was brave enough to say. 'I would like to review all of my accounts and perhaps look to rationalise my affairs. If I could view all of my recent transactions and get your advice on how best to proceed.'

Brunner smiled weakly and turned his eyes from her to the ledger sitting on his desk. His reaction made her feel uncomfortable.

'You do know, Alex that this could have been done without you having to come to Zurich?'

'Yes, I know, but I have other business in the city to attend to.'

'Of course. Let us proceed.' He typed on a keyboard then inspected the information displayed on his screen. From the open ledger, he entered an account number. Then he slid the keyboard across the desk and swung the monitor to face her. 'Now please, your access code.'

She froze.

'Access code?'

'Yes. You have a code for each account and for your safety deposit box.'

'Yes, of course.' She knew she didn't have any such codes in her possession that she could recognise, but she fumbled in her handbag feigning a search. She realised that the spreadsheet she had inside her bag probably held the correct code, but she could hardly go through each number until she found the one she needed. It would take hours. Brunner watched, smiling patiently. She felt herself flush.

'I'm so sorry,' she said, her voice quivering, 'but somehow I have managed to leave home without them.'

'No matter, Alex…'

'I so seldom have the need to use them.'

'I understand perfectly. We can go through a few security questions, and I can retrieve the codes from our side.'

How the hell could she answer questions that only Alex would have known the answers to? She felt the urge to run, to get out now before this man rumbled her and she was arrested. But Brunner appeared unruffled by her predicament and simply retrieved the keyboard, turned the monitor to face him and began to enter information on the bank's computer. She could only look on, praying she knew the answers to whatever questions he presented to her.

'Firstly, your full name?'

'Alexandra Harriet Chase.'

'Date of birth?'

'27 July 1980.'

'And the last address you registered with us?'

She assumed it to be the address in Bayswater, the apartment she and Alex had shared. She couldn't help a sigh of relief when it proved correct.

'First four letters of your mother's maiden name?' She had to think for a moment. Alex had never mentioned her father, nor had she ever said that her parents had been married to each other. But she knew her mother had always used the surname Harper.

She tried to sound confident with her reply. 'H.A.R.P.'

'The name of your favourite teacher at school?' She hesitated. This time she had no clue.

'I'm sorry, but I can't remember ever providing an answer to that question.'

Brunner stared. Now, she thought, he had her sussed.

'The approximate date of your last transaction with this bank?'

She could hardly believe that he had continued. Now she had to think. It was a guess, but she hoped there was good chance that Alex had been doing something with her accounts at least a few days before they'd gone to the Lake District.

'I can't recall the exact date, but I did contact the bank in November last year.'

There was silence in the room, aside from the faint whirring of the fan within the computer.

'Good,' said Brunner. He swung the screen back to face her and offered the keyboard. 'You may log in using one of your account numbers.'

She smiled nervously. Brunner had all of the relevant numbers. She could choose only the one account number that had led her to this bank. From her bag, she produced the small diary belonging to Alex. She found the number and entered it using the keyboard. At last, she would see exactly what her lover had been doing with all the money she had extorted from their clients.

CHAPTER 33

She could feel Brunner's eyes upon her, studying her, perhaps trying to convince himself that she was the Alex Chase he'd met previously. Before her on the screen, and to her dismay, she saw only two accounts registered at Banque Honziker in the name of Alex Chase. One account corresponded to the number she had found on the email and that she had first attributed to this bank. It was a deposit account, showing a current balance of 112,768 CHF. Surely this was not the total fortune that Alex had hidden away? A quick calculation in her head told her it was roughly £84,000. The second account number had a space after it followed by the letter B. She glanced at Brunner. For some reason, she felt he was aware of all of her thoughts.

'Do you require access to your safety deposit box this morning?' he asked.

She guessed then that the second account number, without a balance stated against it but with the suffix B, referred to such a box.

'Yes,' she replied. Immediately her mind addressed the issue of a key for the box. Hopefully, it was among those keys on the bunch she had taken from the cottage.

'Okay, good. When you have finished here I can take you down. You do have your key?'

He smiled, and she realised he was joking since she had already forgotten to bring along her access codes.

A short while later, she stood in a room the colour of gold, the walls with thousands of little brass doors. Behind each one was goodness knows what—the secrets of many people, she presumed. She waited for Brunner to check the account number on a printed sheet and then upon a computer terminal set on a desk in the centre of the room. Then he went to a set of metal drawers, and with an electronic swipe he unlocked the second drawer down. From there he removed a simple mortice lock key and walked to a row of numbered doors in one of the many walled units. He stooped to a door, just one row off the floor, and placed the key into the lock.

'When you are ready, Ms Chase,' he said. She removed a set of keys from her bag, trying to see the type of key Brunner had inserted in the lock. The bunch she held had at least a dozen keys. Some were keys to the flat in Bayswater, some to their office in Soho, one from the cottage in the Lake District and of the remainder she had no idea. Eventually, she found one similar to the one Brunner had used. She made to hand it over, but he stepped back.

'Please, Ms Chase, you must open by yourself.'

Pushing the key into the lock, she twisted and was amazed that it turned over in a single movement. Brunner stepped forward once again; he opened the slim door and pulled out a long metal box.

'This way, please.' She followed him into an adjacent room that contained four wooden stalls. He placed the box on a bench within the first stall and stepped away.

'Please, take your time, Ms Chase. I will be outside when you are ready.'

'Thank you,' she said.

Once he had left the room, she made an attempt to open the box. It soon became apparent that she required her same key to unlock it. When she drew back the lid, she felt nothing but confusion.

CHAPTER 34

Inside the box she found a leather-bound notebook, A5 in size, a loose-leaf folder with several sheets of paper within, and a small black box she assumed was an external storage device for a computer. She hoped this hard drive held all of the information she would ever need to unlock the secrets of Alex Chase. Perhaps it would give her access to the fortune and to the world her mysterious lover had built. Conscious of the bank official waiting outside the room, she quickly glanced through the notebook. There were names, addresses, phone numbers, email addresses and other numbers, messages, dates and financial figures written in no particular order. Inside the folder were a few letters and lists of names, some with numbers set against them. She opened her bag and placed the folder, the notebook and the hard drive inside. Then she closed the metal box, locked it and went to the door. Brunner was standing patiently outside.

'I'm finished,' she said cheerfully, confident now that she had achieved all that she came to do. Brunner fetched the box from the room and returned it to its place in the wall. He invited her to lock the door of the locker, before doing the same with his key. She couldn't help a sigh of relief when the operation was complete.

'Was everything to your satisfaction, Ms Chase?'

'Perfectly, thank you.'

'If there is nothing else, we can return to my office.'

'That won't be necessary, thank you for your help.'

'You are most welcome, Ms Chase. I hope to see you again very soon. Please enjoy your stay in Zurich.' He led her back to the foyer and reached out his hand.

'Good day, Ms Chase.'

'Goodbye and thank you.'

She strode confidently from the Banque Honziker. She had no further business in Switzerland. It was too much of a risk to play the same game with another bank, on the off chance that Alex had accounts there. It was clear that her former lover had spread her wealth and her secrets far and wide. For now, she was impatient to get back to Port Grimaud and to begin work on the information she had acquired.

She was sure that Brunner had his suspicions of her, but what could he do? She presented most of the information he had asked of her. She had account numbers, and she had the key to the safety deposit box. In the end she had walked free from the building, despite her fear that an alarm might sound and a security guard would come after her.

The same day she caught a flight back to Nice, and by late evening had locked herself into her apartment in Port Grimaud. She prepared some coffee, cheese, olives and bread and sat on her balcony with her laptop. The evening was slowly dying of noise from the restaurants below, and the air was warm and still. Despite her anticipation of what she was about to discover on the hard drive, she felt relaxed, drawing on a Marlboro and sipping her strong coffee. She was about to find out if she was set for life. Inserting the USB lead of the external hard drive into the side edge of the laptop, she waited for a list of files to appear on the screen.

There were several named folders visible. She smiled when she noticed the music folder, and she double-clicked the icon to open it. She was moved to see some of the music displayed that she had shared with Alex during their years together. They both had eclectic tastes, from pop to classical, folk and rock. Alex loved the great piano pieces of Chopin, Grieg and Tchaikovsky, while she preferred Mozart, Schumann and Haydn. They had spent hours dancing to Robbie Williams, Michael Jackson and the Backstreet Boys in their bedroom at Bayswater. Amongst their favourite live performances they had seen together were U2, The Foo Fighters, The Rolling Stones, Liam Gallagher and countless others. She couldn't help tears welling in her eyes, and it prompted her to move onto another folder. Viewing the pictures they had taken together on their travels didn't help to stem the tears. Photographs of them in New York, LA, Paris and Spain evoked tender memories, but it was all too much to bear. She grew impatient with herself to find what she really wanted. When she clicked on a folder marked 'property', she drew a sharp breath.

CHAPTER 35

She instantly realised the significance of the folder. There were three sub-folders within it. One was named 'clients', another 'correspondence' and the third folder had no name. She double-clicked on the 'clients' folder. She expected it to contain details of each of their clients, but she wondered if it would also have information relating to Alex's other business activities. Each file name within the folder corresponded to a client's name, and she marvelled at the list they had accumulated. Many of them, most of who were men, although there were at least a dozen women, were well-known people. There were several MPs, a former cabinet minister, dignitaries from the Middle East, Russian millionaires and billionaires, celebrities, clergy and legal professionals. Most of the people on the list were the low-profile rich—they had money to spend, but lived their lives below the media radar.

Within each file, there were personal details of the client, including their preferences for women, men, voyeurism, domination or simply the company of an escort. Many services were, of course, purely of a promotional nature, where girls or boys were provided to populate a party or an event simply to enhance its glamour, or to work at front-of-house. Those clients with more sordid requirements drew Alex's attention—those were the people, she believed, who were ripe for the picking. Sheena had always thought it remarkable that despite being blackmailed by Alex, such clients continued to use her services. Alex, of course, never referred to what she was doing as 'blackmail' directly. She merely offered security and confidentiality as an additional service, and while many seemed content to pay, those that did not would discover to their cost that their guilty secret had found its way into the press. Sheena had never known it to happen, but she put that down to Alex's ability to convince clients they were doing the right thing by paying extra for a discrete service. Alex chuckled and called it data protection.

Apart from the basic details of each client, Sheena could find no information in these files on the financial arrangements between them and Alex Chase. The folder named 'correspondence', however, provided interesting reading. Mostly emails, these files contained sleazy details of what some clients intended to do with their escort. There were also several emails directed at Alex. These had a very different tone. Some expressed dissatisfaction that the service provided by the escorts did not fully satisfy their needs. Some emails were threatening, angry and full of warning. She stopped reading after one email had asked Alex if she knew what acid could do to her smug little face. This brought Sheena to think again of what Alex had been trying to do when she closed down the business. Was she frightened? Had she been trying to run? The horrible image of her lover lying naked and bleeding on the kitchen floor of the cottage once again flooded her mind. Had she killed someone who was simply trying to escape her fears? Maybe this Ella was only a bluff, an easy way for her to break up their relationship by pretending she had found someone else. Suddenly the night air felt stuffy and warm. She felt closed in, trapped by her own raging thoughts. From what had Alex run away? She flipped down the lid on the computer and went straight to bed.

The morning sunlight streaked through the window, and as she blinked awake the sudden brightness stung her eyes. Her throat was parched; the last thing she had done the night before was smoke. She had eaten only once since leaving Zurich and had drunk only coffee when she got back to the apartment. She felt nauseous. It was hard to believe that she felt worse now than when she had struggled through deep snow in the Lake District and almost drowned in a freezing river. A fear she had not felt since that night returned, tightening her stomach and leaving her head in such turmoil that she couldn't think straight. Guilt, fear, unease and uncertainty: she couldn't say what bothered her most, but this morning, for the first time, she didn't feel comfortable living in Port Grimaud.

After a shower, she put on a long, off-the-shoulder beach dress, gathered her bag and laptop and ventured outside. At Café Avellino, as was her habit, she chose a table close to the edge of the quay where the breeze was more apparent. She needed to rid herself of the claustrophobia she had felt the night before. The table was under the shade of the café's awning, and there were only three or four other customers. She ordered a breakfast of goat's cheese, figs, honey, courgette, toast and strong coffee. By the time she had finished eating, she was feeling more relaxed. A cigarette and a second cup of coffee helped dispel the paranoia that had swept through her. When the waitress had cleared away the plates, Sheena set the laptop on the table, switched it on and connected the external hard drive. Immediately, she returned to the set of files she had opened in her apartment the night before.

She opened the folder marked 'property' and then the sub-folder that did not have a name. Within this folder, she was presented with an array of more than twenty sub-folders, each of them labelled with a client's name. The first one she opened held a large number of jpeg images. Out of curiosity, and realising that she had known so little of the business Alex had been operating, she opened the photo browser and looked at each of the images. She ordered another coffee, resigned to spending her morning here with her computer and her confused thoughts.

Many of the images were pornographic. They didn't shock her. What surprised her was that Alex had arranged for them to be taken. She had spied on their clients' liaisons with the escorts she had supplied. Alex had used these pictures in order to sell 'data protection insurance' to her clients. It was blackmail, pure and simple. There were several older pictures, taken in the early days of their partnership, where she or Alex had been the featured girl in the company of a treasured client. The images were sufficiently revealing so that there would be no mistake if ever they were made public. Among the picture files, she came across several video clips recording clients in the company of an escort. Some of these were very explicit, but in each and every one the identity of the client was clear. Alex had been very cunning.

Sheena grew bored scrolling through the decadent activities of rich people, and of those hired to pander to their sexual proclivities. She guessed that there were hundreds of these files stored on the external hard drive. If all of them had led to blackmail, it was no wonder that Alex had made so much money. It was clear also why she had hidden the evidence in the vault of a Swiss bank.

As she lit another cigarette and ordered another coffee, Sheena found a collection of more personal photographs within the client files. No doubt Alex had simply dumped them there in order to keep them together, as one might do with physical prints by putting them in an album. Many of the pictures were of Alex alone, professionally taken, looking much younger and very pretty. She smiled at the few of her with Alex, some quite explicit, snapped on a mobile phone, and others of the two of them at parties. She was about to abandon this folder when she spied a number of pictures of Alex, again quite explicit, but none that Sheena could recall having seen before. Her mind raced with possibilities of who could have taken them. She thought of the woman Alex had finally told her of that morning in the cottage: Ella. She checked the date associated with one of the jpeg files. It was less than a year old. The month was September, which meant they had been taken only a few weeks before Sheena and Alex had stayed at the cottage in the Lake District. The memory brought tears to her eyes as she gazed at several more of the pictures. She looked at a beautiful woman seated beside Alex in a restaurant, then another of the same woman alone, posing and laughing, and finally, the most hurtful of all, Alex and this girl lying on the bed in the flat in Bayswater that Sheena had shared with her. It was humiliating to learn that Alex and this girl had slept in her bed. She had known nothing of the affair until that horrific morning in the Lake District.

Sheena was shaken from her thinking by a woman's voice.

'Pardon, Madame, vous avez une lumière?'

CHAPTER 36

Sheena was scarcely aware of the person to whom she was handing her lighter. Her mind was still concentrated upon the images on her laptop screen. When she looked up, the girl was smiling, her mouth wide and her teeth perfectly white. She had a thin face, not well-tanned but showing a touch of sun, a long nose and dark eyes. The most striking feature of this girl—in her mid-twenties, Sheena guessed—was her long mane of frizzy dark brown hair. At first Sheena was reminded of a Hollywood actress, but for the moment the name eluded her. The girl lit her cigarette and set the lighter back on the table.

'Merci,' she said, staring into Sheena's eyes.

Sheena smiled weakly and quickly averted her gaze. The girl returned to her chair at the next table but one. Only then did Sheena begin to observe her. She sat nonchalantly, her feet resting on a chair, a thick novel in one hand and the cigarette in the other. When she thought the girl wasn't looking, she continued to look at her. She had not seemed tall when standing by her table, but now Sheena saw that her legs were long and slender. Her denim shorts were cut to her crotch, and her faded orange vest covered the merest swellings of breasts. Sheena couldn't help feeling attracted. Very soon, though, her mind returned to the computer screen. She had tired of the compromising images of former clients and quickly browsed the other folders in the hope of finding information that would be more useful to her. Periodically, she glanced over the girl as she read her book. She saw that the novel had an English title and concluded that the pretty girl who had spoken to her in French was probably not French. Anne Hathaway, Sheena thought—that was the actress she resembled.

Once again, Sheena tried to concentrate upon the information she was scrolling through on her computer screen, but she couldn't help herself from watching the girl. Just as Sheena lit up a cigarette, the girl left her table and came towards her once again.

'Sorry, can I get another light?' she asked in English with the hint of a foreign accent.

Sheena smiled warmly this time and handed over her lighter.

'You can keep it,' she said. 'I have another.'

'Thank you, that's very kind.' The girl lit her cigarette, but remained by the table.

'Working hard?' she asked.

Instinctively, Sheena folded down her screen. Then she forced a smile. The girl returned the smile. Sheena felt a strong physical attraction, and with it came her innate shyness.

'I'm just browsing,' she replied. 'Are you enjoying your holiday?'

'Not really on holiday,' said the girl, taking a pull on her cigarette. 'Perhaps a holiday, but a prolonged one.'

Sheena noticed the girl's slightly awkward phrasing. She sounded American, and yet she didn't feel that English was the girl's first language.

'I am a writer,' she added. Without invitation, she sat down opposite Sheena. 'And you? A writer also?' She nodded towards the laptop.

'Oh me, no. I'm just looking through a few old files. Do you write novels?'

'No. I am a scientist. I write mainly on the environment.'

Sheena beckoned the waitress and ordered another coffee. She felt nervous; it was something to do other than to stare at the girl and ask dull questions.

'Would you care to join me?'

'Thank you.'

'Two coffees please,' said Sheena to the waitress.

The girl smiled and went to fetch her bag and the book she had been reading.

'I am Verity,' she said on her return.

Sheena was surprised by the girl's very English name.

'A lovely name, but am I right in thinking you are not English?'

'I am half French-Canadian, but I have lived in London for five years. My father works for a Canadian Bank. The name Verity was given to me by my English mother. My grandmother was called Verity. It is Old English; it means truth.'

Verity paused and smiled brightly. Only then did Sheena realise that she hadn't given her name.

'Pleased to meet you, Verity. I'm Alex.' With a bit of a giggle the two women shook hands across the table.

'Are you on holiday, Alex?'

'Like you, I suppose, a rather prolonged one.'

'And what do you do?'

Sheena hesitated. What did she do, now that her business with the real Alex Chase was no more?

'Nothing much at the moment. I've just sold my business, and I'm considering doing something new, something different, perhaps.' She felt her heartbeat rise. Already, she was sharing more than she wanted to with this girl.

'What kind of business did you have?'

'I was a partner in an employment agency.'

Verity did not look particularly impressed by the reply. To most people it would not sound that exciting, but she was not about to reveal that her agency had supplied escorts and prostitutes to the wealthy. Sheena did not yet feel in control of the conversation, and she needed to be in order to protect her true identity. Too many pertinent questions required the telling of too many lies.

'You're not working today?' she asked Verity.

'No. I'm waiting for some data to come from London. From Imperial College.'

Their polite but trivial conversation continued over coffee and more cigarettes. Sheena was taken by this girl. The tinge of disappointment when Verity rose to leave was something she had not expected to feel. She should not be doing this. She should not be looking for a companion.

'If you're free this evening,' she said, 'I usually eat at Restaurant Desailly about eight o'clock.'

'Thank you,' Verity replied. 'That would be great. I'd love to have some company for a change.'

She watched Verity stroll away, her denim bag swinging from her shoulder. She was soon out of sight at the end of the quay, turning right into the next channel. The flutter arising in her stomach could not be helped. Sheena could hardly wait for the evening.

CHAPTER 37

She spent the remainder of her day getting nowhere with the files and folders from the external hard drive. Her mind was fixed on something else. At first she was unaware of her daydreaming, but after she had smoked the last of her cigarettes and could stomach no more coffee, she realised that her thoughts had wondered, on each occasion settling upon her new acquaintance, Verity.

She called Celine, the waitress, paid her bill and chatted for a while, mostly about Celine's new boyfriend. The girl was little more than eighteen. She had smooth tanned skin and short cropped black hair. Aside from waitressing, she spent her summers water-skiing and her winters snow skiing in the Val D'Isère. Boyfriends came and went, all a part of her care-free life. How Sheena envied her. Feeling quite upbeat following their chat, she left Celine and wandered off to browse the gift shops around the main square. She had a silly notion that she should buy a small gift for Verity. Soon, she realised that she knew so little about this girl that it was impossible to choose anything for her.

When she got back to her apartment, the afternoon sun had warmed her lounge to an unbearable heat and she quickly opened the doors onto the balcony. She had no mind to continue working on the laptop. Instead, she pondered just what to do about the beautiful girl who had simply strolled into her life of solitude. Verity was hot—of that she had no doubt. She hoped, for her own sake, that she was also interested in women like her. Since they had parted at the café, she tried to conjure up signs that perhaps were not there; she was searching for something to convince her that Verity was up for a relationship. Was there something to the manner in which Verity had looked at her over the rim of her coffee cup? It had felt as though Verity was trying to absorb every inch of her. Or was there something to the way she held her cigarette, aloft in her right hand, her elbow resting on the table? Verity appeared confident, even bold. Sheena hoped that she was available, certain that physical loving was what she needed. It had been months since that last time with Alex, and there had been no one else during her time in France. She wanted sex. The consequences could be dealt with later.

Her bedroom was less stuffy than the lounge, but she threw open the windows to gain some fresh air. Feeling a peculiar sense of foreboding, mixed with her eagerness to see Verity again, she lay down on her bed in the hope of some sleep.

When sleep did come, it was a sleep still troubled by her darkest dreams. The knife slashing across the naked Alex, her blood spraying over them both. The look of terror in Alex's eyes, realising that Sheena was intent on killing her. Soon her passion was swamped in a wild-flowing river, the figure of Joe reaching out his arms to save her.

She awoke floundering, gasping for breath. Her throat was parched, her tongue stuck to the roof of her mouth. Rolling off the bed, she padded to the kitchen and opened the fridge, removing the first bottle she saw. The dregs of a Bordeaux, a Semillon. She raised the bottle to her mouth and felt the liquid purge it of dryness. Immediately, she gagged and pulled the bottle away. Coughing brought tears to her eyes and prompted sobbing. She sat down at the table, resting her head in both hands, and allowed herself to cry aloud. She felt so alone, so desperate for what had befallen her. Right now, she and Alex should have been enjoying their life together. Instead, she was wracked with guilt over what she had done and, paradoxically, fuelled with anger over what Alex had intended on doing to her. She thought of the day when they first met.

She had stepped out of a lift at the Lanesborough Hotel at Hyde Park and noticed a glamorous woman rise from her seat in the foyer and stare at her expectantly. Alex wore an expensive business suit in black and a white silk blouse. Her hair, even then, was a rich auburn styled in a bob, and her face was expertly tended with makeup, and yet she did nothing by way of a smile to show off her obvious beauty. She looked sombre; at best, she looked business serious.

'You must be Sheena,' she said, in a silky voice, with her hand outstretched. 'I'm Alex.'

Sheena knew she wasn't looking her best. She had just left the bed of a wealthy hotelier from Dubai. Her evening clothes were stuffed inside her overnight case, and she now stood before this elegant woman of around thirty-five wearing a wrinkled green blouse over a pair of black jeans and flat pumps. She wore no makeup, and her hair was still wet from the hastily taken shower in the hotel suite, before escaping the clutches of her overweight and over-sexed client. He was one of her four filthy-rich tricks; all of the others could only be described as middle-class with a healthy disposable income. Leaving her Arab client satisfied, she was richer by two and a half thousand pounds. Quite startled by the greeting, Sheena reached out her hand to meet the one offered by Alex Chase.

'I got your name from a mutual friend,' said Alex. She threw a glance at Connor, the concierge, a thirty-year-old Dubliner, tall, stick-like, with a bony face and moussed fair hair. His head was lowered as he checked the hotel's computer. Immediately, Sheena realised that this woman would already know everything about her. Connor was the person who arranged Sheena's business with the richest of her clients, taking his ten percent cut in the process. She knew that Alex understood what she was doing in the hotel, and now she also realised why Alex was taking an interest in her.

Alex invited Sheena to join her for morning coffee. She explained that she had a business proposition for Sheena to consider. All the while, however, Sheena couldn't help feeling an instant attraction to Alex Chase. Her brown eyes, separated by a narrow bridge, looked serious, and yet when she spoke in her rather posh voice she gave the impression that nothing in life was serious at all. As she was talking her arms often parted in wide flamboyant gestures, and frequently she placed her hand on Sheena's knee.

'I want to offer you the chance to work for me,' Alex explained, tipping some espresso into her mouth.

'Why would I want to do that?'

'Because the man whose room you've just left... I can offer you that type of client every time, not just once in a while. I can guess what you earn at the moment. Peanuts. In our world, Sheena, this is your chance to make it big.'

Until that morning, Sheena had believed she was already living the big time, the high life. She had left school, a dull comprehensive in Hertfordshire, at sixteen. Soon afterwards she had also left home. With three sisters and a brother, she didn't think her parents, always busy with their careers in sales, would really miss her. Very soon, though, she found the going tough in London. She had little choice but to turn tricks, first hanging round King's Cross, then hotel foyers in the hope of attracting richer clients. Within two months, she had started waitressing in bars and clubs in the West End. When she spotted an opportunity, she provided personal services to clients that she had selected rather than them choosing her. Eventually, she had sussed out a few regulars, but she continued to seek richer clientele until she was making, by her standards, a decent living, decent enough to give up her bar work. She first met Connor in the Lanesborough after an evening spent with a rich Chinese businessman. With Connor's input, she established a client list of rich men and one rich widow, all of them regular guests at the hotel. All the while she had been slowly coming to the realisation that she preferred sex with women, and merely endured sex with men. Now she was sitting next to a beautiful woman who was offering the opportunity of advancement and wondering whether, just maybe, Alex was attracted to her too.

There were few similarities between Alex Chase's background and Sheena's. They could hardly have been further apart on the social scale. Alex, born to a lawyer father and rich mother, had been educated at boarding school. There she had learned how to look after herself and to be confident in her abilities, and she had discovered whilst at finishing school in Gstaad exactly what she needed to do to become successful. In Alex, Sheena saw a woman who could offer her another step up the ladder. But could she trust her?

CHAPTER 38

The cool water on her face revived her. She hoped it would reduce the swelling below her eyes after her latest session of crying. The anticipation of a romantic evening with Verity encouraged her to make an effort to impress. With the exception of her visit to Zurich to meet with Josef Brunner, she had not applied makeup to her face in months. She had a healthy tan and did not require foundation, but she applied some eyeliner, shadow and mascara. A pleasant crimson lipstick plumped her lips. All the clothing and jewellery she had was once Alex's. She chose a long, sky-blue dress, a gold necklace with a jade, pear-shaped stone and a fine gold bracelet. The length of the dress allowed her to wear a pair of flat sandals. Standing before the mirror, with the evening sun streaming through the window, she was happy to realise that the dress was see-through. She wondered if Verity would be impressed. This version of Alex Chase, she hoped, would bring her some luck tonight.

At seven forty-five she left her apartment, went downstairs and stepped onto the quayside. A brief walk around the corner of her building brought her into the Place du Marché, and on the opposite side of the square sat *Restaurant Desailly*. The outside tables, beneath the awning, were busy with tourists, but she managed to attract the attention of the head waiter, Eric, who was always delighted to see her. He raised his eyes to intimate how busy he was, but regardless he pulled a chair from under a table that sat at the threshold to the indoor section of the restaurant.

'Bonsoir, Madame Alex. You look wonderful this evening.'

'Thank you, Eric. I may have a guest tonight.'

He set two leather-bound menus on the table.

'I can recommend the hake and, to start perhaps, some oysters.'

'Thank you. I'll wait for my friend. You can surprise me with a nice bottle of white wine.'

'Of course.'

Eric meandered his way around the tables to the bar. She immediately spied Verity standing in the square gazing towards the restaurant. It seemed, at first, that she did not recognise the woman she had met earlier in the day. Verity's appearance, also, came as a pleasant surprise to Sheena. Firstly, that she had turned up at all sent a thrill coursing through her. Secondly, the way Verity was dressed told Sheena everything she needed to know. She stood in a pair of cropped, black, shiny leggings, a white, over-sized blouse, loosely belted at the waist and black ballet pumps. The irony to Sheena was that, while she was dressed in the manner of her former lover Alex, her guest was wearing the style of clothes that she herself usually favoured. Verity's hair was in some disarray, long strands crimped and pointing in all directions. Her face was darkened by makeup, heavy eye-shadow and liner. Huge gold rings dangled from her petite lobes. The frivolous image sent another thrill through Sheena's already tingling body. She decided there and then that this woman, who had coolly intruded upon her solitude was, at the very least, up for sex. Her impression was confirmed when Verity held her hand as she passed her the cigarette lighter. It was a moment, a telling moment, before she released it.

'You look stunning,' said Verity, then took a long pull on her Gitanes, exhaling high into the air.

'I was thinking the same of you.'

Both women smiled conspiratorially, but Sheena could not prevent her nerves taking hold and she retreated to the safety of the menu.

'What's good here?' Verity asked.

'Well, the seafood is always great, particularly the langoustines with garlic and lemon. If you prefer meat we can share the chateaubriand?'

Verity leaned over the table, pondering the choices before her. Sheena couldn't help noticing her tiny breasts beneath the white shirt; Verity was not wearing a bra. She imagined she could feel their heat rising. She longed to touch her, to hold her, to feel her skin and smell her scent and the rawness of her breath as she exhaled her cigarette.

'No, I'm going to be good,' said Verity. 'I'll have the langoustines.'

Sheena poured her new friend some wine. Verity sat back and raised her glass.

'To us,' she said, her eyes sparkling, 'and getting to know each other.'

Sheena clinked her glass to Verity's, and they both took a brief sip.

The lively chatter around the restaurant had subsided by the time they were finished their meal and a second bottle of wine. Sheena had listened with interest as Verity flowed with details of her life and career, punctuated by copious anecdotes of her romantic relationships. Her stories of romance confirmed for Sheena that Verity was a woman who preferred to share the lipstick. She was aware of being more guarded in what she revealed to Verity about herself. Until she got to know her better, she didn't consider Verity worthy of knowing even the most trivial of her secrets.

Sheena insisted on paying for dinner, and the two women finished off with coffee and more cigarettes. As the evening grew quieter around the Place du Marché, with only a few groups of people here and there still enjoying their drinks, Sheena and Verity ambled to the hump bridge over the canal. Their bare arms touched frequently, deliberately at times, but neither one ventured to hold the other's hand. They paused to look around the peaceful scene of the harbour and canals, where street lights cast wonderful displays of neat buildings with balconies draped in bougainvillea and fuchsia.

Sheena was peering over the bridge into the dark water, wondering how far things might go on this first date. Verity turned to face her, but to Sheena, she sounded a little unsure of herself.

'Well, I really enjoyed the evening, Alex. Thank you for dinner. Maybe we can do it again soon.'

'I would like that,' Sheena replied, and could not help her sheepish expression. For a moment the two of them were lost for words or actions. Finally, Verity stepped towards Sheena and slipped her arms lightly around her. She placed a brush of a kiss on her cheek.

'Goodnight, Alex. Sleep well.' She backed away slowly, her head cocked to the right and with a coy smile.

Sheena wasn't sure if she should push for more, but her rational brain decided that she had gone far enough for one night. She was confident now that there would be others. Soon, she would give Verity the time of her life.

'Goodnight, Verity.' She forced herself to turn away.

CHAPTER 39

Four weeks after her first encounter with Alex Chase at the Lanesborough, Sheena was sharing her bed. Within six months, she was no longer turning tricks, even with those rich clients that Alex had promised her. She no longer had to. She and Alex were building an empire. On the surface, it was a respectable, high-end escort agency providing, for the filthy rich, all of their passionate desires under the guises of elegant companions who could accompany them to formal gatherings and quiet dinner-dates, and who could perform as attractive bed-partners. No cash ever changed hands. This was a discrete service. Clients had accounts with an inconspicuously named company, AS Management, and most had their personal assistants take care of all transactions. This made it easy for Alex and her new partner Sheena to fleece their customers on a humongous scale. It was unlikely that the wealthy clients would audit their expenditure in such detail as to take notice of their spending on 'bedroom' matters. The personal assistants of such rich men and women were even less prone to bring such matters to their boss's attention. As long as clients were satisfied with the services rendered, no one questioned that the escort was on an hourly rate with appropriate extras depending on what was asked of them. When Sheena had the idea of introducing a retainer fee in order for clients to secure a particular escort or a specific service, it increased revenue by another thirty-five percent. As far as Alex was concerned, there were no losers in this business. Her clients were happy and seldom questioned the prices they were charged, her carefully chosen employees were very well paid for having to endure some of the lurid habits of the clients, and the business flourished. On the second anniversary of their partnership, Alex and Sheena celebrated by hosting a party on board a luxury yacht in Puerto Banus. They invited all of their staff, a handful of their clients and several celebrities. It set them back nearly a quarter of a million pounds, but the end result was the acquisition of some new clients and yet another idea to further their business.

By this time Alex was devoting much of her time to the accounts, and her ever-widening and imaginative financial practices. This left Sheena to handle the day-to-day operations of rostering the staff, customer services and taking bookings. The personal relationship between the two women was strong and loving. They spent as much time together as the business permitted. They travelled, they moved into a luxury apartment in Bayswater and they shopped in the best stores and dined in the best restaurants in London. Sheena, understandably, couldn't help taking stock from time to time on how she had made a great success of her life. Her family in Hertfordshire were ignorant of the details of the business and to Sheena's delight, they expressed their pride in her. She had every reason to believe that her life was wonderful. With the success of the company, however, came the eventual pressures on their time. She and Alex were spending less quality time together, although they remained, so Sheena believed, very much in love. What was more dangerous, and something that Sheena had been largely unaware of, was the adventure upon which Alex was embarked concerning the financial background to their business. Sheena knew of all the up-front money coming in—the direct payments from their clients for services provided. What she was less familiar with was exactly what Alex was doing with the capital, and how she was accruing even more money from other sources. Much of their profit was conveniently sent off-shore to avoid tax and the prying eyes of the police. After all, while it might have been a high-end agency, at the heart of the business it was nothing more than prostitution. Alex never worried about their security. They had several high-ranking police officers and members of the judiciary as customers who were happy to keep their activities well under the radar. Nevertheless, Sheena did start to wonder where this extra income was coming from. It took an apparent cosy weekend in a cottage in the Lake District to discover that Alex had been scheming behind her back. By then it was too late. Their partnership was finished. It was certainly too late for Alex Chase.

CHAPTER 40

Frustrated, Sheena slammed the lid of the laptop closed. The plastic chair on the balcony toppled over as she pushed it away and stomped into the kitchen where she picked up the wine bottle. It was only ten-fifteen in the morning, and she had smoked eight cigarettes and drunk half a bottle of Chablis. Not having eaten, she felt wretched. She didn't dare inspect herself in a mirror; she knew it would not be pleasant. Having made little progress with the files on the hard drive that she had brought from Zurich, she was beginning to think the whole exercise was futile. Alex had been smart. Smarter than her. It was never going to be easy to work out what all the numbers meant, or to what they referred. Were they really bank account numbers? If so, then why could she not find reference to the banks involved? Other than Banque Honziker, she had found nothing, and yet she knew that Alex had had dealings with other Swiss banks—a bank in Jersey and at least one in the Caymans. But none of the spreadsheets made sense to her. She had no experience with computing or accounting, and she realised now that Alex had taken advantage of that. It made it easy for her to bury the things she wanted to keep from Sheena. One thing she was sure of, however: there was a lot of money hidden somewhere, much more than the few thousand she had so far uncovered. From what Alex had admitted to her, there were millions hidden away. It was supposed to have been for the two of them to enjoy together. Then she had discovered that the two in the picture were Alex and a woman named Ella. She, Sheena, had not featured in the plans.

Around lunch time each day, she made a point of sitting in her favoured seat at Café Avellino, close to the water's edge, in the hope that Verity would show up. They had not made definite plans to see each other after that first dinner, but Sheena had assumed they would. Even if Verity was not interested in having an intimate relationship, the vibes she picked up had seemed favourable towards meeting again for coffee or lunch. Five days went by, however, and there was no sign of this delicious woman. After the horrific ending of her relationship with Alex, Sheena had not thought much about meeting someone else. She had spent so much of her life moving on from one experience to the next, there was seldom time to develop real friendships. Alex had been the undoubted exception. For nearly five years, Alex had been all that mattered in her life. Since her world had come crashing down, she had reverted to self-preservation mode. It always kicked in when times got hard. This woman Verity had piqued her interest, but as each day went by with no sign of her, she began to think that one date had been enough for the writer. Or perhaps she was busy working. Sheena shouldn't have been so presumptuous, so needy.

With her life largely inactive and with such a basic routine, the days began to merge into one. Sheena rose from bed, she smoked, she drank coffee, she attempted to unlock the secrets to Alex's computer files, she showered and then she went to sit in Café Avellino hoping for Verity to appear.

Ten days had passed since they had met, and Sheena dined alone with some pasta, prawns and white wine. She was startled by the accent.

'Excuse me, would you have a light?' Verity stood over her, beaming a wide smile. Sheena could not disguise her delight and reached for Verity's hand. Verity responded by taking a seat at the table then, reaching across to Sheena's plate, she stole one of the prawns. Sheena could only watch as the girl savoured her mouthful of succulent food. She was also aware that they remained holding hands.

Verity had her hair brushed back and held in a ponytail, and her face, arms and legs showed an improved tan. She wore a white camisole top and a pair of very short and tight denim shorts.

'Have you been busy?' Sheena asked her.

'Very. I received the data from London that I'd been waiting for. I've been number crunching for the past nine days.' Verity helped herself to another prawn.

'You're good with computers?' Sheena asked her.

'I suppose so. I haven't really considered it before. It just seems a necessary part of my job.'

'Maybe you could help me?' Sheena ventured.

'Sure, what's the problem?'

'I'm having difficulty understanding some spreadsheets—financial stuff.'

'I can take a look for you. Can't promise anything.'

She smiled at Verity, who was now dipping a piece of bread into the lemon cream that accompanied the pasta.

When Sheena had finished lunch it soon became clear to her that they would not be lingering in the café for the entire afternoon. They strolled through the resort but always heading towards the apartment where Verity was staying. They couldn't help their haste when they reached the steps leading up to the apartment door. Suddenly there was an urge to rush inside. Within seconds they were making love on the bed.

CHAPTER 41

Verity spent an evening sitting on Sheena's bed, a laptop before her, its light casting a glare on her face, the room otherwise in darkness. From her chair in the corner of the room, Sheena held a glass of cool white wine in her left hand, a cigarette in her right. The balcony doors were open, the air still, the sounds of laughter and chatter rising from the restaurants and bars around the Place du Marché. Both women were naked, having spent another afternoon together in bed. For reasons that Sheena could not explain, lovemaking in the afternoon suited both of them. It may have been that, after lunching together in the café, neither of them could wait until evening, but for two weeks their routine had not waivered.

Sheena was content to watch Verity work. Her presence in the room was sufficient to cast a wonderful spell of serenity in Sheena's thinking. She felt so lucky, so blessed, to have found this woman, just when she was feeling at her lowest since that dark day when she had killed Alex.

Periodically, Verity lifted her eyes from the screen to smile at her. The eyes of both women sent little telepathic messages of love across the room. This evening, though, she tried to let Verity work undisturbed. At last she hoped that Verity might be getting somewhere with uncovering the financial secrets of Alex Chase. She had told Verity a story, with an element of truth, of course, of how her former business partner had done a bunk with most of their money, leaving her, Alex, with nothing but a few thousand in cash. She had managed to gain access to a bank account in Switzerland, where she had found the spreadsheets.

Two days earlier, Verity had taken a first look at the spreadsheets that Sheena had shown her on the laptop. These were the files extracted from the external hard drive that she had taken from the safety deposit box at Banque Honziker in Zurich. Verity, after a cursory look, had said that the information could be deciphered given a little time. She had borrowed the laptop for a couple of days, and this evening had pieced together spreadsheets containing information that resembled bank statements with lists of transactions, account numbers and the identities of the banks involved. Sheena was astounded that Verity had untangled the information that to her was nothing but gobbledy-gook.

'How did you do it?' she asked. Verity looked chuffed to have helped her lover.

'I've seen this kind of security before,' Verity replied. 'None of the files had passwords as such, but your friend had applied a sort of personal encryption to the data. Pretty amateurish really.' She pointed at a row of numbers on a spreadsheet. 'All that she did was to unsort columns and alter column alignments. Once you figure out which columns have been tampered with and, assuming you can recognise real account numbers when you see them, it's easy.' Verity hovered the cursor over a column, clicked once with the mouse, then dragged the cells to the right on the spreadsheet and inserted them beside another column of numbers. 'See? Take the four figures in column F with those now in column G and you have a list of account numbers.'

Sheena looked on as Verity continued to adjust rows and columns in a worksheet, un-hiding cells and inspecting any formula or code ascribed to them. 'It will take ages to unravel the whole thing. Your friend may have also linked these worksheets to other files. But maybe we can find enough information for you to make contact with the banks involved.'

'That's wonderful, Verity. I can't believe it. I would never have sussed that in a million years. We're going to have a wonderful future together.'

Verity gave a wry smile, and Sheena suddenly realised just how presumptuous she had been.

She allowed Verity to continue working in silence, while she sipped at her wine and finished her cigarette. Then the light from the laptop screen faded, and Verity closed the lid.

'I don't know about you, but my eyes are closing. I'll do some more work on it tomorrow.'

In the two weeks of their sizzling affair, Verity had never stayed overnight, nor Sheena at Verity's apartment. After dining together and the afternoon sex, they parted each night.

'You could stay, if you want?' Sheena suggested. She realised how sheepish she sounded.

Verity rose from the bed and pulled a flowery mini-dress over her head. She smiled wistfully at Sheena, as if staying the night was a step too far. But Sheena couldn't see the problem. They already shared a bed each afternoon, why not overnight?

'Thanks, Alex, that would be lovely, but not tonight. I've got some emails to send before I get to bed, and I want to do some writing first thing in the morning. It's my best time of day to work. I'll see you tomorrow at the café?' She pushed her feet into a pair of flip-flops then stepped towards her. A brief kiss on the lips was all Sheena was going to get.

'Thank you,' Sheena whispered. 'I didn't mean to put pressure on you, talking about the future.'

'I know,' said Verity. 'Get some sleep. I'll see you tomorrow.' Verity opened the door and was gone before Sheena could add anything more.

Noise from the streets had subsided, but Sheena didn't feel like going to bed just yet. Instead, she poured another glass of wine and lit another cigarette. She resumed her chair in the corner of the bedroom and gazed at the spot on her bed where, only a few minutes earlier, Verity had been sitting naked and working on the computer. Sheena thought her new lover very clever to have worked out how Alex Chase had jumbled the columns on the spreadsheets. She supposed it was like assembling a complicated machine without instructions. But she could not help wondering, also, how it was that Verity had accomplished it with such ease.

CHAPTER 42

Sheena felt nervous. More nervous than she had felt walking into Banque Honziker in Zurich and meeting with Josef Brunner. The headquarters of PB Wealth Management Services was located in a brand new office development on the Esplanade in St. Helier on the island of Jersey. The building overlooked the car park, where Sheena and Verity were sitting in their hired BMW.

Sheena had realised that as Verity deciphered more information from the spreadsheets she would soon discover that the name associated with the bank accounts was actually Alex Chase. She had decided, therefore, to reveal to Verity that her real name was Sheena Bateman, and that the name of her former partner was Alex Chase. The only reason that she had been using the name Alex, she told Verity, was so that she could get her hands on the money she was entitled to. Of course, although she had shared some of her secret, she had not told Verity that she had killed two people, Alex and the taxi driver, Joe.

'What if they realise I'm not the real Alex Chase?'

'They won't.'

'I really don't know if I can pull this off, Verity.'

'You'll be fine. Just be confident. It's not like you're going in there to steal from them. All you're doing is closing one account and opening another at the same bank. You have the account number, and the access code is one of the two numbers I gave you. If the first one is wrong, it's bound to be the second. It will just look like a simple mistake. It won't arouse suspicion.'

Sheena was dressed in a dark business suit, a tailored-fit jacket, a pencil skirt and patent black heels. At that moment she could not have looked more like her former lover on the day they had first met in the foyer of the Lanesborough Hotel. Her hair was styled just as Alex had worn hers, in a longish bob, and the deep auburn colouring was an exact match. She had just to believe completely that she was now living the life of the woman she had killed.

'Thank you, Verity.'

'What for?'

'For everything.'

'No need.'

'You'll stay with me, won't you?'

'I'll be right here.' Verity leaned across and gave her a peck on the cheek.

'I mean when it's over, when everything is settled. We'll stay together?'

Verity smiled in a way that looked sincere yet frivolous, in keeping with her apparent attitude to life in general. Sheena had learned that much in the few weeks they had been together. While she believed they had grown close, there were times when she suspected that Verity was still keeping some distance between them. Her refusal to stay overnight was one of the things that caused her to wonder, as was the fact that she was never available before lunch each day, claiming that it was her time for writing. Sheena didn't fully buy that. Today, she was nervous about entering another bank in the guise of Alex Chase, but in the back of her mind she was still thinking about how long she could keep a hold of Verity.

Her motive in performing a transaction in another bank was to attempt to rationalise all of Alex Chase's accounts. She was no financial whizz-kid. She could not play interest rates and investment portfolios off against each other. She simply wanted all of Alex's money in one place, where she had access to it.

Verity, without being asked, had suggested that she should first rationalise the accounts so that there was one single account in each of the banks Alex had used. Then, a short while later, she could pull all the accounts together in a single bank. Hopefully this way she would avoid any suspicion from the financial institutions.

Sheena stepped from the car and, taking a deep breath, walked purposefully toward the entrance to the bank. Her mind was focussed on what she had to do, but she couldn't help the nerves in her stomach. What if the people in the office saw right through her?

In the end she needn't have worried. Everything went as she had hoped. A friendly and efficient accounts manager had accepted her ID without question. The young lady led her to an office at the rear of the building and attended to Sheena's requests without fuss. This was not the ordeal she had endured at Banque Honziker. It was a simple clerical process that was completed within forty-five minutes.

Verity watched as Sheena approached, walking smartly and with a big smile emerging on her face. She opened the passenger's door and got in.

'Well? How did it go?' Verity asked.

'No problems.'

'Told you.'

'They understood my need to "condense my portfolio", as they put it. But they hoped that I would continue to invest with them.' Verity started the engine and drove from the parking space.

'No one suspected that you aren't the real Alex Chase?'

'Don't think so. I produced ID, signed a few forms and the deed was done.'

'What was the balance?'

Sheena winced in disappointment as Verity drove onto the Esplanade and headed for the airport.

'Not what I'd hoped,' Sheena replied. 'I'm beginning to think that Alex deliberately spread her funds far and wide in case someone came snooping.'

'How much?' Verity asked.

'One million, two hundred and twenty thousand.'

'Maybe that's all of it.'

'No. I don't think so. There's a lot more. We need to keep working on those files.'

'I'm not sure we can do any more with them.'

Sheena was a little surprised by Verity's attitude. She had uncovered the access codes to the Jersey bank accounts with apparent ease. Why was she suddenly so sure that she could not do the same with other accounts? Alex Chase had amassed a fortune, and one million, two hundred and twenty thousand pounds was certainly not all of it.

Sheena had registered the change in tone of Verity's remarks, and she knew precisely why. For now, though, they were catching a flight to Gatwick, then a connection back to Nice. She had grown fond of Verity, but she hadn't yet come to trust her. If Verity was unable or unwilling to uncover any further information from the computer files then, Sheena thought, she may have out-lived her usefulness.

As the plane lifted off from the island she began to regret divulging what she had to Verity. Her one consolation was that she would not have got as far as the bank in Jersey, and access to over a million pounds, without her. She would still be trying to piece together information she could never understand. And, another thing: Verity was fabulous in bed.

CHAPTER 43

Verity's reluctance to work on the accounts and coded files persisted and Sheena was hardly surprised, also, by Verity's sudden lack of interest in having sex or even in spending time together. She was talking about her returning to England. They were lying on sun loungers on the sandy beach at Port Grimaud, children charging around, in and out of the sea, screaming their excitement, splashing through the waves. Both women wore bikinis and had lathered each other with sun lotion. Verity was engrossed in a novel by George Saunders, *Lincoln in the Bardo*. Sheena was frustrated. She wanted answers. She wanted to know what Verity was intending to do. So far, Verity, despite having alluded on several occasions to returning home, was keeping the details of her plans to herself. The not knowing was eating at Sheena: this morning she had chain-smoked her way through half a pack of Marlboro. It was all getting too much.

'How long will you be gone?' Sheena blurted out the question, startling her companion. Verity lowered the book from her face, but did not turn to Sheena.

'I don't really know.'

'Are you coming back?'

Sheena watched the smile—a conceited smile, she would have said—emerge on Verity's face. If it weren't for the sunglasses, she would have seen her friend laugh at her.

'Em, I don't really know.'

'But you must know, Verity. Don't you have more writing to do? And what about us?'

'I've just told you. I don't really know.'

Verity resumed her reading, and as Sheena lit yet another cigarette she began to consider what she must do.

Sex in the afternoon was no longer sought by either woman, but the day after the episode on the beach Verity, to Sheena's surprise, agreed to have dinner at Restaurant Desailly. Sheena had decided to step back from confrontation and instead set about trying to win Verity over. She realised that tonight might well be her only chance before Verity left for home.

'I was hoping,' she began, as they sat over dinner, 'That if you have time before you go home, we could spend a few days together.'

Verity had developed a kind of smugness in Sheena's company. She seemed to enjoy seeing her lover squirm and crawl. She cocked her head to the side and dropped her voice to a sultry tone.

'What do you have in mind?'

'I found this wonderful hotel in a beautiful village in the mountains. It's not that far away; we can drive up there. The mountain air will be cool and fresh, we can go for walks and the food and wine is great.'

Verity looked pensive; she fiddled with the silver ring on her right hand.

'What do you think? You've done so much for me, Verity. I love you, for goodness sake. If you're not coming back to me I'd like to give you something, to repay a little of what you've done for me.'

'I never said I wasn't coming back. I just said that I didn't know when exactly.'

'Does that mean you'll come with me?'

'I've already booked a flight to London.'

'When?'

Suddenly, Sheena was anxious. She imagined her thumping heart could be seen through her cotton dress. The thought that she might already be too late gnawed at her stomach. She had eaten little of her meal.

'Thursday.'

If they left tomorrow that would give them two days in the mountains. She had to make it work.

'Great. We can leave in the morning and get there for lunch. We'll be back in time for your flight.'

Verity looked doubtful, and her dark eyes seemed to search for something in Sheena's expression.

'OK.'

Sheena lifted her glass and clinked it to Verity's.

CHAPTER 44

Sheena hired a silver Renault Megane Cabriolet from a car-hire office in Port Grimaud. By ten o'clock she had roused Verity from her apartment and the pair of them were on the road to Nice, the car roof down, morning sunshine and a breeze on their faces, French house music blasting from the radio.

Skirting around the city on the A8, they headed north, passing through La Trinité and Cantaron before taking a minor road into the mountains. The views were magnificent: tree covered hilltops, winding roads and elegant villas. Soon they drove along a much narrower road that wound and zig-zagged up the mountain, and eventually it led them to a spot by their hotel, adjacent to the hilltop village of Peillon. The view made both women sigh as they stepped from the car. Peillon looked medieval, perched on top of a narrow rocky peak with a compact assortment of houses in grey stone. The only thing to interrupt the tranquillity was the sound of hammering from a building under restoration. Sheena thought the surroundings were perfect for their stay.

They checked into the hotel and, after leaving their belongings in their room, they had lunch on a terrace overlooking the valley. The air was fresh and clear and it helped them relax—both women were edgy in each other's company, as if they had only just met. Sheena, in an effort to lighten the mood, beamed a smile at her companion.

'What?' said Verity.

'Your hair. It must have caught the wind in the open car.'

'I know, I must look a sight.'

'Actually, it's beautiful. You're beautiful, Verity.'

Verity didn't respond but looked away from their table across the hills.

'Penny for them?' said Sheena.

Verity shook her head, avoiding a reply. Sheena felt deflated. For a while they ate in silence.

'What are we going to do this afternoon?' Verity asked, an attempt from her to restore a light-hearted mood.

'We could go for a walk,' Sheena replied. 'There are lots of trails around the village.'

'A hike, you mean?'

'We don't have to walk far. There are a few spots with scenic views.'

Verity wore a short cotton dress in navy blue with large pink flowers and a pair of leather sandals. Sheena was dressed in a pair of khaki shorts and white vest. They strolled through the narrow streets, winding up and down through low, vaulted passages and at times encountering steep stairways. It was enough to sap their energy, but Sheena was determined to venture from the streets out into the hills. They walked side by side up a winding path behind the hotel. It wasn't long before they were looking down on most of the buildings in the village. Verity, however, struggled with their pace and the late afternoon heat. She soon lagged several paces behind Sheena, who had to pause to wait for her lover to catch up.

'We don't have to do this now, if you're feeling tired?'

'I'm fine,' said Verity, breathless. 'Lunch is still weighing me down.' Sheena threw her arms around her and pulled her close. Their lips met in a brief kiss, but Sheena did not release her hold. She looked into Verity's eyes.

'I love you,' she said. 'I want you to know that.'

'Love you, too.'

'I want us to be together.'

'We are together, silly.' Verity kissed her again, her hands resting on Sheena's shoulders.

'Permanently, I mean. I want you to move in with me.'

'But I can't stay in France indefinitely, Sheena. My work is back in London.'

'I'll go back with you. We can find a flat. What do you think?'

Verity kissed her. It was a clever stalling tactic.

'Sounds wonderful,' she said without conviction.

'Oh, Verity, I'm so happy. I really don't deserve you.' They hugged each other. Now, Sheena believed that she had Verity back onside—she had her trust. That was all she needed.

'You go back down and have a rest,' said Sheena. 'I'll stroll about up here for a while.'

'You don't mind?'

'Of course not.'

'We'll talk later. Be careful,' said Verity, waving as she began picking her way back down the trail.

Sheena watched Verity descending the hill, and when she disappeared from sight, she turned and resumed her climb. The air felt thin, her breathing laboured, but she needed to continue. She had to find a suitable place. The path narrowed, becoming more of a rocky trail at times swallowed by trees and shrubs, then suddenly she would glimpse the entire vista of the valley below her before it was obscured once again by the trees. Not only did she have to find the right spot; she also had to figure out a way of coaxing Verity back into the hills. She was surprised by the girl's lack of energy. Verity was younger and slimmer than she was, although she did smoke an inordinate number of cigarettes.

After thirty minutes or so, she came upon a viewing spot where the path widened and had been flattened into a clearing. From here she could look upon the entire valley below, although the sun now shone directly into her face. She could feel her skin burning from the heat.

From this position the hotel was hidden by trees, but peering over a low stone wall, she decided it was the perfect place—the very spot she had been searching for. On the other side of the wall, the land fell away steeply for more than fifty feet into a darkened ravine.

CHAPTER 45

Verity lay asleep on the bed when Sheena got back to their room. She pulled off her vest and shorts and padded to the bathroom. A cool shower was just the thing to wash the dust from her hair and the perspiration from her body. Her legs, shoulders and face were burning with the effects of the sun. For more than ten minutes, she let the water cascade down her body. Her skin tingled as she stepped from the shower and reached for a towel. Wrapping it loosely around her, she quietly entered the bedroom and made her way onto the balcony. She lit a cigarette and sat down on a wrought-iron chair with her feet resting on the lip of the railing. In her mind, she ran over her plans for the following day. She was disappointed not to have settled matters this afternoon, but seeing her companion's exhaustion, she thought it wise to be patient rather than to make rash judgements that might scupper her plans. She hoped that tomorrow Verity would be more amenable to a stroll in the hills.

As the sun dipped below the mountains, they enjoyed a dinner of rump steak and buttered potatoes followed by crème brûlée. They finished a second bottle of red wine and, after cigarettes and coffee, they strolled hand-in-hand to their room. They watched each other undress then lay naked on top of the bed, for a time simply holding each other close, before passion overwhelmed them and they made love until both of them had delighted in rapturous climax.

It was approaching midday before either woman ventured to the bathroom and finally dressed. To her amazement, Sheena, still comfortably in bed, looked on as Verity stood waiting, full of energy, itching to be out and doing something.

Without wasting any further time, Sheena rose and got dressed. Verity drove them down the valley to a little café they had noticed the day before. It was set against a sheer cliff face by the side of the road. A mauve-flowering clematis strangled a wooden awning, and hanging baskets on each supporting post were rich with petunias, lobelias and geraniums. There were only four tables outside, two of which were occupied. Verity parked the car close into the cliff at the side of the road, and they took their seats at one of the free tables. Two men in their mid-thirties, dressed similarly in white shirts and dark slacks, were drinking coffee, smoking and chatting. The other table was occupied by an elderly couple, a silver-haired woman in a flowery dress, and a bald-headed man with a thick neck and bulging stomach. Both were ensconced in their newspapers.

Sheena and Verity ordered orange juice, coffee, bread and cheese, and for a while they sat in silence browsing their mobile phones. Sheena tried to mirror exactly what Verity was doing. If she was content to stay on her phone that was fine with her. If Verity wanted to chat, that was fine, too. All the while, however, Sheena was toying with how best to entice Verity for another walk in the hills. The vision of the beauty spot she had found the previous afternoon shone in her mind. Today would be her only opportunity.

'Any thoughts on how we should spend the day?' Sheena ventured when they had finished eating. She handed Verity a lighter for her cigarette; the girl never seemed to have one to hand. She was astonished by the reply.

'I don't mind attempting another walk. Seems like the only thing to do around here.'

'We could just get drunk and go to bed?' Sheena said it deliberately, knowing that Verity was less likely to be keen so soon after their last session of love-making. It had the desired effect; Verity re-iterated her desire to go for a walk.

'It *is* an idyllic place. We're only here for another day; we should make the most of it. Besides, it's cooler today. I'm less likely to flag out.'

Sheena was bubbling inside, amazed that it had been so easy to nudge her friend into going for a walk. This time, though, she would take things easy. No point in exhausting the poor girl before they reached the right spot. She didn't want Verity to tire out again and return to the hotel without her. This time, she hoped, things would be very different.

Holding hands, they meandered through the gardens of the hotel and as if by accident happened upon the same trail they had followed the previous day. Sheena thought that Verity could not have looked more stunning. She wore sky-blue culottes and a white T-shirt with short, frilled sleeves. Her hair raged in all directions, although they had not gone far when she stopped to tie it back with a rubber band. Sheena kept hold of Verity's hand as if for affection, but really she did it to prevent her lover from dropping behind, or perhaps giving up once again and retreating to the hotel.

'I am really not fit,' said Verity, panting and wiping her forearm across her brow.

'You need to stop with the ciggies, we both do.' Verity halted. Rather than release her hand, Sheena stopped, too, and waited for her lover to catch her breath.

'Right, let's try again.' Verity, with renewed vigour, attempted to pull Sheena along.

'Take it easy. We've got all day.' Inside, though, Sheena couldn't wait until they reached the place she had chosen.

It was late in the afternoon when they emerged at the tiny clearing where, a day earlier, Sheena had gazed over the valley and the village of Peillon. Now she was keen to show Verity the same view. From her previous wanderings, she had encountered few people around on this path. There had been more on the lower regions, close to the village, but she had not seen or met anyone at this high point. As Verity took in the scenery, Sheena glanced around for signs of life. She could not afford witnesses.

Verity was standing by the low wall. She turned to face her lover. Sheena reached out her hands and took Verity's in hers.

'It's beautiful up here,' said Verity, still panting, perspiration beaded on her forehead. 'I'm glad I lasted the pace.'

Sheena moved closer and drew her into a long passionate kiss. She felt Verity's slight frame in her arms. There was little flesh on her bones. Her own body trembled. Despite the blazing sun, she was suddenly chilled. Verity eased herself free of Sheena, turned and looked out across the valley. She stood close to the wall. Sheena's right hand hung in the air, an inch from Verity's back. Silently, she eased herself behind her. She was ready.

'It's been wonderful, my darling,' Sheena whispered. Verity turned slowly to face her.

'Goodbye... Ella!'

Sheena thrust both arms forward, striking Verity on the chest. Verity, a terrified look on her face, tumbled backwards. Her calves scraped on the rocks of the wall as she toppled over. She reached out her hands to Sheena, but Sheena stepped back. Verity's arms flailed desperately in the air. She screamed as she fell.

'Sheena! No!'

Only five feet into the descent, her head smashed on a rock. Her unconscious body somersaulted and bounced down the cliff. In a flash, it lay broken among the leaves and boulders in the ravine. Several small birds fluttered skywards.

Sheena peered into the dim cavity but could not see her. It was not a sheer cliff face, but nonetheless, the chances of surviving a fall from this position were surely remote.

She turned and walked briskly away, the afternoon sun beaming on her face.

Chapter 46

At breakfast the following morning Sheena had coffee, croissants and a final cigarette. She had decided that, from today, it was a habit she must quit. Sleeping had been easy. She thought she might struggle after what she had done, but her conscience was surprisingly clear, undaunted by the horrible death she had inflicted upon a woman who had so recently shared her bed. Verity, or Ella, or whatever the hell her name was, had fallen into her trap.

Around the hotel there had been no signs of alarm or news of a body being discovered in the hills. No one had commented that she had dined alone in the evening or had breakfasted on her own. She had packed all of her belongings and Verity's into the car. She had made the reservation at the hotel, so she had simply settled her bill and departed. No one had looked at her with suspicion. No one enquired after her companion. If, and when, Verity's body was found, the authorities would have nothing with which to identify her. Perhaps one of the hotel staff might recognise her, but if she lay undiscovered for long enough there wouldn't be much left of her after nature had taken its course. She had nothing to worry about.

She kept the roof of the Renault down, allowing the chill of morning air, not yet warmed by the sun, to fill her nostrils and revive her after a night's sleep. As she drove swiftly towards Port Grimaud, the niggling thoughts she had had since first meeting Verity surfaced once again. How had this woman found her? How did she know who she was? Most importantly, why had she come after her? One spine-chilling notion sat with her, but she kept telling herself it could not be. It was impossible.

She knew that she would miss the physical relationship she had shared with Verity. There was no doubt that she had been a wonderful lover. A sensuous lover—more so than Alex Chase had ever been. But, while she had always trusted Alex when they were together, she could never have the same trust in Verity. The motives of the woman in seeking her out would have always been there between them, a gaping chasm that no leap of faith could ever bridge. Besides, Verity had been intending to leave her and return to England. She always knew they never had a future together.

On the journey back to her apartment, she stopped at several places and deposited Verity's belongings. Her clothes went to a textiles bank on a civic amenity site on the outskirts of Nice. Her washbag, perfume and jewellery went into a large bin in an alleyway beside a restaurant near Antibes. Anything relating to the identification of Verity, or Ella Mason—her handbag, purse, bank cards and drivers' license—were casually tossed over a wall and down a steep slope by the side of the road on the drive down from Peillon. When she arrived at Port Grimaud, she returned the car to the hire company then spent the evening in her apartment going through each room, making sure there was not a trace of Verity left in the place. All of her toiletries, she placed in the bins outside. She wiped down the bathroom, kitchen, bedroom and all other furniture with disinfectant wipes. Finally, she dumped all of the clothes she had worn whenever they had been together. It didn't leave her with much, but she would soon kit herself out with a whole new wardrobe. After all, with over a million pounds in a Jersey bank account, she was a rich woman.

Over the next few days she kept an eye on the apartment where Verity had stayed. She had the keys to the place, having taken them from Verity's handbag before disposing of it. But she had yet to summon the courage to venture inside. She knew there were several things belonging to her within the apartment. More importantly, she wanted to have a look at the laptop that Verity had been using. Maybe there was information on there about her. She also hoped to find some background on who this Verity or Ella had been and how she had come to meet Alex Chase.

Despite her coolness in dispensing the girl to her death in the hills above Peillon, Sheena experienced strange pangs of nerves when it was time to go inside the empty apartment. Although she understood only a little French, she could not find anything in the press regarding the discovery of a woman's body lying in a gully in Peillon. All signs were favourable. There would be no better time than now for her to enter Verity's apartment and take what she needed.

CHAPTER 47

Summer weather on the Côte d'Azur encourages the outdoor life: relaxing in the sunshine, lying on a beach or by a swimming pool or, in Port Grimaud, to sit in the early morning outside a quiet café drinking coffee and watching those with keen maritime interests venture out on their expensive cruisers. Sheena quickly returned to her pre-Verity routine of lounging at Café Avellino, at the same table each day, drinking her coffee, resisting the urge to smoke and trying to plan some vestige of a future life beyond this paradise. She had to admit to feeling lonely since the demise of Verity, but she contented herself in the knowledge that she was now a reasonably well-off woman with the ability to go anywhere and do anything she wanted. At least, she was thankful to Verity for that. If she had not deciphered the accounts on the file from Alex's hard drive, Sheena could never have marched into the bank in Jersey and performed a funds transfer on a grand scale to a new account. Verity had been more of a help than a threat but, still, she had to go.

Sheena switched on her laptop and sat back in her chair at Café Avellino. A faint breeze ruffled her freshly washed and blow-dried hair. This morning, she mused, she not only looked like Alex Chase, but she felt as though she had adopted her attitudes to life. Her face was nicely tanned and, now thinner, she even more resembled her former lover. She still wore clothes that she had taken from Alex's wardrobe in their London flat. She felt comfortable in a loose cotton dress with pink and blue bands. She had all of Alex's ID; she had control of some, though definitely not all, of her bank accounts. She had seen off a major connection to Alex by killing Verity. She was inching closer and closer to wholeheartedly becoming a woman whose name was Alex Chase.

Opening her handbag, she retrieved the small, leather-bound notebook she had taken from the safety deposit box in Zurich. Inside

she had written four words and four codes, each one providing access
to the accounts in Zurich and in Jersey. The main accounts in each
bank were in the name of Alex Chase, and now that Verity was gone,
only she had the means of accessing them.

She entered the website of Banque Honziker and clicked on
the client login tab. When the login screen appeared, she typed her
username and was prompted for a password. Double-checking the
notebook, she typed in the eight characters. Next she was prompted
for a numerical code which she had to verify by selecting one of the
six-digit codes that she had written in her notebook. Once entered,
she gained access to the brand new account that she had set up in the
name of Alex Chase when she had visited the bank headquarters in
Zurich. She clicked on a drop-down menu to view recent transactions
and the balance on the account. Her blood froze. There had to be
a mistake. She must be looking at the wrong account. The account
that she had closed, perhaps? She cross-checked all the numbers that
she had scribbled into her book. Everything was correct. There was
no mistake. Why then did the account balance read 1.00 CHF? The
last time she had checked, it had showed a balance of 112,768 CHF.

Without logging out of the Banque Honziker web page, she
navigated on a second tab to the website of PB Wealth Management
Services in Jersey. As soon as she had logged in and gained access
to her account, she stared in horror at the stated balance of £1.00
Sterling. She blinked back tears. Her mouth was dry. She knew she
should be looking at a balance of £1.22M. Her heart pounded, beads
of sweat emerged on her forehead; she couldn't believe what she saw
in front of her. She had set up the new account when she and Verity
had visited Jersey. She had noted the balance then. Now the money
was gone. She had nothing. She was finished. Only Verity knew how
much money she had and in which accounts. Verity had known all
of the account numbers, the passwords and the access codes. It could
only have been Verity who had taken her fortune—and she was dead.

CHAPTER 48

No longer thinking straight, Sheena rose from her chair, toppling it backwards. It hit the ground with a clatter. She grabbed her bag and rushed away. Customers in the café looked on inquisitively. The laptop, still open to the accounts of Alex Chase at Banque Honziker and at PB Wealth Management Services, remained on the table. It didn't matter. She must get to Verity's apartment. Maybe on Verity's computer she could find exactly what had happened to the money. Her money. As she ran along the quayside, over the bridge to the building where Verity had been staying, she felt her entire world crashing down around her. She had nothing—all was lost. She had felt the same on that snowy morning, waking in bed to the sound of a telephone conversation between Alex and Ella. It was that dreadful morning when she had learned that Alex was leaving her—taking all of their money, leaving her with nothing. It was the time she saw how the knife had ripped at the soft white flesh of her lover and how her blood had splattered over her naked body. It was the evening when that creep of a taxi driver had climbed on top of her in his car—when he had pinned her against the tree, when she had fallen into a swollen river, when she'd let go of his hand and watched him rush away in the swirling waters. She had thought then that she would not survive. But she had. Now she must do it all over again.

Her eagerness to get into the apartment made it all the more difficult to slide the key into the lock. Her entire body trembled, her hand unable to hold the key steady. When at last the door opened, she thrust it to the wall and rushed inside. It was an open-plan space, similar to her own apartment: the kitchen and lounge were one, and there was a bathroom and one bedroom, directly off the lounge. She didn't find the laptop in the lounge, but when she thundered through the bedroom door she saw it lying on the unmade bed. Diving onto the bed, she pressed the ON button of the laptop and waited, sobbing and sniffing back tears. In an instant, her frustration turned to absolute devastation. Access to the laptop was password protected. In vain, she tried a few words that may have meant something to Verity. She typed VERITY, then ALEX, LONDON, PORT GRIMAUD. Every attempt failed. She had no clues as to what to do next. She sat staring blankly at the empty screen. What more could she do? Verity had screwed her over. But why? It was only Verity and her who had access to the new accounts set up in Switzerland and Jersey. Only they knew the account numbers and the access codes. Verity had stolen all of her money, cleaned her out. She should have checked the accounts before killing her. Now it was too late.

Suddenly, she heard a sound from behind her. Someone was in the apartment. She braved herself to turn around.

'My God! You even look like me.'

CHAPTER 49

Sheena clutched the laptop across her chest as if it could afford her protection. Protection from a ghost. Her heart pounded and her tongue snagged in her mouth. The colour drained from her face. She couldn't summon the words to say. She could only think that a ghost stood before her now.

'No! It can't be you.'

'Oh yes, Sheena. I'm afraid so, darling.'

The woman stood, leaning against the door frame, her arms folded, a sinister smile on her scarred face, her hair now much longer and strawberry blonde. She grinned mischievously at Sheena languishing on the bed nursing a laptop computer.

'Find anything interesting on there?'

Sheena could only manage to shake her head. Her bloodshot eyes were fixed upon her visitor. The shock value of the apparition before her was not wearing off quickly.

'But?'

'I know, I know. You killed me. I was dead. You left me lying in a pool of blood—in a lonely cottage in the middle of winter, blah blah blah.'

'You *were* dead. I was sure of it.'

'Oh, Sheena, don't be so bloody stupid. Did you even check that I was still breathing? Did you decide that with all that blood I just had to be dead? When you started swinging that knife, I knew my best chance was to fake it. Isn't that what we call-girls are good at? Faking it? I could hear you stomping around the house, taking my things, my clothes, my money and my files. Not once did you stop and look at me—not until you pulled the ring from my finger. You made sure you took everything. As far as you were concerned, I was dead. Self-preservation kick in, did it? Just look at what you did to me.'

Alex Chase raised her linen beach dress over head and pulled it away. She stood before Sheena in a black bikini and sandals. Sheena gasped when she saw the wounds she had inflicted on her former lover. A red scar stretched from her left shoulder and across her chest, disappearing below the bikini top at the right breast. Another ran horizontally across her abdomen, resembling a scar from a surgical procedure. Several shorter lines were noticeable around her bust, but the most shocking of all was the gash that had opened Alex Chase's beautiful face, from her left ear, down her cheek and under her chin on the right side. There were numerous marks on both her forearms, several on her upper thighs and multiple smaller scars on her face, neck and chest. Sheena had no detailed memory of the moments when she had inflicted such pain. She had struck out in anger and fear. She had lost control.

She closed her eyes now, momentarily, but saw only flailing arms and splattering blood.

'Lucky for me you managed not to sever any major arteries, although I don't think you were being particularly careful on that score.'

'Alex, I'm…'

'Sorry? Save it, Sheena. Let's go have a drink.'

CHAPTER 50

The two women walked with determined stride, although Sheena, her head bowed like a schoolgirl about to be scolded, lagged a few steps behind Alex Chase. When she realised that Alex was not headed towards Café Avellino where, a few minutes earlier, she had abandoned her computer and ran to Verity's apartment, she called out.

'Can we go in here? I've left my things inside.'

Alex didn't appear bothered by the suggestion. She turned right and strode into the café. Thankfully, Sheena saw that her laptop still sat upon the table in the corner beneath the awning. They took a seat on either side of the table and, within a few seconds, Celine, the waitress, appeared and Alex ordered two beers.

Despite her scars, Alex looked well. Her face was bright, although it lacked her usual affectionate smile.

Sheena had so many questions she had no clue where to begin. She guessed that Alex was enjoying the moment, relishing the shock she had just inflicted on the woman who had believed she was dead.

'This is nice,' said Alex. 'How did you find it?'

Sheena, still processing her disbelief at encountering Alex, was unnerved by her making trivial conversation. She didn't know whether to engage, or to beg Alex to get to the point of telling her what was going to happen next.

'When I left London,' she replied, her voice quivering, 'I was just running. I had an urge to be somewhere warm. I remembered you once mentioned Port Grimaud when you were talking about a client.'

Celine returned with two half-litre glasses of Stella. She smiled at the two women and set the beers on the table.

'Sisters?'

Sheena couldn't summon a reply.

'Just close friends,' Alex replied.

'Ah, you look so alike.' Celine shrugged and smiled as she wandered off.

Alex lifted a glass of the beer and held it out towards Sheena.

'Cheers,' she said, taking a long drink. Sheena could do little but watch; she was in no mood for drinking, her stomach was gurgling. Instead, she lit a cigarette, one of Verity's Gitanes, and drew in a lungful of French tobacco smoke.

'When did you start smoking again?'

'First day I arrived here.'

Alex looked unswervingly at Sheena.

'Why, Sheena?'

'I just felt the urge for a good smoke after all that had happened.'

'I don't mean the bloody fags, I mean, why did you try to kill me? Did I really deserve that?'

Acting from nervous instinct, the need to pause, the need to compose herself, Sheena lifted her glass and took a sip of the cold beer. She was aware that her hand was still shaking and that Alex could see it. She replaced the glass on the table and tried her best to look Alex in the face.

'I was angry, I suppose. Frightened. I felt betrayed. I loved you, Alex. I fucking worshipped you, and when I heard you on the phone talking with her, something broke inside me. I panicked. Why were you leaving me, Alex? What had I done?'

She had tried hard not to shed tears. She had been strong enough to kill Alex, or at least thought that she had. She had been strong enough to dispense with Verity. Now she needed to be strong to face down the challenge before her at this table. Despite her efforts, her tears flowed. While Alex looked content and confident, Sheena was a train wreck.

'It wasn't you, it was me,' said Alex. She reached a tissue to Sheena.

'Huh! How very original of you.'

Alex laughed heartily. Sheena saw how the colour rose in the scars across her body. Her work with the knife had ruined a once-beautiful face.

'What are you laughing at?' Sheena asked.

'Ironic, isn't it? I was the one planning to run, and yet you were the one to get away. Isn't life wonderfully strange?'

'You still haven't told me why you were planning to leave me. Was it simply because of Ella? Or should I call her Verity?'

Sheena thought that Alex was startled by the question of names.

'Her name *is* Ella,' Alex replied. 'Although Verity is a lovely name, don't you think? It means truth.' She laughed again, her nose scrunched, and her hand went to her mouth to stifle the sound of a snort.

Sheena felt a sudden pang of guilt, then a feeling of exhilaration. She had felt the same way when she was about to push Verity over the wall to her death.

Alex had spoken of Verity in the present tense. Sheena realised that Alex did not know what had happened. She did not know that Verity lay dead in a gully.

'No,' Alex said, recovering from her outburst. 'I wasn't leaving you because of Ella. We are in love, I suppose, whatever that means. Wasn't it Prince Charles who said that when he got engaged to Diana? What a peculiar thing to say at such a time.'

Sheena couldn't help thinking the same thing. Alex was skirting around the subject, and yet she was the person with all the answers. Sheena had only a growing number of questions. Uppermost in her mind were the problems she was bound to face once this conversation had ended. What was she going to do? Where could she go? What about money? She was tiring of Alex's dispassion.

'If not for Ella, then why were you leaving?' Sheena had channelled every serious tone into the question. She wasn't smiling or laughing. Alex had to know that she demanded answers. Lives had been ruined, and yet this woman, once her lover and mentor, was reducing the experience to frivolous giggles.

But then suddenly Alex's manner changed. She reverted to the purposeful woman who had confronted Sheena in Verity's apartment thirty minutes earlier, and had removed her dress to reveal the scars she had to live with every day.

'I was in trouble, Sheena. A lot of trouble.'

Sheena cocked her head to the left and looked directly into Alex's eyes. Alex used to find it an endearing trait in her.

'What sort of trouble?'

'I suppose you could call it financial trouble.'

'You weren't broke, surely?' Sheena leaned forward, alarmed by the thought that maybe there had never been any money when she had expended such effort in searching for it.

'No. Quite the opposite, in fact. I had all the money I would ever need. It's how I came by it that landed me in the mire.'

'Why didn't you tell me? I could have helped you. We were partners as well as lovers. We could have faced it together.'

'There it is, there's my wonderful Sheena. But it was my problem, darling. I'd brought it upon myself. It was up to me to deal with it.'

'And leaving me was how you were going to deal with it?'

Alex leaned across the table, her face drawing closer to Sheena's. She smiled a dry smile. Ironic, Sheena would have called it.

'I was leaving you in order to protect you.'

The words hung between them for a moment. Sheena's eyes darted back and forth. She was trying to process this revelation. In her wildest thinking after she had believed that she had killed Alex, she never reasoned that Alex had been trying to protect her. She searched for truth in Alex's eyes.

CHAPTER 51

They ordered two more beers, and for a time sat in silence. Alex browsed on her phone, and Sheena looked once again at her laptop and the zeros on her bank accounts. She was certain now, of course, that Verity, on behalf of Alex, had been responsible for taking all of her money.

'Why did you send Verity?'

'Oh, come on, Sheena. You're brighter than that. I had to get my money back. I wasn't sure how much of it you'd managed to get hold of, so Verity checked it out for me. It was my money, Sheena, not yours.'

'Why didn't you come earlier, instead of waiting until…?'

'Until what?'

'Until now, damn it.'

'Is that what you really mean? Until now?' Alex glared coldly at Sheena. It caused Sheena to look away. 'I know what you've done to Verity. I'm no fool. I know you've done her some harm. Is she still alive, please tell me that?'

Sheena dropped her head and sobbed.

'Spare me the tears, love. They mean nothing to me. What a demented soul you really are.'

'What are you going to do?' Sheena asked, wiping tears away. She was aware of the people around them. She felt that all eyes were upon her.

'There's that self-preservation kicking in again. To hell with the rest of us, eh Sheena?' Alex reached her another tissue. 'Wipe your nose for goodness sake. You're a mess.' Alex lit up a cigarette and passed it to her.

'What did you mean earlier, when you said that you were trying to protect me?'

Alex seemed to inspect her. Sheena felt wretched. Her eyes were red and swollen, her cheeks smudged with tears and her hair tussled beyond any style. Her throat ached, and the cigarette was doing little to ease her discomfort. She felt desolate. Her fear was rising, afraid of what Alex may have in store for her. Did she intend handing her over to the police for killing Verity? Or for attempting to kill her at the cottage in the Lake District? Twenty-four hours earlier, her life was sweet. She had her hands on a fortune, and Verity had been removed from the situation. She had been free to go anywhere, do anything. Now, she didn't dare speculate on a future. A brief thought flashed through her mind. Could she win Alex Chase over once again?

'You were nothing more than a prostitute when I met you,' Alex said with deliberate spite. 'You had some class, of course, otherwise you'd have been a non-starter, but you were still a prostitute. I bloody made you, darling. I gave you a life you could never have imagined. Look at me now. Look at me, damn you.'

'I loved you, Alex. I still love you.'

Alex scoffed and drank some beer. She continued with her rant.

'While you were turning tricks and organising escorts for our clients, I found another way to make money. I skimmed and I blackmailed.'

'Skimmed?'

'These ultra-rich clients of ours, they had staff, underlings, to handle the financial side of their indiscretions. I added a little to every bill, and it was never questioned. What menial was ever going to raise the subject of their master's bizarre sexual proclivities in a business meeting? No one, if they wanted to keep their job. Sometimes, I added up to forty percent to the client's bill. For some, it was money well spent; for others, it was a hell of a lot to pay for a straight blow-job.'

'And the blackmail?'

'You know that some of our clients, particularly those in the public eye, were understandably secretive regarding their associations with our company. If word got out, careers, marriages and families could be destroyed. I targeted these people and made sure they paid a high price for my silence. It didn't come across as blackmail—more of an insurance policy. I made millions, Sheena. 4.8 million, to be exact.'

'What happened?'

'Cadoc Fedorov, that's what happened.'

'The name is familiar. Was he a client?'

'Of course he was a bloody client. A very smart client. He comes from Moscow. Billionaire. He lives in a bloody palace in Surrey. And that's where I made my mistake. A billionaire doesn't give a shit about reputation as long as he's not likely to fall foul of the law. When I suggested the "insurance policy" to his personal assistant she went for it, no problem. But Cadoc is the rare breed of man who still enjoys counting his own money, every damn penny of it. He questioned his account with me. My God, I even slept with him twice. He wasn't pleased to discover how I had been ripping him off. He can hardly speak two words of English, but he managed to utter that very phrase: "ripping him off". There's a rumour that there's a plot in Mitinskoe Cemetery in Moscow with the graves of people who dared cross Cadoc Fedorov.'

'What did he do to you?'

'Nothing. I never gave him the chance. He sent two of his assistants to see me at the office. They made it clear that Mr. Fedorov was not amused by my methods of taking his money. That should have been the end of it. I should have learned my lesson and cut all ties with the Russian. Instead, I opened my big mouth. I suggested to his lackeys that Mr. Fedorov might prefer it if his super-model wife did not find out that he got his thrill from fucking old women under a full moon in the middle of a damn barley field. Something relating to his childhood, I imagine. I even had him recorded on video. They seemed to take my threat seriously, and I thought they might continue to pay up and keep Fedorov in the dark about it. The following morning, as I was leaving our flat, a black Bugatti Veyron pulled up beside me. A shaven-headed man wearing an earpiece got out and handed me a package. I didn't think for a moment that it could be anything sinister. I went back inside the flat and opened the parcel. There was a little gold carriage clock and an envelope inside.

When I opened the envelope and pulled out the letter, I knew that my time was up. I'd gone too far.'

'What did it say?'

'The words *"tick-tock, tick-tock"* were printed at the top of the page. Beneath that, it said, *"get out of London today. Next time it will not be a clock."'*

CHAPTER 52

'I had already agreed to the purchase of the cottage,' said Alex. 'So I caught a train from Euston the following day. Staying in the Lake District gave me time to organise my leaving the country and hooking up with Ella. Once that was done, I called you and told you to come up.'

Sheena moved her hand across the table and placed it on top of Alex's, but she was quick to withdraw it. For the first time since showing up in Port Grimaud, tears appeared on her scarred face, and she wiped them away with a napkin. Sheena longed to comfort her, to hold her close, to right all wrongs. If only she could get inside Alex's head, maybe she had a chance to save herself from the misery she had begun to imagine. Trouble lay ahead for her, with no money, no home and no friends. She needed this woman back in her life.

But Alex maintained an indifference towards her. Not even for a moment had she dropped her guard.

'You were saving me from a Russian billionaire?' said Sheena.

'Yes, if you like. By close of play on that day, a Thursday, I had most of my money transferred off-shore.' Alex laughed. 'Do you know, I even called that Russian pervert and apologised for the trouble I'd caused him? He told me that if he ever laid eyes on me again he would take me to a field under a full moon and personally slit my throat. Then he lost it completely. He told me that his guys were coming for me. I was a slut, a whore, blah blah blah.'

'That doesn't explain why you were leaving me, Alex. I could have run away with you. I could have helped you. We could have been here, together, all this time. Why leave me for Ella?'

'Fedorov knew nothing about you. Your life was in danger if you stayed with me. Like I said, I was protecting you.'

'But you had already found someone else. A new lover.'

'Ella was a friend. I'd known her a few years, and I knew she was good with computers and figures. She arranged all of my finances from Jersey.'

'You mean, she wasn't a scientist?'

'No, she worked for PB Wealth Management Services in Jersey. She was my financial consultant before she became my lover.'

Sheena recalled how Verity, or Ella, had insisted on staying in the car on the day they visited PB Wealth Management Services. Now Sheena realised that Verity had to avoid being recognised by her colleagues in the bank. But Verity had set the whole thing up, creating a new account and transferring money, when the whole time she intended that the money would be moved back again when it suited Alex and her.

Alex's words were hurting. All this information was overwhelming. Firstly, to discover that the woman she thought she had killed, the woman she loved more than anything, was still alive, had survived and had recovered from her wounds. Secondly, to sit in this café, this peaceful relaxing place, and listen to a story of deception, threats and danger. Finally, to learn that Alex claimed to have been protecting her from a mad Russian billionaire. It was too much for her to process in her already flustered mind.

'That day,' Sheena began, 'when you were intending to leave the cottage for London. What were you planning to do?'

'I was booked on a flight to Malaga. When Ella had finished her business in Zurich, on my behalf, she was to join me there. We intended to lie low for a while and make plans for the future. There would be no rush. After all, I was a rich woman.'

Sheena couldn't dispel the vision of her holding the knife and confronting Alex in the cottage, swiping and slashing at her pale flesh, shocked by the sight of blood spraying across the room, the screams and cries of her lover begging her to stop, begging for mercy until she fell to the floor, still, and apparently lifeless. She must have closed her eyes for a few moments. When she opened them, Alex was staring coldly at her.

'And what about me, Alex? What was I supposed to do?'

A snide grin spread across the face of Alex Chase. She had no trouble matching the challenging stare of Sheena, who had made such an effort to look so like her.

'Seems to me you took matters into your own hands, darling.' With one finger she pointed to the scar across her face. 'I had made arrangements for you, too, but you wouldn't listen to me.'

'You were fucking dumping me, Alex. How was I supposed to feel?'

'If only you'd let me explain. Instead you ruined both our lives and now, it seems, you've killed Ella.'

'I knew who she was the minute she walked towards me, right here, and asked for a light. You left a picture of her on that hard drive I took from the safety deposit box in Zurich. I was bloody staring at it as she lit her fag. Ella was never coming out of this smelling of roses. She was doomed the day you sent her to me.'

'It was her idea to go after you,' said Alex 'I was prepared to let you go. I never wanted to see you again.'

'Then why didn't you stop her?'

'I thought I had stopped her. I had convinced her not to bother with you. Then we realised you might get your hands on my money when you raided my safety deposit box in Zurich. Ella wanted to put a halt to it.'

'Was she intending to kill me?'

'Don't be ridiculous. She was merely going to fleece you for every penny you had.'

'Did she tell you that we slept together?'

Alex's stare was colder than ever. Sheena baulked. It sucked her confidence.

'It can't have meant that much. After all, you killed her.'

'She was better than you, Alex.'

'Still lashing out at me, Sheena?'

'You're getting what you deserve.'

'Such wonderful people we are, don't you think? I tried to explain, but you picked up the knife. Before you arrived at the cottage, when Ella was sorting out my money, I had her place one third of it in your account. I considered it a fair settlement. Just think, right now, you could be living a comfortable life on £1.6 million.'

'You're lying! You weren't giving me a penny.'

Alex lifted her soft leather bag from under the table and opened the zipper. From within, she produced a brown envelope and tossed it across the table.

'See for yourself.'

Sheena removed two pieces of paper from the envelope and unfolded them. It was a printed statement from two accounts in the name of Sheena Bateman: one, a current account; the other, a savings plan. She was drawn immediately to the deposit of £1.6 million in the current account and the subsequent funds transfer of £1 million to her savings. Beyond that, she noticed the balance as she had last seen it, containing £278K. She knew also that since her attack on Alex—and having stolen her identity, abandoning all of her own possessions—she had no means of accessing these accounts. But now she considered the possibility that she would be all right. When she finally parted company with Alex Chase, she might be able to take back her own name, and her own money.

CHAPTER 53

The sun was setting, casting an orange stain upon the sky, and a light breeze whispered through the streets and quays of Port Grimaud. Tourists were enjoying early dining in the restaurants, and the noise of chatter and laughter gradually increased. Sheena was in no mood for eating, but her lack of appetite did not dissuade Alex from ordering mussels and a light Grenache Blanc. Sheena looked on with increasing unease. Alex, it appeared, had a conscience sufficiently clear to allow such indulgence. Arrogantly, she continued with her story as she ate.

'Do you know, Sheena, it was the cold that nearly killed me that day, not your handiwork with the knife? I had to lie still on the floor, while you went about the house stealing my life and leaving yours behind. I think that I passed out for a while, but I can still hear you rushing about, talking to yourself, trying to justify what you thought you had done. A word of advice, darling: if you're going to kill someone, you really should make sure they are dead before you run away. It only causes more problems if you don't.'

Sheena sat uncomfortably, smoking yet another of her Gitanes, her throat raw and her stomach in knots. Despite the warmth of early evening, she felt cold. She wondered how much longer this torture would last, and feared the outcome of this bizarre reunion. She couldn't summon anything to say, not even in her own defence. She was reduced to a passive listener, and what she heard seemed more a work of fiction than the truth, a strange acerbic tale that was gradually clawing away at the fabric of her life.

'As soon as you left,' Alex continued, 'I scrambled my way to the bathroom. Most of the bleeding had stopped, except for this one.' She drew the top of her dress away from her chest to reveal the scar that ran from her shoulder to her breast. 'It was the deepest cut. I thought I was going to bleed to death. The weather was really bad by then, and

I couldn't phone for help; there was no signal. I pressed a towel onto the wound for two hours before the bleeding finally stopped.'

Alex paused from eating and glared at Sheena. Her expression was harsh and filled with loathing.

'You may not like hearing this, Sheena, but you're going to listen to every word. Drink some more beer and smoke another fag, darling.'

Celine removed the dish of empty mussel shells, and soon after she returned with a plate of hake fillet in parsley and lemon butter. There were two side dishes also, one of mixed green vegetables, the other of French fries.

'You have to have chips with fish,' said Alex, while Celine was present. 'It's the English thing to do, don't you think?' Celine smiled politely at Alex and glanced at her companion. She could see that Sheena was not looking well. Before walking away, she placed her hand gently on her shoulder. Sheena smiled weakly. Alex noted the interchange between the women but did not react.

Alex's insouciance blossomed again. Sheena could tell that Alex was enjoying every minute of her retribution.

'It didn't take me long to realise,' she continued, 'that not only did you believe that you had killed me, but you'd also thought it a great idea to steal my identity. You took everything: my clothes, my bags, shoes, even my underwear. Were you really so intent on becoming me?'

'I wasn't thinking straight, Alex. I panicked—it seemed like a good idea.'

'It was a rhetorical question, Sheena. I really don't give a shit what you were thinking.'

Not for the first time on this day, Sheena experienced deep fear. This was no 'clear the air' speech so that both women could move on. Alex Chase was exacting her revenge, and Sheena realised that there would be worse to come. Maybe it was time for her to run. Alex was staring gravely at her.

'So, I had to wear your clothes,' said Alex, derisively, 'although I didn't manage to do much. Once I got the bleeding stopped in all of the cuts, I managed to use a flannel as a pad to put over the stab wound in my back. Fortunately, it wasn't deep; you managed to strike bone. I wrapped myself in a blanket, turned up the heating and sat on the sofa for two days, unable to do anything or go anywhere. Eventually, I managed to call Ella. She was in a real panic that I hadn't met up with her in Malaga. Bless her heart, she thought maybe I had changed my mind. When I told her what you'd done, she caught the next plane to Manchester and drove up to the cottage. She cleaned my wounds and bandaged them. She wanted to take me to a hospital, but I didn't want to explain what had happened to just any doctor. They would have involved the police. Besides, I was still in hiding from Cadoc Fedorov. Ella, it turned out, was rather nifty with a needle and thread. She filled me with wine, and then, with a lot of antiseptic, she stitched up the worst of my wounds. She did a good job but, unfortunately, it was always going to leave me with scars.'

'Alex, I am so sorry for what I did to you. It was the heat of the moment. I was distraught that you were leaving me.'

'Save it, Sheena. I don't need your apology or your tears. Just shut up and listen.'

'But what are you going to do? Please, don't hand me over to the police.'

'Oh, Sheena, listen to yourself! You're pathetic. I can't think why I was ever interested in you.'

Alex summoned Celine and ordered two cognacs. By this stage, she had abandoned her meal and Celine removed her plate. When she had gone, Alex leaned over the table and whispered in a venomous tone.

'By the time I'm finished with you, Sheena, you're going to wish I had called the police.'

The two women stared into each other's eyes. For Alex there was hatred and anger, for Sheena fear and self-pity.

'Where was I? Ah, yes, what did I do next? I spent another week with Ella at the cottage, discussing with her what our best option would be. I had to find out how you were intending to go on living as me. I see now that you went all the way. You even got the right shade of hair, and you're still wearing my clothes. But really, Sheena, you weren't so clever. You should have kept your own identity, too. I was left with little access to my world. I risked going back to the flat in Bayswater, but you'd cleared the entire place of me. My God, you even took my books and my music. For a while, I had to wear your clothes. Not my taste at all, as you well know. I couldn't access my bank accounts. Not my own. But I could access yours. After all, you'd left everything of yourself behind when you quit London for here. And as I've told you, I'd put a tidy sum into your bank account. I was now you, Sheena Bateman. All I had to do was take the money back that I'd given you, while you were helping yourself to my accounts in Zurich and Jersey.'

'But Alex, all of that money is gone. Your accounts have been emptied. It must have been Verity.'

Alex smiled conceitedly.

'Well, I must say, it's been a very tiring day. We'll talk some more tomorrow.'

She drained the cognac from her glass and stood up.

'Night, night, Sheena. Sleep well.' Alex strode from the café and headed towards the exit of the port complex.

Sheena remained seated, forlorn and once again wiping tears from her eyes. She could hardly believe that she had any left to shed. For a moment she considered following Alex to see where she was staying, but she couldn't think what she would gain by it.

CHAPTER 54

Sheena bent double over her toilet. Her stomach heaved, but little came away. She had eaten nothing and had drunk only two beers and a glass of cognac. Her head pounded, a deep pulsing, like the sound of a heavy Japanese gong. How could she have been so careless? Why hadn't she made sure that Alex was dead? She had been in too much of a panic, that's why. She had been so concerned about how to get away that she paid little attention to what she was leaving behind. At the time, she believed the sensible thing was to take Alex's identity and disappear, leaving her own behind. If Alex had died then so, too, would the name Sheena Bateman.

She coughed phlegm into the bathroom sink and wiped her mouth across her forearm. She had to think quickly. What should she do now?

It was late. She couldn't sleep. No chance. Every sound of the night fired shock waves through her body, forcing her eyes wide open. Each voice she heard from outside had her leaping to her feet and peering through the window. All of her instincts screamed at her to run. Now. But she had to know what Alex had planned for her. She had to know exactly what she was running from. Wise or foolish, she must wait till morning, and she must see Alex one more time. Throughout the night her mind punished her over and over with visions of what Alex might do. Maybe she was planning to kill her, but was she capable of such an act? All of the money, presumably, was back in her possession. Why couldn't she just go away and leave her alone? She had made her point.

As Sheena's mind battled the need for sleep, she longed for a time when she was happy in her life. But she struggled to recall any period when she had truly felt that way. Largely ignored by her parents, save for feeding and clothing her, and ensuring that she went to school and did her homework, she had no happy memories of growing up.

In her teenage years she hadn't considered herself pretty, yet boys lined up to take her out, or to 'have a go at her', as they most often put it. By the time she had left school, and before departing Hertfordshire for London, she had discovered that her body could be the pathway to earning money. Several men in her area, well-off and supposedly happily married, were easily parted from their cash in return for her favours. Why bother with boys of her own age when she could have experienced men and money in her purse? Married men were always turned on by the idea of having the babysitter.

She had never been in love until Alex found her. She had never known real heartbreak until she discovered that Alex was leaving her. Verity, though, remained a puzzle to her. Having known from the outset who Verity really was, she never pictured a lasting relationship with her, and yet the sex was so fulfilling she realised that she was in love. Never did she believe herself capable of killing someone, but she had managed it twice—three times if she included her failed attempt with Alex.

The night seemed darker than she had ever known in Port Grimaud. She didn't much care for seeing daylight ever again.

By morning she felt such confusion that at first she was unaware of the buzzer sounding at her door. The caller was persistent, and the buzzing continued in long urgent bursts. Sheena hadn't undressed from the night before. Her dress was stained in vomit, her hair was matted with sweat and she reeked of cigarettes. She was in no state to greet visitors. Fear rose in her gut, suddenly realising who it must be calling at this hour. It was barely seven o'clock.

When she opened the door there could have been no greater contrast in the two women. While Sheena looked desolate, forlorn, Alex was immaculate in a pale blue suit with matching court heels. Beneath her jacket she wore an ivory silk blouse and a dazzling necklace of gold with ruby-coloured stones. Her hair sat perfectly, dangling blonde curls tumbling over her shoulders. The style suited her; it made her look younger. Her face, too, was brighter from makeup, successfully masking some of the scarring on her cheeks.

Alex marched right past her, four-inch heels clicking on the tiled floor. Sheena closed the door and followed her nemesis into the lounge.

'Good morning, Sheena. I don't have much time. I'm catching an afternoon flight to London. I've just come to finish off our little chat from last night, and to tie up any loose ends. I won't keep you long. I realise you'll soon have a lot to do.'

Sheena looked quizzically at her former business partner and lover. She could neither understand nor cope with Alex's nonchalance.

'What do you mean, I'll soon have a lot to do?'

'You might want to sit down for this.'

With doubts spilling over like a pot of soup on a stove, Sheena did as she was told and sat on a chair close to the open balcony doors. Alex remained on her feet, pacing slowly around the room. Her tone was blunt, her expression determined. She had come to pronounce sentence on the woman who had once tried to kill her, on the woman who had killed Ella and shown no remorse.

'Yesterday, I explained what happened to me after you left me for dead. Since you had taken my identity it seemed logical that I should assume yours.'

Alex looked her in the eyes. Her confidence gave her words a fiercely dominant tone as she paraded before the pathetic creature Sheena had become in so short a time.

'I also told you that I had been trying to protect you from Cadoc Fedorov. I knew he was coming after me. That's why I fled London, first for the Lake District, and then I was intending to go to Malaga. Of course, you scuppered that plan.'

Sheena attempted to speak, but Alex cut her off.

'As far as I am aware, Fedorov is still on the hunt for Alex Chase. He has people everywhere—in several countries, I believe—and as I told you, he is not a man to cross. Fortunately, I have nothing to fear from him, as I am no longer Alex Chase. You are. My name is that of a nobody, a woman who goes by Sheena Bateman. I'm free to go anywhere I wish, and I have the money to do so. You, darling Sheena, haven't a bean. If I were you, I wouldn't stay here for much longer. It won't take Mr. Fedorov long to find you once he gets an anonymous tip-off.'

'Alex, please! Don't do this. Can't you forgive me?'

Alex stood over her with a sardonic smile on her meticulously painted ruby lips.

'Let me see. Firstly, you tried to kill me. Then you stole my identity and tried to get your grubby little hands on my money. Finally, you murdered a young woman of whom I was particularly fond. So, the answer is no, Sheena. I can't forgive you. You were nothing but a cheap whore when I found you; I should have left you in the gutter. One piece of advice you can have for nothing...'

'Advice?'

'If you still have in your possession the hard drive you took from my safety deposit box, I wouldn't hold onto it for too long. It contains video recordings of what Mr. Fedorov gets up to in a barley field under a full moon. That's why he's so angry. He wants it badly. Badly enough to kill anyone who stands in his way. And, of course, as a business man, he has realised that I must also hold incriminating details on other clients. Just think what he could do with that.'

'Please, Alex, they'll kill me. I have no money; how can I get away?'

'Lie on your back and open your legs, darling. I'm sure some randy Frenchman will consider you worth twenty Euro.'

'Goodbye, Sheena darling; I mean, Alex.'

She laughed as she strode proudly from the apartment.

Sheena sprawled across the chair, unable to contain her despairing sobs. She heard the door closing. The sound of it spurred her into action. Still in tears, she stepped onto the balcony and peered down to the quayside. She waited for Alex to emerge from the building, eager to call out to her, to berate her, then to beg for her mercy. But the words wouldn't come. They were lost in her sobs.

As if to inflict one final thrust of the knife, Alex, when she reached the hump bridge over the canal, stopped and turned around. Sheena met her gaze, but she was still unable to summon any pleas.

With a wry smile, Alex calmly resumed her elegant strides across the Place du Marché and was soon out of sight.

Sheena's hands ached from gripping the balcony railing, her knuckles turning white. All hope had vanished that somehow Alex would forgive her. Already, her mind had switched to survival mode. Her next move was to get away from here. If this Russian billionaire was coming after a woman named Alex Chase she could no longer stay in Port Grimaud. If Alex was intending to tip off the Russian, it wouldn't take his men long to get here.

CHAPTER 55

She bolted her door. Mentally, she prepared a list of things to be done before she made her escape. Twenty-four hours had passed since she had eaten anything. Her stomach gurgled. She found a stale baguette in the kitchen and fetched some cheese and tomatoes from the fridge. Every mouthful became a struggle and was punctuated by spontaneous bursts of crying. After ten minutes, she darted to the bathroom where all of her attempts at eating were regurgitated in the toilet.

Pulling off her soiled clothes, she stepped into the shower and, with the warm water pouring over her weary body, was soon able to relax. If Fedorov should come for her now then let him do his worst. She needed this time. When she at last felt vaguely human again, she stood over the bathroom basin and inspected herself in the mirror. She lifted a brush and drew it through her wet hair, wishing, for the first time, that she did not resemble the real Alex Chase. Quickly, she went to a drawer in the kitchen, found a pair of scissors and returned to the bathroom. Peering into the mirror, she began cutting. Handfuls of soft, wet auburn hair tumbled into the basin. In seconds, she was left with only an inch of hair, and she returned to the shower to wash any remaining loose strands away. It was neither elegant nor completely unattractive, but she didn't care if it helped her to disappear unnoticed.

Still wet and naked, she darted around the apartment gathering clothes, shoes, jewellery and toiletries. She dumped it all into a suitcase and forced the zipper closed. Although Verity, or Ella, had been clinical in the clearing of her bank accounts, she had kept some cash hidden around the apartment. From under her mattress, she retrieved €300 in mixed notes. She removed €2500 from the bathroom cabinet, and £520 was stashed in a handbag. She had sufficient cash to get her out of Port Grimaud and, if necessary, out of France. But she had no idea of where to go. Little money, no close friends and a Russian oligarch baying for her blood did not provide many options.

She decided, for the moment, that it was safe enough to visit Verity's apartment. Maybe the girl had left spare cash lying around. She had disposed of Verity's bank and credit cards on the drive from the hotel in Peillon. She realised, however, that she could use the credit card she held in the name of Alex Chase to book flights or trains. It might be her passage out of France.

She pulled a loose cotton dress on over her head and slipped into a pair of flip-flops. As quickly as she could manage, she made her way to Verity's apartment. When she stepped inside, she realised that it would not be long before someone started asking questions about the unoccupied apartment and the whereabouts of its young female tenant. This, she told herself, must be her last visit.

In the bedroom, she found Verity's laptop, abandoned when Alex had made her re- appearance. A few Euros, coins and notes, lay on the bedside cabinet. They amounted to €33.65. She gathered the money in her hand and continued with the search. Although she could not access the laptop, she was hoping that Verity might have left some information in the apartment that would point her to the money. Most likely, Verity had re-directed the funds to an account in her own name, or in the name of Sheena Bateman.

The intention to track Alex down had arisen within her as quickly as her stomach had parted company with her breakfast. She dared hope that a final showdown with Alex would get her the money she was owed from their business. Disappointed in finding little of use, she closed the door of Verity's apartment and hurried back to her own. As she went she was struck by an idea.

CHAPTER 56

Alex had told her that Fedorov, more than likely, was determined to get his hands on the hard drive containing the incriminating evidence against him and many other of Alex's clients. Sheena wondered if he would be willing to pay for it. She had little interest in the sordid contents of the hard drive, and could do with raising a substantial sum of money to get back on her feet. By the time she had reached her apartment, she had come up with a plan. If Fedorov's henchmen came calling under the impression that she was Alex Chase, it might be hard to convince them otherwise. If she could use the hard drive as a bargaining tool, it might just save her life. She realised also that she must not have the drive in her possession. It would be too easy for Fedorov to take what he wanted and then kill her.

After a few minutes spent searching the lounge and bedroom, she found a large, unused envelope within a pile of unopened junk mail. She could think of two places where she might send the hard drive—where it would be relatively safe from the Russian. More importantly, she would be safer without having it in her direct possession. Neither place was ideal. In the end she wrote the address of the flat in Bayswater she had shared with Alex. If Alex had gone back there to live, then she could figure out what to do with it. If not, then she could tell Fedorov where to find it in exchange for a substantial pay-out and an assurance that he would not harm her. Out of malice, she printed the name Alex Chase on the envelope.

The post office serving Port Grimaud lay on the main road outside of the town. There was not enough time for her to walk there, so she hurried down to the café in the hope of finding Celine. The waitress, wearing tight jeans and loose vest, saw her approach and stepped out to greet her.

'Bonjour, Alex. Café?'

'No thank you, Celine. I wanted to ask for a favour.'

'Of course, what can I do?'

'Would you mind posting this letter for me, next time you are in St. Tropez?'

'Yes, I can do that for you.'

She handed Celine a €20 note and told her there was no immediate hurry to post the letter. She reached her the envelope containing the hard drive, which had been folded in half and secured with Cellotape.

'Thank you, Celine. I am going away for a few days. I'll see you when I get back.

'Of course. Have a good trip, Alex.'

Sheena hurried away from the café. Her face flushed in fear when she noticed a man standing by the bridge that led to the Place du Marché. He looked out of place in a light-grey suit, shirt and tie. He was in his thirties, and his hair was short, but he had stubble on his face—the unyielding face of a man who looked well-used to dealing with trouble. She hoped that he had not been watching her when she gave the envelope to Celine.

CHAPTER 57

Intermittently, she ventured a look from her balcony, hoping that the man had gone. She prayed also that she would see Alex striding towards the apartment to tell her it had all been a joke, an almighty cruel hoax. But the man still loitered by the bridge, and Alex was nowhere to be seen. She tried to convince herself that the man had nothing to do with her, that he was merely waiting for a colleague, or a friend, but the coincidence of him standing there looking towards her apartment was too much for her. She must get away, now.

Without a plan of where to go, or even how to escape the apartment without being seen by the man at the bridge, she gathered her belongings. She set her packed suitcase by the door and loaded an overnight bag with her laptop, paper copies of Alex's bank account details and the cash she had gathered.

The sun slipped behind the higher buildings of the Place Du Marché. In thirty minutes it would be dark. She risked another look from her balcony. The man was pacing around on the little hump bridge. All notions of him being an innocent bystander had scarpered. She feared that he would come for her once night had fallen. She wondered also if he had met with Alex. Had Alex really tipped off the Russian billionaire while pretending to be Sheena Bateman? If this man worked for Fedorov, would he be able to distinguish Sheena Bateman from Alex Chase? As Alex had told her early that morning, Fedorov was interested only in Alex Chase and not Sheena Bateman. The fact that she had switched identities solved nothing. Somehow she would have to prove that she was really Sheena Bateman. The next moment she convinced herself that Alex had simply bluffed her. She had arranged for a man to watch her apartment just to frighten her. To make her believe that the Russian was coming for her. There was no one pursuing her. Alex's revenge had been to frighten her, to feed on her paranoia. Sheena's confidence was suddenly restored. She began to rest easier. She could wait for the man to walk away.

By nine o'clock, however, he was still on the bridge. He had disappeared briefly, and she got ready to flee the apartment, but then he returned, drinking from a water bottle. He had taken a comfort break. Still convinced that this was an elaborate hoax staged by Alex to put the wind up her, she had relaxed sufficiently to consider her plans for the future. But the vision of the real Alex Chase striding elegantly from her apartment earlier in the day clouded her thinking. They were not finished with each other. Once she escaped Port Grimaud, Sheena would seek out her former lover and she would fight for what was hers.

When the quiet of the midnight hour had settled on the pseudo-Venetian port, the boats moored silently by the quaysides, the cafés and bars closing and the last of the evening revellers making their way to apartments and campsites nearby, the confidence she had felt earlier evaporated. The man in the grey suit, undoubtedly a patient man, continued his vigil by the bridge, but now he had company. Another man dressed in similar fashion, smart suit, well-trimmed hair and athletic build, stood nearby on the quayside. The pair resembled a detail of American Secret Service agents charged with keeping their President safe from the perils of the night. If Alex had set them up for her benefit, it had worked brilliantly. But it was well past being a sick joke. She was frightened beyond anything she had ever experienced, including her time in the torrential river, trapped against a rock, her rescuer a man who had attacked her twice. Her self-preservation had kicked-in hours ago, but so far it had yielded few ideas on how she could escape.

Lying face down on the cool floor, she slithered onto the balcony for another inspection of the men waiting for her. Peering through the metal railing, she watched them pacing around. The recent arrival was engrossed in his mobile phone; the other smoked a cigarette while staring aimlessly into the dark water below the bridge. Suddenly, as if he had sensed her presence on the balcony, the man who'd been there all day stared right back at her. Despite the darkness, and Sheena's belief that he really could not see her at all, she saw an amused grin on his face. What were their intentions? Were they about to storm her apartment? Would they hurt her? Kill her? Not here, surely. They would take her away to a lonely place in the countryside and put a bullet in her head. She slid back to her lounge. It was time to go before they could act.

CHAPTER 58

She reached for her phone to call for a taxi. Vehicles were not permitted onto the quayside below her apartment, but there was a taxi rank on the road, adjacent to the town. She decided to wait for the taxi until she guessed it had arrived outside the port, then make a dash for it before the men at the bridge could do anything. She hoped also that there were no others watching the rear of her block. Leaving through the back door provided the quickest route to the main road.

The taxi operator told her a cab would arrive in ten minutes. She waited for fifteen. During that time, she doused her face in cold water and wiped away the dried tears that had dripped down her cheeks all day. She dressed in blue jeans, a white T-shirt, a red leather jacket and flat-heeled ankle boots. Her cash was distributed between her handbag and the pockets of her jacket. The Sterling would not be required immediately, so it was placed inside the suitcase.

She didn't have the courage to have a last look from her window. Instead, she gathered her case and bags and opened the door of the apartment. The automatic light in the hallway came on. She hoped it would not be noticed by the men on the bridge. When she stepped onto the landing, a hand gripped her throat and forced her backwards into the apartment. She tumbled over the suitcase, landing on her back, her head thumping on the tiled floor. She tasted blood in her mouth. She had bitten her tongue. One of the men stood over her.

He didn't speak. His stare was cold and menacing as if she had caused him a load of hassle that he didn't need. She lay on the floor, too frightened to attempt getting to her feet.

'Who are you?' she cried. 'Let me go! I'm not who you think I am.'

The man looked impassively at her but said nothing.

'Don't you speak English? I said, let me go!'

She heard footsteps on the stairs. Quick steps but not frantic. In a few seconds, the man who had kept watch on her apartment all afternoon appeared at the doorway. He held his phone in one hand and gazed at the display.

'OK,' he said, stepping into the room. 'You can get up now. Don't make noise, or Jordi will slit your throat, OK?'

Both men watched as she struggled to her feet. Neither one was inclined to lend a hand. She felt light-headed, and she closed her eyes for a second. When she opened them the room had stopped spinning, and she focussed on the man who had spoken.

'I'm not who you think I am,' she said. 'I'm not Alex Chase.'

'OK,' the man replied.

Despite his reply, he did not look convinced by her claim. He maintained an amused grin on his face as he wandered around the room. His sidekick, Jordi, picked through her overnight bag and handed his companion a passport and a purse.

'OK. You say you are not Alex Chase. This passport says that you are Alex Chase. OK? You fuck with me again and Jordi slits your throat.'

Jordi grabbed her under her chin and forced her backwards until she fell onto the sofa.

'Please! My name is Sheena Bateman. My partner is Alex Chase. She has taken my identity.'

'OK. You fuck with me, right?'

'No. Please, you have to believe me.'

Jordi opened a drawer in the kitchen and removed a steak knife. He ambled towards her.

'OK, whatever fuck is your name,' the other man said. 'You have something for my boss.'

'I don't know your boss. I don't know what you are talking about.' The man nodded to Jordi who bounced onto the sofa beside her. His arm went around her head, his hand gripping her chin. His right hand pressed the point of the knife against her neck.

'OK, you talk soon. Jordi likes blood.'

'I am not Alex Chase. My friend took my identity, and she took the hard drive holding the information that Mr. Fedorov wants. Fedorov is your boss, am I right?'

'OK, you fuck with me again,' said the man with no name.

Jordi pushed the blade into her skin until blood appeared. She winced from the pain and watched her blood trickle onto her white T-shirt.

'No! Please, it's true. Call Fedorov. Take my picture; he will know I am not Alex Chase.'

The man looked at his companion, Jordi, who still had the knife pressed against her flesh. They seemed to be considering her idea, she thought. Her body trembled, and her neck stung where the knife had pierced her. The two men spoke to each other in what she assumed was Russian. To her relief, the man aimed his phone at her and took a photograph. Next he called a number and strode away towards the balcony as he spoke. She could not understand a word of what was being said, but she knew her life depended on it.

CHAPTER 59

When the man had finished his phone conversation, he turned to his companion, Jordi, and spoke. To Sheena, it sounded abrupt and strained. Whatever had been said, Jordi released his grip on her, pushed her away and got to his feet. Sheena's hand went to the cut at her throat. Warm blood soon coated her fingertips. She hoped it only looked worse than it was.

'OK, we go now,' said the man.

'Where? I've told you all I know. Did you show my picture to Fedorov?'

'Sure.'

'And what did he say?'

'He say that you are not Alex Chase.'

She felt some relief on hearing that, but her confusion was uppermost.

'Then where are you taking me?'

Neither man said another word, as she was hauled to her feet. Jordi took her by the arm, the point of the steak knife this time jagging into her side. The other man pulled some tissues from a box on the coffee table. One by one, he forced them into her mouth until it was full. She had to breathe through her nose as she felt the tissue soaking up her saliva. She tried to resist by refusing to move, but a violent shove from the man sent her stumbling to the door. With each step on the staircase, she winced as the knife cut into her side. They led her out of the building by the rear door, the route she had planned on taking alone. All was quiet, and only the streetlights illuminated their walk from the building, under the arch and over the bridge to Avenue de la Mer that led out of Port Grimaud. She saw the lights of a car, her taxi, she guessed, sitting a few yards along the road beside a loan palm tree. She was jostled away to the right. A black BMW SUV sat in a corner of the deserted car park. The man went to the driver's

door, while Jordi, playing havoc with the knife in her side, bundled
her into a rear seat. As the engine started up, she attempted to remove
the tissues from her mouth, but Jordi pushed them back in and she
gagged. If they were taking her somewhere to kill her, she had only
her voice to save her.

She noted that they were not headed along the coast road,
either towards Saint Maxime or in the opposite direction to St.
Tropez. Instead, the car drove west, and soon there were few signs of
civilisation around them. All was dark as they rose into the hills, trees
and thick undergrowth lined both sides of the road. The further they
travelled, the more she feared that all their bargaining was done. She
was being driven to a place of her execution.

The car slowed suddenly and bumped to the left, off the main
highway and onto an unapproved trail. The four-wheel-drive SUV
had no problem in countering the potholes and ruts as they continued
into the wilderness for another ten minutes. By the time they rolled to
a halt, Sheena was shaking and tears streaked down her face. She had
to breathe hard through her nose just to remain conscious.

The driver stepped out of the car and came around to the side
where Jordi was trying to pull her out. In the struggle, she managed
to expel the tissues from her mouth, and she screamed for all she was
worth. Jordi lost control of her; she tumbled out of the car and landed
in a heap on stony ground. The man with no name kicked her hard,
his foot striking her in the ribs. She screamed in pain. Jordi grabbed
her arms and pulled her to her feet. In the darkness, she tried to look
the man in the face.

'OK, whatever fuck your name is. We say goodbye. First, Jordi
want some fun. OK.'

'Please, let me go. I can help you. I can help Fedorov. I know how
to find Alex.'

Jordi snatched at her clothes. He pulled her jacket off her shoulders
and away from her arms. He threw it into the bushes. She yelled with
all of her strength as he opened the button and unzipped her jeans.
She fell to the ground, kicking out, as he pulled them down her legs.
She tried to fight him, raining punches on his arms as he mauled her

body. The man with no name pressed his foot on her left ankle to stop her from squirming. She continued punching at Jordi until he pushed her head into the ground, his hand across her mouth and nose. Time swirled in a haze of screams and pain. She had no idea how long it lasted, but when the thrusting ceased, she watched Jordi get to his feet and fasten his trousers. The face of the man with no name was illuminated by the glare of his phone. She longed to curl up in a ball. Her hair and legs were covered in dust, she felt sharp stones digging into her back and she had the abhorrent taste of Jordi in her mouth. But this would be her last chance. If she failed now, she was dead.

'Please!' she begged 'I can help Fedorov. I can get the hard drive. I can get him all that he needs. Names, pictures, videos, even bank account numbers. I know what Alex is doing. I can help you find her.'

'OK. How you know this?'

'Today, before you came to my apartment, I had the hard drive. I posted it to England.'

'OK, where you post it?'

'I'll tell Fedorov. Take me to see him.' She attempted to rise, but Jordi placed his foot down on her chest. 'Please! Let me speak with Fedorov.'

For a few seconds the man seemed to be considering her idea. Jordi kept his foot pressed on her chest.

'OK. You fucking with me again?'

'No. I'm not lying. If you kill me, and Fedorov can't find the hard drive he won't be happy. I'm giving you the chance to please him. I can lead you to the hard drive, and I can lead you to Alex Chase.'

Suddenly, she felt Jordi's hands on her arms once again. She screamed, believing that he was about to slit her throat. He wrestled her to her feet then stepped back, pointing at her pants and jeans still around her ankles. She bent over and pulled them up. Her entire body begged for a shutdown. She ached all over. Stinging from the cuts to her body, at her neck and her side, and throbbing pains at her crotch, her back and ribs, she could no longer look either man in the face. To her relief, she was shoved towards the car and, without further struggle, she climbed inside. She had one more chance to survive.

CHAPTER 60

Sheena had lost all sense of time or place as the car weaved its way down through the hills back towards the coast. She could think only of what she might say to save herself when she came face to face with Cadoc Fedorov. But she had no idea if or when that was going to happen. Was Fedorov here on the Côte d'Azur, or was he in London? She had bought some time for herself, but how much?

Soon, she recognised the surroundings on the road around the bay from Port Grimaud. She assumed that they were headed to St. Tropez.

The Quai Jean Jaurés, in the centre of the town, was quiet and deserted at this hour. They drove by the harbour, which at this time of year was lined with yachts and cruisers of the rich and super-rich, and came to a halt along the harbour breakwater. Jordi ushered her from the car, taking a firm hold of her arm. It was yet another pain to endure. The man with no name, who over-used the word OK, descended some steps on the quayside and, when Jordi pushed her to follow, she saw a small motor launch tied up by a wooden pontoon. Pulsating fear had not left her since meeting her captors, and now fresh doubts only added to it. Was she being taken to meet Fedorov, or was she to be dumped at sea?

Jordi sat next to her on the boat as the nameless man took charge of driving. She couldn't bear Jordi's touch, his hand on her arm, his leg pressed against hers. It made her flesh crawl, knowing that he had been inside her, and she had not been given the opportunity to clean herself. She wondered if the taste of him would ever leave her.

In only a few minutes, the motor boat had sped from the harbour and, several hundred yards into the Golfe de St. Tropez, the engine slowed as they approached a large white yacht. As they pulled in alongside it she noticed the name on the bow in black lettering:

Annushka. Now, it seemed, she would be meeting with Fedorov after all.

They stepped on board the luxury yacht via a sloping gangway, and she was taken immediately towards the stern. An open space under an awning was furnished with ivory leather suites, and a table for six was already laid out for breakfast. In her exhaustion, she longed to collapse on one of the sofas, but instead was forced to stand beside the man who so recently had soiled her. His companion disappeared indoors.

Looking presentable was impossible, yet she straightened her blood-spattered T-shirt and pulled up her filthy jeans, her leather jacket discarded in the wilderness. A light breeze blew off the sea, and she shivered waiting for the man she prayed would spare her life.

A clear glass partition with an automatic sliding door separated the deck from the interior lounge of the yacht. After a few minutes, she saw the man with no name emerge from a corridor. He was deep in conversation with the man she presumed was Cadoc Fedorov. She tried to recall his image from the video clips stored on that damned external hard drive, but she couldn't be certain. He was short—no taller than her—and rotund. He seemed to carry a beer gut, although it was more likely acquired from consuming foie gras and red wine. His hair was dark but covered only the back and sides of his head. Under the yellow lighting in the lounge, his face looked tanned. When he turned to look at her, she saw large and bulbous eyes glaring. Sheena did not have a good feeling about what was going to happen. Nervously, she watched both men approach. Fedorov wore a silk bathrobe in gold and a pair of white bathroom slippers. Her eyes were drawn to his chest, which was thick with black hair. He stood three feet away, looking her up and down. Then he stepped closer, and she felt his stale breath upon her face. He had the look of a man in his mid-fifties, and his breath smelt of whiskey and garlic.

'Miss Bateman,' he said in a calm voice. 'I apologise for the trouble you have endured this evening. A genuine mistake for Uri to assume you were Alex Chase.'

His English, although drenched in a Russian accent, was quite fluent. Alex had told her previously that he could not string a sentence together in English. Sheena tried to hold her breath while he spoke. She didn't want her relief to show.

'It is late,' he continued. 'Uri will show you to your cabin. You can shower, and there will be clothes provided for you. We can talk later.' He smiled briefly then turned and walked away, snapping orders in Russian to Uri.

'OK,' said Uri.

At last she had a name for him.

'Follow me, OK.'

As she followed him indoors, she noticed Jordi making for the steps where they had boarded the yacht from the motor boat. It seemed, to her relief, that he would not be staying on board.

The cabin was sumptuous. The floor was covered with a deep-pile carpet of pale blue, and there was a huge circular bed with mirrors at the head. Several nightdresses had been left upon the bedcovers, one in red silk, the other two in a rich shade of cream. A bathrobe, similar to the one Fedorov had worn, lay beside them. In the en suite there were ample soft towels laid out by a free-standing bathtub. She decided to take a shower, where she tried her best to wash the detritus of Jordi from her battered body. As the water flowed over her skin, she counted the bruises forming on her arms, legs, ribs and around her crotch. The cut on her neck had dried, but the gashes in her side began to bleed again under the running water.

When she had finished showering, she searched the drawers and cabinets hoping to find a sticking plaster for her wounds. She settled for some cotton wool that she held firmly in place over the cut in her side with her hand. Finally, she lay down on the bed. She didn't bother with any of the nightgowns—instead, she just lay with a towel wrapped around her. Exhaustion soon overcame her, but with sleep came dreams, unpleasant visions of flowing water, freezing cold and the sensation of falling endlessly, until she awoke gasping for breath.

CHAPTER 61

Sunlight peeped through the cabin porthole, casting its glare at the foot of the bed where the various nightgowns lay unused. Sheena had no idea of time. There was little movement and no sound of engine noise. She assumed that the yacht had remained at anchor throughout the night. She felt only the sensation of a gentle rising and falling upon a calm sea. Sliding from the bed, she noticed that some clothes had been laid out on a stool next to the dresser. A cotton dress, mainly in white with tiny rose-coloured flowers, lay with a pair of jeans and a blouse. She was surprised also to see a pair of panties and a bra in her size. Someone had entered the cabin, while she slept, and removed her dirty clothes. Opting for the light-blue jeans and white blouse, she dressed and inspected herself in the bathroom mirror. There she also found a fresh hairbrush and a toothbrush. Her hair, after yesterday's severe cutting, was easy to brush but it did not sit well. When she had decided that she looked presentable, she slipped into a pair of flip-flops, also provided for her, and went to the cabin door. She expected it to be locked but, to her amazement, it opened without a sound. Tentatively, she stepped into a narrow corridor. As best as she recalled it, she retraced the route to the open deck at the stern of the yacht. The place was deserted. Classical music played softly from a sound system. She saw the table set for breakfast, but so far it seemed that no one had dined. Once she stepped onto the open deck, she was grateful for the fresh sea air carried on a light breeze.

'Good morning, Miss Bateman,' said a cheery male voice from behind her. She swung round to see a handsome young man, fair-haired, with an athletic build and a wonderful smile.

'Good morning,' she replied, timidly. Self-consciously, her hands fiddled at her hair and then her blouse. She did not feel well turned out.

'If you would care to have a seat, Mr. Fedorov will join you shortly for breakfast.'

The boy—she had decided that he was little more than twenty years old—had an accent from her part of the world. For all she knew, he may have come from the next street over to her family home. It gave her a slightly increased feeling of security. It was hard to believe she was standing on a yacht belonging to a super-rich man of dubious character.

'I'm Josh. Can I get you some tea or coffee?'

She couldn't help examining him. A picture of health: tanned and unblemished skin, denim shorts and pale yellow vest. Her hopes rose when she wondered if Josh might be just the person who could get her off this boat and away from Cadoc Fedorov.

'Coffee would be great, thank you, and I'm Sheena.'

'Delighted to meet you, Sheena. Help yourself to orange juice. I can bring you anything you care to eat.'

He disappeared down a narrow stairway to a part of the yacht she had not yet seen. Scarcely before she'd taken a sip of juice, he returned with a silver pot of coffee. As he poured some into a cup, she ventured some questions.

'What is Mr. Fedorov like to work for?'

'Fine, I suppose. We don't see him that often. He only uses the yacht, maybe, twice a year. The rest of the time, we just keep her at the ready.'

'And what of the others on board, do they all work for him?

'*Annushka* has a crew of five. Two guys look after the sailing, another looks after the engine and maintenance, and there are two of us to do the cleaning and catering. We live on board.'

'What about Uri and Jordi?'

He shrugged before answering.

'I can't tell you much about those guys. They travel with the boss. Keep themselves to themselves, if you know what I mean?'

At that point, two girls emerged from the inside lounge, and Josh's attention fell immediately upon them.

'Good morning, ladies. Sleep well?'

The pair had the obvious look of siblings. Both had long blonde hair, exquisite bodies and expensive smiles. One of them spoke in perfect English.

'Darling, Josh, why didn't you come to my cabin last night?'

The other girl threw her arms around Josh's neck. Josh smiled and delicately slipped the girl's arms back to her side.

'You know I can't do that, Katya. Your father wouldn't approve, and besides, you're too young.'

'I'm sixteen,' said Katya 'I can do whatever I want. Sasha is too young, of course, she is only fifteen.'

'Katya, Sasha, allow Josh do his work, please.'

Fedorov, wearing navy shorts and a plain light blue shirt, padded onto the deck, and a woman with a long mane of chestnut hair and glaring bosom walked by his side. The two girls released Josh, who bade everyone a good morning, took their orders for coffee and retreated below. Fedorov grunted as if he had only just remembered that he had Sheena, an impromptu and mysterious guest, on board.

'Miss Bateman, I trust you slept well and that all your needs have been addressed?'

Sheena felt compelled to rise from her seat. Her eyes went from Fedorov to the three women staring back at her.

'Yes, thank you.'

'This is my wife, Masha, and these two incorrigible girls are my daughters, Katya and Sasha.'

Sheena shook hands with everyone, and they all took their seats around the table.

'Thank you for the clothes,' she dared to say. The daughters looked on bemused, but the mother replied.

'It was no trouble.' Her speech was heavy with accent. Of all the family, she looked and sounded the most Russian. Fedorov had better English than his wife, while Katya and Sasha had all the traits of an expensive English education. Sheena wondered exactly what Fedorov had told his family about her. Was she his guest? His prisoner? How did he explain her coming aboard in the middle of the night without luggage, without clothes? Perhaps the women knew better than to ask such questions. She found it difficult to dismiss from her mind the image of this man having sex in a barley field with an older woman, under a full moon, howling like a wolf as he climaxed. What would the glamorous Masha make of that extra-marital pursuit?

Masha Fedorov had a long, thin face, a wide mouth, dark brown eyes and a pointed nose, but she held herself in a stunning pose. Clearly, she was used to presenting herself in a glamorous light. Sheena estimated her age at forty-five, perhaps a year or two older. Her body was lithe, her breasts, Sheena reckoned, had undergone considerable enhancement, and her skin had tanned as if stage-managed by a Hollywood beautician. She was certainly no stranger to the hands of a talented plastic surgeon.

As trivial conversation and family banter played out over breakfast, Sheena relaxed slightly, feeling that she was a tad safer with the Fedorov women on board. When the meal concluded, however, Fedorov dismissed his daughters and his wife in an authoritative tone. None of them seemed the least affronted to be spoken to in such manner.

'Time to talk some business, Sheena,' he said.

Her stomach rose, and all her aches and pains suddenly resurfaced. She waited for the Russian to continue. When he did so, his voice was quiet and deep, and all the more chilling for it.

'You have something that I want, isn't that so?'

Sheena bit hard on her lower lip. He sat to her left at the head of the table waiting for her to answer.

'If you're talking about the pictures that Alex had taken of you...'

'Yes, yes. You know exactly what I'm talking about, Sheena. Your friend, Alex, has gone too far with her extortion. I want her, and I want the pictures.'

'All of the evidence, shall we say, is stored on a portable hard drive. How much is it worth to you?'

Fedorov's unshaven face did not even flinch at the question. His eyes stared intensely at the woman beside him.

'You are in no position to bargain with me for this hard drive. By now, you should already know this.'

'I had no part in any of this business. Alex and I were partners until she closed down the company. I had no idea what she was doing to our clients, including you, Mr. Fedorov. Your men kidnapped me from my apartment, they drove me into the wilderness where one of them raped me. They were going to kill me. For what? I took the hard drive from Alex Chase, because I was trying to get money from her. I was trying to get what I was owed from our business. You can have the hard drive; I have no need of it, but I believe I deserve some recompense for the trouble you've caused me.'

Fedorov laughed.

'You are a very determined woman. Just like my Masha.'

She tried her best not to shake in front of him. If he sniffed her fear, she was finished. She would never get off this yacht alive.

CHAPTER 62

Fedorov was talking on his phone. Sheena couldn't understand a word. Russian, although she imagined it was angry Russian. His voice was loud, impatient, as if he wasn't giving the person on the other end time to speak. After a couple of minutes, he ended the call and discarded the mobile on the table.

'I have more money than I can count, Sheena, but still I cannot get people to follow my orders.'

She smiled sympathetically as he continued to stare in her direction.

'Today, you are my guest. You stay on board, and we will talk again later. In the meantime, please enjoy my hospitality. I have other business to attend to.'

He rose from his chair and shuffled back inside the lounge, disappearing into a corridor. Sheena was alone again on deck, with only her thoughts for company. She couldn't understand this man, who at one point had allowed his lackeys to dish out a disgusting punishment to her, but had now welcomed her as a guest on his yacht. She substituted prisoner for guest. He was holding her until he could figure out what to do with her. If he managed to find Alex and the hard drive without her, then she was of no use to him. Now she regretted putting the damn hard drive in the post.

She gazed around her, at St. Tropez in morning sunshine. Land was little more than two hundred yards from the yacht. Could she swim that distance? She believed that she could if she had to. There was no sign of either Uri or Jordi. It was a good thing for her, but she wondered if the pair had been sent in search of Alex Chase.

There was an upper deck on the *Annushka*. It stretched from the mid-section to the end of the lounge and overlooked the rear deck where she had breakfasted. She climbed a flight of steps and found the three Fedorov women sun-bathing, both daughters isolated from the world by headphones and sunglasses. Masha, also wearing sunglasses, was reclined on a lounger, holding a Kindle in her right hand. Sheena didn't think that she had been noticed.

'You are welcome to join us, Sheena,' said Masha, her eyes had not broken contact with her reading.

'Thank you.' Sheena sat on a lounger next to Masha. She had no intention of sunbathing; for her, this was not a holiday. Her motive was to learn all that she could about Fedorov and his family. After a few moments silence, she asked a question.

'How long have you been married to Mr. Fedorov?'

'Twenty-one years,' Masha replied.

'How long have you lived in London?'

'Twelve years, I think.'

She felt that her questions were viewed as an intrusion, given the clipped answers and no elaboration. She decided not to pry further. Surprisingly, however, Masha had some questions for the guest.

'And you, Sheena, what is your story?'

'What would you like to know?' She felt nerves rising in her stomach, wondering how much this woman already knew about her.

'I do not involve myself in Cadoc's business affairs, but your arrival last night was—shall we say—strange. We do not have many guests on board, especially those without luggage.'

'Staying here was not my idea. I am a reluctant business associate of your husband.'

'And what kind of business are you in?'

Sheena thought carefully before answering. In the end, she decided the truth would suffice.

'I am not in any particular business enterprise. Your husband is dealing with my ex-lover. Unfortunately, I seem to have become embroiled in the matter. May I ask how your husband made his money?'

'A family business, Sheena. Cadoc and his two brothers invested in the new infrastructure in Russia—construction and transport. Now it is a global operation. I hope your dealings with my husband are concluded successfully. Then you can relax and enjoy your time with us.'

Masha resumed her reading, but her words left Sheena with more to think about. It was hard to reconcile this luxurious setting and family bliss with the activities of Fedorov and his employees. She had been raped and was close to being killed. Only her scheming brain had saved her. Now she had to find a way off this yacht and somehow get back to London. That's where Alex would be, as well as the valuable hard drive. Only then would she be in a position to bargain with Fedorov. If she stayed on board, Fedorov would eventually find Alex and the hard drive for himself and, to him, her life would be worthless.

CHAPTER 63

Sheena left the women to their sunbathing and set about exploring the yacht. It seemed that, for now, it wasn't going anywhere. She made her way below to the cabin where she had spent the night. On the way, she noted that there were five more cabins along the narrow, wood-panelled corridor. At each door, she paused to listen for signs of activity, but all was quiet. With the women up on deck, that left Fedorov and the crew below, assuming that Uri and Jordi had been sent ashore.

Retracing her steps, she soon found herself in the palatial lounge that opened onto the rear deck. There were several doors off this lounge. She thought they might lead to areas of the yacht where she would not be welcome. Fedorov's private quarters or his study, perhaps. There could be an operations room where he conducted all of his business. If so, she wanted to see it. She traversed the lounge and tried the handle on one of the doors. It was locked. The next, to the right, opened silently onto another narrow corridor. She proceeded along it until she reached another door at the top of a short flight of steps. She opened this door to be faced with the surprised stares of two men. One of them, she was relieved to see, was Josh. The other, in a smart white shirt and slacks, smiled warmly.

'I'm sorry,' she said. 'I was just wandering around. I didn't realise this way led to the bridge.'

'It's fine, don't worry,' said Josh. 'This is Max, our skipper.'

'Hi, I'm Sheena.'

'G'day, Sheena. Good to meet you.'

Max's accent was from Australia or New Zealand. Sheena was thankful for another friendly face. She couldn't help wondering, though, how loyal these employees were to Fedorov. Maybe she could explain her predicament, and these guys would take her off the yacht to safety.

Max was tall and swarthy and his head was shaven, giving him a similar appearance to Uri and Jordi. For now, she thought that she would work on Josh. And she must work quickly. She wasn't looking forward to the next meeting with Fedorov.

'Where is this yacht usually moored?'

'Monaco,' Max replied, slurping coffee from a large mug. 'We're sailing back there this evening.'

'Mr. Fedorov is heading off on a business trip,' said Josh. 'Not that he ever stays on board for long.'

'And what about Masha and the girls?' Sheena asked.

'They'll probably stay until it's time for the girls to go back to school.'

'Do they ever go ashore?'

'Sometimes in the evenings they go to a restaurant or a nightclub.'

She was conscious that while both men willingly answered her questions, it was beginning to seem like an interrogation. She wondered also if the men had been in a private conversation before she had barged in.

'I think I'll get some coffee now,' she said. 'Great to meet you, Max.'

'Likewise, Sheena. See you later.' She closed the door and re-traced her steps.

Learning that the yacht was soon to leave St. Tropez made her fearful of what would happen to her if she didn't escape before they departed. She needed to speak with Josh alone. When she reached the open deck on the stern, she found one of the daughters, Katya, drinking orange juice and talking to a young woman with short, fair hair, who wore denim shorts and a T-shirt. Katya smirked when she noticed Sheena and tried her best to ignore her, but the other woman spoke first.

'Hi, you must be Sheena. Josh told me about you. I'm Lucy, the housemaid and cook. Can I get you some coffee?'

'That would be great, thank you.' She was grateful for another friendly face, an English, female one. Lucy rose from her chair and went to a coffee machine set upon a counter beneath the awning.

'So, what brings you on board?' Lucy asked above the noise of the coffee maker grinding beans.

'I have some business with Mr. Fedorov.' Sheena noticed the look on Katya's face. Another smirk.

'You don't seem very busy,' said Katya.

'I believe your father has more important things to do this morning. No doubt, we'll speak later.'

'Are you one of my father's other women?'

The question hung between them for a moment. Sheena tried to fathom the motives of the precocious girl. Katya's expression was perfectly serious, her sky-blue eyes unwavering. For a teenager, she had self-confidence in abundance.

'I'm not quite sure what you mean?'

'I mean, is he fucking you?'

CHAPTER 64

Sheena studied the impish smile on Katya's face. Was this question even worthy of an answer? But why should she care? Fedorov was her captor. She owed him nothing but a heavy dose of revenge for what Uri and Jordi had inflicted upon her.

'Your father has affairs?' Sheena asked.

'Not affairs, more like—liaisons.' Katya nodded towards the shapely Lucy, who was pouring coffee, and whispered. 'She has fucked him several times. At least once while my mother was on board.'

Lucy set a cup of coffee and some milk on the table.

'Would you care for anything to eat?' she asked.

'No thanks, but I'd love a cigarette if you have one?' said Sheena.

'Sure, no problem.' Lucy strode across the deck and retrieved a pack of Camels from a drawer within a side cabinet. When both she and Sheena had lit up, the conversation resumed.

'Well? Is he?' Katya asked.

'What are you hoping to hear, Katya?' said Sheena.

'What do you mean?'

'Would it please you to hear that I'm sleeping with your father, or do you merely carry tales to your mother?

Lucy's face coloured, but she remained silent. Sheena felt she was under scrutiny from this employee of the Russian.

'It's purely for my own interest,' said Katya. 'I like to observe how my father conducts his business.'

'Well, if you must know, I'm gay. I sleep with women, not men.'

'Sounds like fun.' The girl finished the remainder of her orange juice and smiled provocatively at Sheena.

'Not today, Katya. When you're older, perhaps.'

Katya's expression suddenly turned sour. Without another word, she rose from the table and strutted off.

'What an obnoxious young girl,' Sheena felt able to say.

'They come in twos round here,' said Lucy. 'Sasha is exactly the same. If they were boys they'd be setting fire to the place. Instead, they try their best to create scandal. If they're not flirting with Josh, they're trying it on with Max. I think they're bored, but one day soon they're going to get someone sacked.'

'Or worse.'

Lucy looked puzzled by the remark, but Sheena didn't elaborate. She wanted to get to know more about this young woman, enjoying a smoke with her.

'How long have you worked here?' Sheena asked.

'Couple of years. Since I finished university and couldn't find a proper job.'

'What do you think of Fedorov?'

'He's okay. Exactly what you'd expect from a foreign billionaire. The good thing is that we only get to see him twice a year. The rest of the time we keep everything in order and ready to receive him at a moment's notice.'

'Have you ever noticed anything sinister occurring on board?'

'Sinister?'

'Strange, violent maybe?'

'Can't say I have, why?'

Sheena took a long draw on her cigarette and blew the smoke high in the air.

'I'm his prisoner,' she explained. 'Last night I was snatched from my apartment, driven into a forest and raped by a man called Jordi. Then I was brought aboard this yacht. I have no luggage, and no clothes of my own.'

'Oh my God. But why?'

'I have something that Fedorov wants to get his hands on.'

'What is it?'

'Let's just say, it's evidence of his infidelities that he would prefer that Masha did not see. Also, similar evidence on other individuals that I'm sure he can use for his own ends.'

'What are you going to do?'

'I was hoping to do a deal with him, but he's holding all the cards. I need to get off this damn boat. Can you help me do that?'

'I'll try. I may be able to get you on the launch when it delivers our supplies. We're sailing back to Monaco this evening, so we'll have to do it this afternoon.'

'That would be great, Lucy. Thank you. I hope I don't get you into any trouble.'

'It'll be fine, don't worry.'

As Lucy went below, Sheena noticed that Katya had not gone far when she had left them. The girl was lying on a leather sofa just inside the lounge, and the sliding door had remained open. Sheena hoped that Katya had not overheard the conversation with Lucy. She felt some relief when she noticed the headphones on Katya's ears. The girl looked vacantly towards her. Sheena could not rest easy until she had made her escape. For now, she was completely dependent upon a woman she hardly knew.

CHAPTER 65

Sheena smoked another cigarette while she drank her coffee. She couldn't help gazing towards the harbour breakwater, hoping to see the approach of the motor launch. There had been no sign this morning of Uri or Jordi. She hoped that their absence would ease her departure from the yacht. Savouring the last of the cigarette, she noticed Katya rising from the sofa and disappearing through one of the doors at the rear of the lounge. She felt nervous that this girl, a daughter of Fedorov, may have heard of her intention to run. She wondered, too, if it had been wise to reveal herself to Lucy. Maybe she should have waited and spoken to Josh. Either way, she had to take someone into her confidence if she was going to escape. Without help, and the chance of leaving on the motor launch, she would have no option but to jump overboard and swim for it. Once the *Annushka* set sail, she didn't believe that she would survive the voyage.

She was startled by the tall, slender frame of Masha sweeping by, making for the juice bar sitting next to the coffee machine.

'My husband says he will meet with you in your cabin in five minutes.' The woman looked coldly in her direction. It didn't seem like a message she was happy to convey.

'Thank you.'

Masha had already turned her attention to pouring fresh orange juice. She did not respond. Sheena rose immediately and found her way below to her cabin, her mind in a rush, her hands trembling. Why her cabin? Why not his study or simply up on deck? She stepped inside the plush surroundings of the room where she had spent a peaceful end to the previous evening. The bed had already been made, presumably by Lucy, she thought. The nerves in her stomach rose as she waited for Fedorov. She went to the en suite and examined her face in the mirror. She looked a mess but that was the least of her worries. Thoughts of what the Russian was going to say had her hands shaking. She heard a click at the door and assumed that Fedorov had entered the room. Stepping from the bathroom, she saw the cabin deserted. She went to the door to look outside. It would not open. She pushed and pulled on the handle, but the door was locked.

'Hello? Can anyone hear me? My door has locked! I can't get out!'

There was no response. She pulled again on the handle. A sudden realisation swept through her. Did Fedorov already know of her intention to escape? She was certain now that Katya had overheard her conversation with Lucy and had played the faithful daughter.

She sat on the edge of the bed. Her skin oozed a cool sweat, and her heart pounded. Her one hope of escape had vanished. Her anxiousness to know what would happen next set her mind racing to all manner of scenarios. Surely, someone would come to her soon. Even if it was Fedorov himself, she could at least attempt to engage him once again, persuade him to do business. She noticed the telephone built into the console above the bed. She had no idea how it operated. Could she dial direct to anywhere? Was there a switchboard controlling the calls on the yacht? Placing the receiver to her ear, she at first listened for any activity. Within a few seconds, there was a click, and she heard a man's voice.

'Hi, Ms. Bateman, how can I help you?' It was Max, the skipper of the yacht.

'Max, I can't open the door of my cabin. It appears to be locked.'

'OK, Ms. Bateman.' There was silence, and she was about to set the phone down when Max spoke again. 'Eh, sit tight, Ms. Bateman. I'll get someone down there.'

'Thank you, Max.'

'No worries.'

Perhaps it was simply a misunderstanding. She had jumped to the conclusion that she was locked in the cabin on the orders of Fedorov. If this was not the case then where was he? He was supposed to be meeting with her.

CHAPTER 66

Feeling helpless, she lay across the bed, shedding tears every few minutes. She had no idea of the time. She no longer had the Cartier La Dona watch that she had stolen from Alex. Jordi had snatched it from her wrist after he had finished raping her. She was surprised that an animal like him could even tell the time.

There was a single porthole in the cabin. From her position on the bed she saw only sky, and a few clouds floating by as the day grew longer. She dozed off for a time, and when she awoke with a start that same sky had darkened. It was dusk, and she had no idea just when the *Annushka* was to leave St. Tropez for Monaco. No one had come to her. There had been no further response from Max. She assumed that he was acting on Fedorov's orders. Stay away from Sheena Bateman—she means trouble.

But why hadn't Fedorov come to speak with her? Did he not believe her claim that she could get him what he wanted? She could obtain video evidence that people, who might be of use to him, had sleazy secrets they would prefer to hide. She realised, having spent a day locked in a cabin on his yacht, that Fedorov was playing a waiting game. If Uri and Jordi could track down Alex, then Fedorov might get hold of the hard drive without her help. She would no longer be of use to him, and she had no doubt that he would have her killed. If Uri and Jordi failed, only then would Fedorov consider doing business with her. Until then, she was his prisoner.

Another doze was interrupted when she heard the cabin door open and Fedorov shuffled in, dressed in cream slacks and a loose shirt. He reeked of cologne, expensive perhaps, but still too much. He looked down his reddened nose at her and grunted. His eyes never left her cleavage, and Sheena was revealing too much because of her dishevelled state sprawled out on the bed. Feeling insecure, she sat up and fastened two of the buttons on her blouse. She could hardly believe that a man would find her attractive in her present state, and yet she thought he looked on the verge of dropping his trousers. He had no inhibitions about fondling his groin right in front of her. Instinctively, she reeled back when he sat beside her on the bed, his left hand firmly taking hold of her thigh.

'Sheena, I hope you understand that it was necessary to detain you for today. Until I know the whereabouts of this hard drive I cannot allow you to leave my yacht. If it cannot be found then I will ask you to retrieve it for me, in exchange for your life.'

'And how much will you pay me?'

Her question brought a cynical smile to his face.

'I consider sparing your life more than sufficient payment.'

She attempted to look at him eye to eye, but his hand moved to her face, brushing her cheek gently. He looked at her with a pleasant grin and continued stroking her face. She thought he was about to kiss her. Her mind buzzed with options. Should she comply? Would she get her way if she gave herself to him? Swiftly, with force, he grasped her neck and drove her down upon the bed. Her mouth and nose were pressed against the bedcover; she couldn't breathe.

'Be warned, Sheena, if I do spare your life, that if I ever see or hear of you again then I will let Jordi and Uri do their worst. You will wish then that it was merely rape.'

His hand released her, and she drew a lungful of air. When she dared look, Fedorov was back on his feet and heading for the door.

'We will be leaving for Monaco after dinner. You are welcome to join us on deck, or you may dine here alone. I will not lock the door.'

'I'll eat here,' she said curtly. She longed to add that she would not eat with an animal like him, but thought it best not to rile him. A vision of what he could do in a barley field under a full moon filled her head.

'I'll have Josh bring you something.' The cabin door closed behind him.

In one respect she felt better. There was no way that Uri and Jordi would get their hands on the hard drive. They might track down Alex, but she would not have it. Alex would be careful. She would never return to the flat in Bayswater, and even if she did, and found the hard drive among the mail, she would soon get rid of it.

Sheena rose from the bed and went to the bathroom. She examined her tired and stressed face in the mirror. She looked ten years older, and yet, only a few days earlier, she could not have felt or looked better. She had had a fortune in the bank, a peaceful existence in Port Grimaud and all of her troubles were behind her, having dispensed with the scheming Verity. Now, she would be lucky to get off this damn yacht alive. There was a gentle tapping at the door, before Josh entered holding a tray.

'Hi, Sheena, I've brought you some food.'

'Thank you, although I don't really feel like eating,' she said stepping from the bathroom. Placing the tray of coffee and sandwiches on the bed, Josh rushed towards her. He took her in his arms. At first, she tried to fight him off, trying to push him away. She was under attack from another sexed-crazed animal. He was strong and held her tight, pressing his mouth to her ear.

'Don't say anything,' he whispered. 'We have a boat alongside this one ready to get you out of here. Follow me.'

She felt a surge of exhilaration. Josh took her by the hand and led her out of the cabin. When they stepped outside on deck, they did not make for the stern, where small inflatables and jet-skis were usually tethered. Nor did they go to the portside, where the gangway was situated, and from where she had first boarded the yacht. They stood on the starboard side, out of sight of the rear deck, where the Fedorovs would soon dine. A short rope ladder with wooden rungs was draped over the side. Below was a small speed boat that the family used for water-skiing. Sheena drew a sharp breath when she saw who was at the wheel.

'But…'

'Shush! Climb over,' said Josh. 'Katya and Sasha will take you ashore.'

'Thank you, Josh.' She kissed him on the cheek.

'Take care, Sheena. Stay out of trouble.'

As she clambered down and onto the speed-boat, she couldn't hide her shock at seeing Fedorov's daughters. Sasha put a finger to her mouth as a warning to keep quiet. Then she caught the rope from Josh and pushed the boat away from the side of *Annushka*. Katya sat at the steering wheel. She gently eased on the throttle until they were a few yards off the yacht. Then she gave it full power, and headed towards the open sea.

'We have to make it look as though we're just a boat coming into port from out at sea,' said Sasha above the noise of the engine. 'We don't want our father to see us coming from *Annushka*.'

'But I thought it was you who had told your father about me wanting to escape.'

'Not me, Sheena,' Katya said, turning around with a glorious smile. 'That was Lucy's pleasure. I told you she was fucking him.'

'You'll get into trouble for helping me.'

'We're his daughters. What can he do?' Both sisters giggled like naughty school girls.

After a few minutes of bouncing on the sea and heading away from St. Tropez, Katya turned sharply on the wheel, and the boat made a sweeping turn until the bow pointed back towards port. It was now dark, and only a single light shone from the stanchion at the stern of the boat. Sheena felt relief just to be breathing fresh sea air and to be moving towards the myriad of lights in St. Tropez. They crossed the bow of *Annushka*, fifty yards off, and Sheena prayed that Fedorov had not seen them passing by. Once they had rounded the harbour breakwater, they lost sight of the super yacht, and Katya slowed the engine, motoring to a set of steps at the wall of the quayside.

'We'll leave you here, Sheena,' said Katya. 'Here is some money. Enough to get you well away from St. Tropez.' She handed her a bundle of Euro notes.

'How can I ever thank you girls?'

'Don't give father what he wants,' said Katya.

'Don't let him win,' added Sasha. 'We know some of the bad things he does to people.'

She hugged both girls and, on impulse, took pleasure in giving Katya a taste of a woman's kiss. Katya's eyes sparkled in response. Sheena then climbed the steps onto the quay.

'Thank you so much.'

'Have to go, we're late for dinner,' said Katya. They set off, whooping and cheering. Sheena couldn't help smiling at their revelry. With the girls still waving, she hurried from the harbour and found a taxi parked close to the tourist information office.

CHAPTER 67

She realised that it was risky, but she instructed the driver to take her to Port Grimaud. It would not be a long stay. She would collect her things—her suitcase and handbag, her laptop and her files.

When they arrived at the entrance to the town she asked the driver to wait. She had a sufficient amount of money scrunched up in her hand to pay him. Cautiously, she stepped from the taxi, glancing around her for any signs that someone was watching, or that someone had followed her from St. Tropez. She wondered how long it would take before Fedorov noticed that she had fled. Once he had discovered her absence, he would quickly set one of his lackeys on her trail. Aside from collecting her belongings from her apartment, she wanted to check with Celine, at the café, that she had posted the parcel containing the hard drive. If so, it would be well on its way to London by now.

As she hurried across the Place du Marché, she saw the café in complete darkness. Surely, it was not so late. Café Avellino was usually open until midnight. When she reached the door she noticed a tape strewn across the entrance and a sign hanging from it. She realised it was a police sign, but there was no information to explain why the café was closed. Quickly, she ran to Restaurant Desailly, in the adjacent quay, and sought out Eric, the head waiter. He emerged from the kitchen, a plate of food in each hand.

'Good evening, Alex. Are you dining with us tonight? I have not seen you for some time.'

'Not tonight, Eric. Can you tell me please, why is Café Avellino closed?'

The waiter, slim and dark-haired, with a pleasant face, suddenly looked grave.

'A murder has taken place.'

Sheena froze. She feared she already knew the answer, and shock waves throbbed through her body. Still, she asked the question.

'Who, Eric?'

'Celine,' he said. 'Very bad. She was raped, and her throat was cut.' He continued to a table where he set the plates before two female customers.

Sheena walked away but soon broke into a run. Now she had no way of knowing what had happened to the parcel. If Celine had managed to post it, then she could pick it up in London. If she had not posted it, then where was it now? Still in the café? At Celine's home? She had no doubt that the murder was the work of Uri and Jordi, but why? They must have witnessed her giving the parcel to Celine on the day they had kept watch on her apartment. When she claimed to have something that Fedorov wanted, Uri must have realised that the package she'd given to Celine contained the hard drive. They had gone after her to get it. But if Fedorov already had the hard drive in his possession, she would be dead, too. The two evil thugs had killed Celine for nothing.

Sheena no longer had a key for her apartment. Jordi and Uri had dragged her from the place. She never had the chance to bring anything with her. There was no time to contact the rental agent to get a spare. The only way to get in was to break the lock. She wore only light pumps on her feet but, regardless, she kicked at the door. It made little impact. She hurried to the foot of the stairs, removed a fire extinguisher from its stand and hurried back to her door. She had barely the strength to lift it high enough, and the first strike became a mere push and a thud against the wood. Seeing the door give slightly from the impact raised her hopes, and rallying all of her energy, she thrust the cylinder forward once more. Two further strikes, and the wood surrounding the lock splintered. She threw her whole body against the door, but it remained closed. Crying punctuated her continued attempts with the fire extinguisher until, finally, the door swung open.

She gathered the contents of her suitcase, her clothes having been scattered across the room by Jordi. Her movements were panicked, with her thinking that by now Fedorov would be aware of her escape. The Russian would waste no time in sending someone after her. If they caught her again they would show no mercy.

She changed into a pair of jeans, a light jumper, a denim bomber jacket and brown knee-high boots with three-inch heels. Several times she looked out from her balcony, into the quiet of the port, praying that no one was rushing towards her flat. Thankfully, there was no one loitering on the bridge. With her suitcase again packed with clothes, she glanced around in search of her laptop. She found it lying open in the bath. Hopefully, it was still in working order, but she had no time to check. She packed it into her leather bag.

She didn't bother closing the door behind her but hurried down the flight of stairs and thrust her shoulder against the rear door of the building. It failed to open. She pushed harder, without success. She fought to control her breathing. Why wouldn't it open? It was always open. There was a simple internal lock without a key. She turned it one way and then the other and then heard a click. Finally, she shoved the door open and stepped into a calm and silent darkness. The wheels of her case rumbled on the pavement as she traced the perimeter of her building. Once clear of the path, she emerged into open space and had to climb the rise of the hump bridge beneath the archway, where the port met the main road. To the right, the road led to the beach, and to the left, it led away from the resort toward the main highway.

She dared a final look behind her and couldn't help crying out. A figure of a man was walking her way. It may have been quite innocent, but still her panic rose. Then she heard his shouts, followed by his running feet on the pavement. She ran, her suitcase rolling unsteadily behind her until, bumping over cobbles, it became uncontrollable. Pushing down the handle, she managed to lift the case and run. When she reached the road she saw her taxi, twenty yards away. Glancing behind her, she saw the man coming over the bridge. She opened the rear door of the taxi.

'Allez, allez!' She thrust her suitcase into the back seat and climbed in after it. The driver at first hesitated then reacted to her pleas. The man reached the taxi as it pulled away. She urged the driver to keep going. Her door was still open, and the man reached for her arm. But the car was gaining speed. He couldn't keep up. She scratched at his hand to break his grip. He tried to jump inside. His feet couldn't maintain the speed, and finally, he released her arm. He tripped and went sprawling, his face smashing to the ground. Looking back, she saw another man emerge from the port entrance. He could only look on as the taxi sped away.

'Gare de Saint Raphael, s'il vous plait.'

'Oui, madame.' She panted for breath.

'You have trouble?' The driver asked. 'I can take you to gendarmerie?'

'No, thank you. It's fine, really. No police. A jealous lover. He gets angry.'

'Ah, oui.'

She realised that she would arrive at the station much too early to catch a train, but she could think of nowhere else to go. As long as those men were unable to follow her she would be fine waiting in the station. She looked at her watch—the time was 1.25am.

She paid the driver from the cash Katya had given to her. Inside the station building, she read on the departures board that the first train to Nice was due to leave at 6.11. She prayed the two men weren't following. She had not recognised either man, but she knew that it wasn't Jordi and Uri.

CHAPTER 68

Her time spent on the station platform waiting for the train bound for Nice was not wasted. Despite her fear that Fedorov's men would find her, she focussed her mind on staying free of them and on what she would do when she caught up with Alex Chase. The intention to kill her was uppermost. After all, Alex had left her to die at the hands of Uri and Jordi. Over the past six months she had revelled in living the life of Alex Chase and not Sheena Bateman. There was no way she was going back. She would kill the real Alex Chase once she had recovered the fortune that Alex had spoken of.

Amongst the plans and schemes circling in her mind, Sheena couldn't help thinking of Verity, or Ella, or whatever her real name had been. The image of her lying broken and twisted in the ravine saddened her, and she closed her eyes to blink away tears. They could have made a formidable partnership had their motives only merged to the same point where they had love and trust for each other. One thing was certain: she had never known such an amazing lover. She had never imagined anyone better than Alex until Verity came along. It was a damn shame she had to go.

The early morning brought pleasant fresh air as she battled to remain awake. Her discomfort seated on a metal bench on the station platform prevented that final drifting into sleep. Several times she jerked awake and looked around in alarm. She couldn't help the feeling that Fedorov's men were watching her, waiting for the right moment.

At five-to-six, a young man strolled onto the platform and stood a few yards away. At first sight of him, she feared the worst, her heart thumping and her hands trembling. He set a briefcase at his feet and removed his phone from the pocket of his jacket. Not one of Fedorov's men, she concluded. He was casually dressed and handsome; his dark hair was neatly styled, and he had fine features and swarthy complexion. A feeling of security descended on her, which was reinforced when a woman with a suitcase, followed by two middle-aged men and a younger couple, arrived on the platform. Getting lost in a crowd could only be good for her. By the time she boarded the train for Nice, she began to feel more confident of her escape. She recalled Alex's advice: if you're intending to kill someone, make sure they're dead before you leave them. She would recite those words to her when they next met.

At ten o'clock, she departed from Nice on the TGV bound for Paris. Finally, she relaxed. There was no sign of anyone suspicious while she had waited for her train. Either she had given them the slip, or they were putting little effort into keeping up with her.

She turned her attention once again to how she would deal with Alex. But her eyes felt as though they were full of grit. She was hungry and drowsy. Undecided which to address first, she grew more comfortable in her seat as the train sped from the Côte d'Azur. Soon the issue was settled when her eyes closed, and she fell into a restful sleep. She was completely unaware of the man, dressed in a grey suit, sitting several rows behind her in the carriage.

CHAPTER 69

It was approaching four o'clock when Sheena crossed the concourse of Gare de Lyon. She felt relaxed and rejuvenated. A confidence that was absent during the last twelve hours had returned, and she walked with purpose towards the Metro, pulling her suitcase behind her. She had no idea, or any reason to suspect, that she was being followed. She had felt certain that no one was trailing her since her departure from Saint Raphael in the early morning.

She checked the departure boards for the Metro to Gare du Nord. Soon she would embark on the last leg of her journey home. How she relished another showdown with Alex Chase. It would be the last. It had to be. No more mistakes. Once she had her hands on the money, the real Alex Chase would perish together with the name of Sheena Bateman, and she would be free to resume the life she had imagined for herself.

As she stepped onto the underground train for Gare du Nord, a man she immediately recognised entered the same carriage. Her intake of breath was sharp, as if a knife had been thrust into her back. From her seat, she watched him steady himself by the door as the train left the station. Her eyes frantically searched for his companion, searching, too, for someone she might turn to for help. She was certain the man on the train was the same man who had appeared out of nowhere as she'd hurried from her apartment in Port Grimaud. It was the man who had lost his grip on her arm and tumbled to the ground as the taxi pulled away.

He stared at her until he made eye contact. His expression sent a chill down her back and a sweat broke on her forehead. She saw the scratches on the side of his face, presumably the result of his fall when chasing after the taxi. But what could he do now? If he was alone, she decided, then he could do very little. She had no need to leave the station once she arrived at Gare du Nord. From there she was catching the Eurostar to London. Was he going to follow her all the way home? What orders had Fedorov given him? Was she simply playing into his hands, heading for home, for London?

She examined his face. He had a smooth complexion, except for the scratches on his left cheek. His eyes were cold, steely grey, full of devilment, she thought—a man perhaps capable of great cruelty. Was he another animal like Jordi? Once she had looked into his face, and studied him, his eyes never left her. He seemed to enjoy the tease, for his mouth creased to a dispassionate grin. The other passengers had no idea of what was playing out between them. A stout lady wearing a cream-coloured hijab sat opposite, staring into space, a large colourful bag held on her lap. Two young men of middle-eastern origin were discussing something that was on their phones. A couple in their twenties, a boy and girl both in jeans and trainers, stood next to her stalker, gazing at each other without speaking. An elderly man with a bushy, grey moustache, smartly dressed in brown sports jacket and wearing a neckerchief, sat next to Sheena. He read from *Le Figaro*. All were oblivious to her plight, and as the train approached her destination her mind grappled for ideas of what to do next. Create a diversion? But how? Pretend to have taken ill? She reckoned that the man would merely observe her desperate efforts to gain attention.

Her throat dried shut. The train slowed at the platform. Gare du Nord. If she was to catch the Eurostar, she must alight here. The train stopped, and the doors opened. Several people got off, including the young couple who'd been standing next to her stalker. When other people joined the train, her stalker was forced to move further inside the carriage and away from the door. A woman wheeled a child's buggy into the space. He had to move to the far side of the carriage. He was hemmed in. She seized her chance and bolted for the door. A youth stepped into her path as he boarded. She pushed her way around him. The doors were closing. Her stalker barged past the mother and buggy. Another child stood in his path and, in his haste, he knocked her over. The mother cried out, and the child screamed. Sheena stepped onto the platform. The doors closed and the train moved away. She looked over her shoulder. Her stalker peered through the train window, the same wry grin on his face. She gave him the finger and hurried on.

CHAPTER 70

A deep-set feeling of unease plagued her journey to London. She had no doubts now that someone was still following her, despite having outwitted the man on the Metro. What would happen to her on her arrival at St. Pancras? For a moment, she imagined that Alex would be there to greet her. It was more likely to be Uri and Jordi. She wondered if Fedorov was merely allowing her to lead them to the hard drive. What better way to get his hands on it? No bargains to be struck—he simply had to wait until she had it in her hands, then snatch it from her. Beyond that point, she would be of no further use.

She tried to make plans. Firstly, she must return to the flat she had shared with Alex. If Celine had managed to post the parcel before she was killed, then by now it should have reached the flat in Bayswater. She wondered if Alex had gone there, too. Maybe she believed it was safe to live there again, now that she claimed to be Sheena Bateman. If she was in Bayswater it would be a reunion for Sheena sooner than she dared hope. If Fedorov really was baying for blood, she would have to be careful. Nothing mattered to Sheena if she could not get her hands on the money. She must gain access to the accounts, and then deal with Alex Chase. Her mind buzzed with every possibility, but she was wise enough to know that anything she planned would not play out just as she wished it.

She was relieved to climb into a taxi at St Pancras. She didn't see anything to alarm her as she gazed around, looking, in particular, for Uri and Jordi. There was no sign of them. Her stomach cried out for nourishment, yet she did not feel like eating. Instead, she sipped periodically from a bottle of Evian.

She asked the driver to drop her off on Queensway, around the corner from the flat she had shared with Alex. If there was anyone waiting there for her arrival, she wanted to see them before they saw her. At Gare du Nord she had used the remainder of her Euros to book a seat on the train to London. Now she used the last of her cash to pay the taxi driver.

She couldn't think beyond getting into the relative safety of the flat. It would only be for one night. She realised that she couldn't stay for long. Fedorov's men were bound to be searching for her, but she needed somewhere to sleep. Sooner or later they would come to Inverness Terrace.

It was still early, just gone seven-thirty. There were plenty of people around. She felt safe and inconspicuous walking along, blending in, despite trailing her suitcase behind her. When she reached the junction of Queensway with the elegant street where she used to live with Alex, she paused. The flat was halfway along Inverness Terrace. There were a lot of cars parked, but the street was quiet, with fewer people than on Queensway. It was still daylight; she didn't expect to see any lights on within the flat, but instinctively she looked up to the second floor. Before climbing the steps to the front door, she pulled the keys from her handbag. Hopefully, if Alex was living here, she had not changed the locks.

If Alex was not inside, Sheena wondered where she might be hiding. There was no Russian billionaire chasing after her seeking vengeance. At least, that is what Alex believed. When Fedorov found out that Uri and Jordi had not apprehended Alex Chase but had instead found her former partner, he had dispatched his bullies to find the real Alex. She would not be expecting a visit from them. Alex would believe that she was free of danger.

Sheena breathed a sigh of relief as the key did its job of opening the heavy main door to the building. Inside, the hall was no different from the last time she had been there—the day she had bid farewell to London and embarked on her new life in the south of France. The hall was silent. She climbed the stairs, conscious of the hauntingly familiar creaks on each step.

On the second floor there were two apartments, one set to the right of the landing, the other to the left. Both flats extended from the front to the rear of the building. Another of the keys she held opened the door on the right. She smiled at the thought that Alex had not changed the locks. Momentarily, she hesitated before setting foot inside. She listened for sounds to suggest that someone was there, but all was quiet. She stepped inside and parked her suitcase in the dim hallway. To her left, the hallway led to the bedroom and bathroom at the rear of the flat. To her right, there was a door ajar leading to the lounge and another, closed tight, which led to the kitchen. Growing in confidence, she entered the lounge and set her handbag on the sofa. She couldn't help looking around her, searching for any changes since she was last there. Everything seemed familiar and in its place. The paintings of Italian landscapes on the wall above the fireplace— modern versions of an age-old theme, the Grand Canal in Venice and the Basilica of San Lorenzo in Florence—were just as she remembered them. The beige rug on the floor, running from the armchair to the television stand in the corner, was definitely unchanged; the red wine stain that never quite came out was still evident in the centre. The room was exactly as she had left it, nearly ten months ago.

Going to the window, she peered onto the street below. Such a contrast in the view to the one she had left behind in France. She was relieved that there were no men in grey suits loitering on the pavement. But the silence that at first was comforting now felt ominous. She longed for someone to talk to. She had not had a conversation since her escape from Fedorov's yacht. Since the demise of Verity there had been no one with whom to share frivolous chat and laughter. She missed Verity. She missed Alex. One day, she might feel safe and settled again, but would she ever know real happiness, real contentment, without a companion?

A car pulled out from a space below the house. She only saw the driver for a second, and could not be certain as to who it was. Paranoid, she told herself that not everyone she saw could be the man who had followed her across France. She shivered. Drawing herself away from the window, she picked up the TV remote from the coffee table. She found a channel showing an American sitcom. Canned laughter filled the room—it was company of a sort. Now it was time to find something to eat. She hoped that maybe there would be a tin of baked beans or a macaroni cheese in the cupboard. She left the lounge and pushed open the kitchen door. Her cries drowned out the laughter on the television.

CHAPTER 71

Her stomach heaved, but there was nothing to expel. For a second, Sheena was frozen in time, unable to move and unable to react to the horror before her. The kitchen had the metallic odour of blood, not a smell she had been aware of previously, but in here it could be nothing else. The table, which was normally set to one side of the kitchen against the wall opposite the sink, and upon which they usually had their meals, now stood in the centre of the room. Alex lay face-down upon it. Wearing only a black bra, her flesh was deathly white. Her head hung over the edge of the table and her hair obscured her face. Electrical flex had been used to strap her down upon the pine wood table. It was stretched across her back, running beneath the table and tied again on top. Sheena realised that it was telephone wiring; a small phone plug was still attached. A similar length of cable had been used to secure the backs of her legs to the table, and was tied off to one side against a table leg. Both of her arms had been crudely tied with string to a table leg on each side. Directly below the right arm, a plastic wash basin sat on the floor; below the left, there was a stainless steel saucepan. Both wrists had been slit open with several cuts on each, and Alex's deep red blood dripped into the receptacle below. The basin and saucepan were both a quarter full, and there was a lot of blood splattered across the grey-tiled floor.

In her panic, Sheena assumed that Alex was already dead. Fear prevented her from taking even one step closer. She may have tried to kill Alex once and had dispensed with Verity, but to be confronted by a chilling scene for which she was not responsible had dulled her thinking and cut to the core of all her fears.

She jumped in fright when she noticed Alex's head moving. Unable to stifle her scream, she fell to her knees beside the table. Trembling, she placed her hand beneath Alex's chin and tried to raise it. A bizarre grin seemed fixed to her face.

'Help me, please,' Alex groaned. If not for the silence of the room, Sheena would not have heard. She let go of her chin and Alex's head fell downwards. Strange feelings were taking hold of Sheena. Alex was still alive, and she wanted to save her. She couldn't let her die. Not yet. She raced to her mobile phone in the living room. By the time she reached it, a fresh idea had gripped her. She would not be making a call for an ambulance, after all. She went back to the kitchen. By the look of Alex, she didn't have long. Her skin was pale and cold to the touch. Crouching down, Sheena drew level with Alex's head and raised her chin for a second time.

'I thought you'd be dead by the time I reached the airport,' Alex said, in a weak voice. Never thought I would see you again. You lead a charmed life, Sheena Bateman.'

'Who did this, Alex?'

'Fedorov. I didn't fool him that I was you. Please help me, Sheena. I'm so cold.'

'I'll call for an ambulance, but you have to tell me something first.'

'Please, Sheena. Help me.'

'What have you done with the money, Alex?'

She waited for an answer but Alex closed her eyes.

'Come on, Alex, wake up. Tell me what you've done with the money, and I'll call for an ambulance.' Sheena held her mobile phone in front of Alex, but there was no response. She set down the phone, and with one hand cupped around Alex's chin she patted her cheek with the other.

'Where's the money, Alex? Tell me, and then I'll fetch help.'

Her face cradled in Sheena's hands, Alex managed a weak smile, but again her eyes were closing.

'They raped me, Sheena.'

An image of Uri and Jordi flashed in Sheena's head.

'Come on, Alex, the money, where is it?'

'Lakes.'

'What do you mean?'

There was no response, and in frustration Sheena gripped Alex's hair and shook hard.

'What do you mean, Alex? Tell me, and I'll get help.'

'The cottage in the Lakes.'

'Is that it? I can get to the money if I go to the Lakes? Is that what you mean, Alex? Where in the cottage? Alex? Come on, tell me.'

'I'm cold, Sheena. Help me, please.'

Sheena let go of her hair and her head dropped again.

'This time, Alex, I'll do as you told me. I'll make sure you're dead before I leave.'

She returned to the lounge and used her phone to book a train ticket.

CHAPTER 72

Sheena browsed several magazines, old, used copies of *Hello* and *Vogue*. Anything to take her mind off what was happening in the kitchen of the apartment. All was quiet. She had no intention of checking that Alex was dead until she was ready to leave the flat. The kitchen was an appalling scene; it would forever be etched upon her memory.

It wasn't long before sleep overcame her, but it was not a comforting experience. Her dreams were again filled with visions of recent horrors, and each image merged with another. She saw Alex bleeding, her blood dripping onto deep snow, and Verity falling through space as Joe, or perhaps Uri, was carried off by a flood. She awoke startled, glancing about the lounge for reference of time and place. The room was cold. She shivered. She didn't suppose that the heating had been on in the flat for months. It was dark now; only a faint light from a streetlamp allowed her to see shadows and outlines of furniture within the room. She rubbed her arms to encourage some heat then reached for her phone, beside her on the sofa. The time was four-fifteen in the morning. Surely, by now Alex was gone. How much more blood could she have to lose?

Sheena believed that it was best to leave the apartment before people in the area began stirring. It was better not to attract suspicion. The thought prompted an idea. Perhaps she could leave a few clues around the flat that would implicate Uri, Jordi and Cadoc Fedorov.

She wondered why Alex had even returned to the flat. The only plausible reason was that Alex had believed she was now in the clear as far as Fedorov was concerned. She had been passing herself off as Sheena Bateman. What she didn't know was that Fedorov had not been fooled for a second. The Russian's main objective had been to get his hands on the hard drive. He was prepared for Uri and Jordi to kill in order to get hold of it. But when Sheena had posted the hard drive to this flat, she had never truly believed that Alex would return here. She now assumed that if the parcel had arrived then Uri and Jordi had taken it after inflicting a slow death on Alex. It seemed also that Jordi, before leaving, had dished out his perverted brand of humiliation upon her.

Without switching on any lights, and using only the torch on her mobile, Sheena searched the flat for the hard drive, just in case the two Russians had failed to find it. She discovered Alex's handbag lying on the floor in the bedroom they had once shared. Judging by the state of the room, it seemed that the Russians had dragged Alex from her bed to the kitchen. The duvet had been pulled to the floor. Alex's shoes were discarded across the doorway and the contents of her handbag scattered over the carpet. Getting down on her hands and knees, Sheena examined the contents of the bag. There was lipstick, mascara, perfume, a hairbrush, a pair of earrings of silver pear drops, a ballpoint pen, an aircraft boarding card, several tissues and a small, soft-back notebook. The boarding card was for a flight Alex had taken from Nice to Gatwick two days earlier, in the name of Sheena Bateman. Quickly, she leafed through the notebook. Most of its pages were blank. She found several numbers that she assumed were telephone numbers, but there was nothing obvious regarding Fedorov.

Rising from the floor, she went to the bottom drawer of the dresser. Alex had always stashed odd items of correspondence, mainly personal, in here, but Sheena found nothing of interest, merely old invitations to parties and gatherings that Alex had attended around London. She remembered then that she had disposed of most of the drawer's contents when she had been arranging her escape to France, taking with her only what she thought important.

She failed to find anything she could use to incriminate Alex's killer. Giving up her search, she scribbled the name Cadoc Fedorov onto a page in the notebook that she had found on the bedroom floor. Below the name, she wrote the current date and estimated the time when she thought that the Russians had called on Alex.

Remaining in darkness, she went about the flat, wiping down surfaces and door handles, the TV remote and cups and glasses in the kitchen that she had used. Finally, she summoned the courage to check on her former lover. She bent down at the head of Alex Chase and listened for sounds of her breathing. She heard nothing. Next, she felt for a pulse at her neck. Alex's skin was stone cold. With her own fingers trembling, she felt nothing. She cast the light from the mobile onto Alex's face. Her eyes were closed and sealed behind dried tears. Placing her hand on Alex's back, Sheena felt the cold flesh and only then noticed that the saucepan had overflowed with blood. It looked more of a solid mass rather than a liquid. Her blood had clotted inside the pot. Sheena was certain that Alex was dead. This time there would be no mistake.

She gathered her denim jacket from the lounge and quietly stepped from the flat into the landing. She closed the door with hardly a sound and made her way downstairs to the hall. On the way down, she wiped the handrail with a tissue and finally around the front door. She stepped into the early morning chill, holding her overnight bag and suitcase, and walked briskly down the street.

Approaching from twenty yards behind her, a postman took to the steps of the building and pushed a small flat package through the letter box on the door.

CHAPTER 73

She had no chance to run. A car, a large black Audi, slewed to the curb as she reached the junction of Inverness Terrace with Queensway. Two men jumped out and came swiftly towards her. Acting purely from instinct, she brought her arms close in to her chest for protection. It was useless. One strong hand went to her throat, another somehow grasped her short hair, and she was dragged then shoved towards the car. She screamed. Several people close by could only watch as she was bundled into the Audi. The car sped off, her suitcase abandoned on the pavement. She wrestled with the men seated either side of her. Jordi turned briefly, smiled at her then returned his attention to driving the car. One of the thugs still had a firm grip of her neck. She was choking but continued to punch at his arms and face.

'OK, you stop now or we fucking kill you right here. OK?' It was Uri. He emphasised his warning by squeezing her throat. She was close to passing out. Her arms flopped down in her lap, and Uri released his grip.

'Where are you taking me?' Her words were barely audible. The burning in her throat stifled every utterance. 'Is Fedorov in London?'

She got no reply for her efforts as she watched the streets whizz by. If she was not on her way to meet Fedorov then she was headed some place to be killed. How could she save herself this time? These men had caught up with Alex, and now she was dead. If they were still searching for the hard drive, she didn't have it. This time she had nothing to bargain with.

Morning traffic was building up as they drove from Bayswater, travelling east along Edgware Road, Baker Street, Regent's Park and then Euston Station, the very place where she had been going when they snatched her. She had no clue where they were going. Fedorov could be anywhere in the city.

Jordi was impatient with the slow-moving traffic. He muttered, then swore, and waved a hand in the air in frustration. Uri remained silent.

For the first time she took in the third member of the party, seated to her right. A bloody clone of the other two, she thought. Dressed similarly in a grey suit, a white shirt and a navy tie, his head was closely shaven and he had the same colourless pallor on his face. His eyes were staring straight ahead.

Sheena's mind raced with thoughts of how to escape—desperate, foolish thoughts, of crawling over Uri to reach the door when the car next slowed in the traffic, of removing her clothes to let both men ravish her until she could slip away, of creating such a rumpus that the arsehole Jordi lost control and smashed into the car in front. Her scheming resulted only in increased fear and despair. She saw no way out of this, but when they reached their destination it would be too late, even if it were to meet Fedorov. This time, he would show her no mercy. He had said as much when they last spoke on the yacht.

They drove through Whitechapel and the surroundings became less familiar to her. She gradually slid down in her seat. The bookends to either side of her didn't seem bothered by her movement. The car picked up speed with the thinning out of traffic. For brief periods, she feigned sleep, while her mind was edging her closer to a strike for freedom.

The interior of the Audi A8 was roomy and plush, with leather upholstery, video screens mounted on the back of the headrests and, crucially, quite a wide space between the two front seats. Her feet now rested upon the raised floor, above the drive shaft, in the centre of the car, her knees as high as her head. She eased her feet closer to the central console. No one spoke. No one took notice of her efforts to get comfortable. The car was moving fast now. Surely, there couldn't be much further to go.

Her knee-high boots had three-inch block heels. It would be better if they were stilettos. Calmer now, Jordi drove in relaxed fashion, one hand on the steering wheel, an elbow resting on the door. She didn't think she could reach him. Slowly, she eased her bottom forwards, off the seat. Her head was below the level of the car windows; she could no longer see outside. Uri and his companion looked straight ahead. Russian metal blared from the stereo. With all her strength she thrust her right foot at Jordi's head. Her heel struck the back of his skull, and he shot forwards, his face striking the steering wheel. It was enough for him to lose control of the car. A loud scraping of metal accompanied the Audi hitting the side of a van, in the inside lane. Jordi quickly raised his head, one hand going to the point of the pain. But it was too late. Uri, and his friend in the back, were powerless to restrain her before she struck Jordi a second time. He yelled and swore. His foot stamped on the brake. The car swerved to the right. It hit the crash barrier of the central reservation and slid along, smashing into the rear of a car that was slowing in a queue of traffic.

She shot forwards; her head hit the roof, and she landed face down between the front seats. Neither Uri nor his companion had been wearing seatbelts. Their heads slammed into the video screens mounted on the seats before recoiling and pounding into the rear headrests. The car had come to a halt, but in a flash a heavy vehicle ploughed into the back of them. The two Russians shot forward, and she heard a crack of bone.

She threw up, spewing onto the front passenger seat. Her chest ached, and her head felt woozy. The taste of blood was on her tongue, but at least she was conscious, still breathing, and still alive. Carefully, she pushed herself upwards. One of the guys in the back was sprawled across her legs. She was trapped under his weight. Turning her head to the right, she saw Jordi, semi-conscious, moaning, and blood trickling from his nose. Right then she wanted to place her hand over his mouth and smother the bastard. But there wasn't time. She had to get out of the car. She had to get away.

Her legs were trapped under Uri's head and shoulders. She slid backwards until she was in a sitting position on the back seat. Uri's head slid from her legs. He looked like he was sleeping, but she realised the Russian was in a much worse state. His companion was slumped forward, his head pressed against the video screen on the headrest of the front seat. It lay at a peculiar angle, flat upon his shoulder. She realised the crack of bone she'd heard was the breaking of the man's neck.

Crawling behind his body, she reached for the door handle. At the same time, a man on the outside opened the door to greet her.

'Are you all right, Miss?'

'Yes, I'm OK.'

'We need to get you to a hospital. Someone's calling for an ambulance.' He was a thickset man in his mid-fifties, greased hair, dressed in navy trousers, a short-sleeved shirt and a company tie. 'Sorry, I couldn't stop in time. Never seen anything like it. You swerved to the left and right, hit the barrier and then bang!'

She eased herself from the car, wincing from the pain in her chest.

'My friends need help,' she said, hoping the man would cease fussing over her and turn his attention to the others. Traffic was at a standstill. People emerged from their vehicles and hurried to the scene of devastation. No one appeared seriously injured in the other vehicles. Jordi had driven into the back of a red Mercedes. A Range Rover had ploughed into the stricken Audi, a collision that had sealed the fate of Uri and his friend. A white van sat in the adjacent lane, the side panel badly scraped from the Audi's first impact. The Russians had come off worst; at least one of them was dead. As rescuers milled around the stricken Audi, she eased herself away from the centre of attention to a place where she passed as an onlooker rather than the person who had caused the mayhem. She wanted to get away, but her head throbbed and her vision was blurred. Moving from one vehicle to another, she leaned on the side of each one, trying to recover her senses. Then she saw him emerge from the car. Her heart raced. He was looking around in search of her. She froze, her bottom resting against the wing on a small hatchback. He had seen her.

CHAPTER 74

Fortunately, she had managed to drag her overnight bag from the car. Within it she had enough money to get away, to catch a train to Penrith and finally get her hands on the fortune Alex had stashed away. But Jordi, barging his way through the onlookers around his car, was coming in her direction.

She tried to situate herself in her surroundings. Nothing seemed familiar until she looked behind her and saw the high-rise buildings of Canary Wharf. She knew there must be a station nearby. Beyond the scene of the crash, the road became an elevated section under which the River Lea eased through its final bends before pouring into the Thames.

Jordi was getting closer to her, unsteady on his feet, blood still dripping from his nose. Her attempt to run soon became a brisk walk; the shock of the crash was taking hold. She searched for a place where she could leave the road and make for cover. Weaving her way through the halted traffic on the left-hand carriageway, she came to a slip road on the right. Cautiously, she climbed over the barrier of the central reservation and waited for a gap in the free-flowing traffic on the right-hand carriageway. Briefly, she lost sight of the Russian, but when she dashed across the road, she glimpsed him as he struggled to climb over the crash barrier. Once off the main road, Sheena reached a pavement and noted the sign, which read *East India Dock Road*. There was a row of trees to her left, and she hurried under their cover, hoping to lose Jordi, but she saw him reach the same stretch of pavement that she had done seconds earlier. When he staggered into the trees she knew that he had never lost sight of her. The recent plantation came to an abrupt end next to the premises of a vehicle testing centre. Now, she had nowhere to go. Jordi, twenty yards away, saw his chance. She saw the blood on his teeth when he sneered.

Her choices were to run and hope that she was in better shape than him after the crash, or to stand and defend herself, praying that she was also stronger. Her only weapon was the overnight bag containing her laptop. She gripped the straps tightly. With her back against the metal railings of the testing centre, she watched the dishevelled Russian approach. Ten feet away, he stopped, grunted and wiped a sleeve across his bloodied nose. The look on his face was the same as the night he'd raped her in the wilderness of the South of France. She vowed he would not have another opportunity. Her confidence sagged when he produced a flick knife from his trouser pocket. He grunted and smiled sadistically. Then he lunged at her.

She swung her bag. It caught him on the side of the head. The weight of the laptop sent him staggering to the side. For a second, she thought she had done enough. Then he laughed and lunged again with the knife. Again she swung the bag. The strap snagged on his hand and the knife dropped onto the rough ground. He could only move slowly, but she didn't give him another chance. She dived to the ground and grasped the knife. When she attempted to regain her feet, he was standing over her. She could hardly believe his complacency. He allowed her to get to her feet. She made it to her knees, but he gripped her hair, pulling hard, and forcing her to rise. She didn't hesitate. She thrust upwards with the knife. It pierced his trousers at his crotch, and he cried out. He released his hold on her hair, and fell backwards. Now, she could run, she thought. This time he wouldn't follow her. With luck he would bleed to death. Standing over the stricken Russian, she panted for a calm breath. Her mind clouded with visions of her slashing at the naked body of Alex Chase, and releasing the hand of a damned taxi driver named Joe. She saw Verity topple over the wall, as clear as if she was standing beside her, her head smashing on the rocks, and the saucepan filled with the blood of the woman she had once loved.

Jordi writhed on the ground, moaning and swearing, his hands red with his own blood. She stared coldly at him; she pictured him inside her, grunting as he pressed her into the earth, his stale breath on her face, his mouth rasping across her lips. She saw the satisfied smirk on his face when he had stood over her, fastening his trousers, while she lay used and dirty. She had seen that same look an hour earlier when he'd smirked at her from the driver's seat of the Audi. She had no doubt that he had intended to repeat his act before he killed her. And still he writhed in agony, his grey trousers stained dark red.

She crouched beside him and peered into his face. There was no mischief in his eyes now, only a plea for help. He reached a blood-soaked hand towards her, but she slapped it away. She dropped to her knees beside his head. She should cut his throat. Finish him. But for some reason, she failed to understand, she searched for remorse in his steel grey eyes. Was there even a hint that he was sorry for what he'd done to her? She decided there was none. With a scream of anger, she raised the knife above her head with both hands. She rammed it downwards. It pierced his right eye and then his brain.

CHAPTER 75

The train pulled out of Euston Station into a dull morning. The sky was heaped with dark grey clouds, trees by the side of the tracks willingly shedding their leaves in the strengthening wind. She had a peculiar feeling, not of *déjà vu,* but more that her life wasn't quite straightened out. She was still dealing with a recent and turbulent past. And here she was, returning to the place where for her the trouble had all begun.

She had bought several morning papers in the station. She had little interest in world events as she perused the *Daily Telegraph.* Politics, economics and the posturing of one nation before another left her indifferent. She tried *The Express* and read, with slightly more interest, about the fortunes of a new female celebrity in her romance with a Premiership footballer. On page four she noticed a short article reporting the death of a financial consultant, twenty-three-year-old Ella Mason from Surrey. Mystery surrounded the discovery of the woman's body in a steep ravine near the picturesque village of Peillon in the south of France. That was it. The news sent a tingle down her back, but her mind told her that no one would ever connect the death to her. Her main concern now was that she could not be linked to the murder of Alex Chase, the road accident involving the Audi or the murder of its driver, a Russian named Jordi. It would be exciting, she thought, to hear what the police investigation would conclude. Would the body of the woman found at a flat at Inverness Place be identified as Alex Chase or as Sheena Bateman? That would determine who she was to be in future. Would a Russian billionaire be helping police with their inquiries? Surely the car crash involving Uri, Jordi and a third unnamed accomplice would be traced back to Fedorov. And what would the billionaire make of the death of his man Jordi? A shiver swept through her, realising that she was still not free of Fedorov. If the police failed to deal with him, she would be on the run for a long time to come.

As the train rolled northwards, having discarded the newspapers, she was left with her thoughts and, in particular, her lack of remorse over the death of her former partner. It had not been a difficult decision to allow Alex to die when she might have saved her. She realised now that what really had driven Alex Chase was her love for money. What Alex had told her in Port Grimaud, about how she was to have been destroyed at the hands of Alex and Verity, still induced pain. And it had worked brilliantly for the pair of them until she had pushed Verity off the cliff. If she had saved her life, how long before Alex would have amassed another fortune and moved on? She hadn't even expressed her sadness for the death of Ella, a girl who lost her life because of Alex's pursuit of money. How could she have been fooled for so long? How could she have remained oblivious to what really made Alex Chase tick? Years ago, when they first met in the hotel foyer, Alex had bought her with money and then used her to build a financial empire. She, on the other hand, knew only how to survive. Self-preservation kept her going.

Alex's reply when she had asked her how to get hold of her money sent a wave of trepidation coursing through her. Now, sitting on the train, the thoughts of returning to the cottage in the Lakes filled her with dread as to what awaited her. She felt her fears rise again, as they had done when Uri and Jordi first came calling.

CHAPTER 76

It was late in the afternoon when Sheena stepped off the train onto the platform at Penrith Station. For a moment, she stood watching as the train pulled away, feeling a similar emptiness inside as the station minus a train. Rain was pelting down, pattering on the roof and bouncing on the tarmac concourse outside. Beyond the station stood Penrith Castle, a bleak edifice against a heavy sky. Taking shelter in the hallway of the old station building, she peered outside, hoping to catch sight of a taxi. Two minutes later, she was on the road. The surroundings were not so familiar, but once into the hills she knew she would recognise the stone cottage at the end of the long and steep lane. She squeezed the door keys tight in her hand as if they gave her courage to face her return.

Soon, the taxi veered off the main road and onto a narrower carriageway, climbing gradually into the mountains. She was startled to recognise the tidy cottage by a bridge as they drove by. It was the house where she had sought refuge on that snowy night and met Sandra and Richard. She pictured the woman now with her baby and the changes it would bring to her life.

It was almost a year since she had last breathed the air in this corner of the world. Today, mist covered the highest peaks and rain, incessant rain, fell on the moors and found its way into the rivers and lakes. Already the streams and brooks were swollen but, thankfully, it remained too warm for snow. It was cold, uncomfortably so, but the dismal weather was unlikely, on this occasion, to prevent her swift return to London and beyond to a new life.

She paid the driver when he had pulled onto the gravel drive by the front door of the cottage. He was a middle-aged man with little charm or chat—just what she wanted from the journey. She noted, too, that he worked for a different taxi company to that of Joe. This driver had no interest in her business, nor she in his. She stepped from the taxi and inspected the house before her. The car reversed onto the lane, and she heard it roar away down the hill. For a second, she looked at the keys in her hand, suddenly unsure what they were doing there. Rain trickled down her face and under the collar of her jumper, another item of clothing that belonged to Alex. The slight discomfort prompted her to action. She slid the key into the lock and pushed the door. It did not open all the way, and she recalled how it had scraped at the bottom edge and required a shove. Finally, with her shoulder against it, the door creaked open and she took a few tentative steps inside. She was struck by a strange notion that, somehow, Alex would be there waiting for her with a warm fire blazing in the hearth and a glass of wine sitting on the table. But the house was as it should be: cold, smelling slightly of damp, of being isolated from the surrounding fresh mountain air—and there was silence. She pushed the door closed and ventured from the tiny entrance porch into the kitchen and lounge. All appeared as she remembered it to be on that day when she had awoken to find Alex talking on her mobile phone.

She had brought only her overnight bag. Her suitcase had been left by the roadside in London when the Russian mob had bundled her into the Audi. She had no intention of staying any longer in the cottage than she had to. It should take one night to retrieve the files and be on her way to London. With her hands on the money, she could start all over again. She pictured a new life in another place, where the sun shone and a clear blue sea lapped gently on a golden beach. Already, she was dreaming of the Bahamas. With more money than she could ever have imagined, she would be free to go anywhere, be anyone. She could be strong and fear nothing.

For now, though, she shivered from the cold and from the eeriness of her surroundings. Without removing her jacket, she filled a kettle with water and switched it on to boil. In a cupboard, she found a box of tea bags and a jar of instant coffee. She could drink either one without milk. It didn't matter. Deciding on the coffee, she placed a spoonful into a mug she had taken from a tree on the workbench, and when the water was boiled she poured some into the mug and gave the coffee a stir. She sat on a stool at the breakfast bar, the very stool she had sat upon naked the morning when Alex had tried to explain why she was leaving her for Ella or Verity. How the passing of time can paper over the cracks, she thought.

Conscious again of her reasons for being there, she glanced around the room and set her sight on the spot where she imagined that Alex would have hidden all of the information relating to her money. She didn't imagine that there was cash to be found. More than likely it was information on bank accounts and probably accounts in the name of Sheena Bateman. She couldn't wait. Leaving her coffee on the bench, she slipped from the stool and went directly to the small oak cabinet supporting the television in the corner of the room. There was a single drawer beneath the shelf that held the DVD player. She pulled hard on the handle, and the drawer came away completely from the cabinet and dropped to the floor. Inside were several DVD cases, a remote control for the DVD player and a paperback novel, Jane Austen's *Emma*. There was nothing else. No files, paperwork or a flash drive that might contain the information she needed.

She scanned the lounge searching for clues. There was nothing out of place in the room. She bounded to the kitchen area and quickly rattled through each drawer and cupboard, her anxiety rising with each disappointment. Frustrated and growing worried, she resumed her seat at the breakfast bar and drank some of her coffee. A harrowing thought struck her. A thought that all of Alex's secrets could be so well hidden in this cottage that she would never find them. She thought of the fields surrounding the house and a vision of Alex digging and then burying the keys to her fortune. Maybe Alex had lied to her. She would find nothing here, because the information she needed was elsewhere. Maybe, as she languished in this dull corner of the country, Cadoc Fedorov not only had in his possession the hard drive but he also had his hands on her money. A few million would mean nothing to him except for the satisfaction that he'd destroyed a woman who'd dared to cross him. She couldn't help falling into self-pity and, not for the first time in recent days, she wept in despair.

CHAPTER 77

Sheena awoke, freezing cold, in darkness. Her shoulders felt stiff from having flopped over the breakfast bar in tears and subsequently fallen into a troubled sleep. Suddenly frightened in the silence and the dark, she darted to a light switch and the lamps in the lounge came on. The fire was already set with coal and logs, and fetching the lighter from the kitchen drawer, she bent down and attempted to ignite a firelighter beneath some coal. It took a few moments for it to finally catch, and then she stepped back and watched as the flames took hold. She was wearing her denim jacket and the remainder of the clothes that she had changed into before her escape from the apartment in Port Grimaud. She had gone more than three days without a change. She felt wretched. Adding to her sorry state, she couldn't bear to venture upstairs, to shower or to climb into the bed she had last shared with Alex. If she had to search up there for the files, it must wait till daylight. She was not moving from the lounge. Removing her jacket, she lay down on the sofa and pulled a throw from the couch around her. She peered into the growing flames, hoping once again for sleep.

When next she awoke, the fire had almost died out, a few dull embers were all that remained. The lamps were still on and, gazing toward the window, she saw to her annoyance that it was not yet daylight. Once again, she was cold, as if she would never again feel warmth in this part of the world. She shivered at the images flashing by of deep snow and wild rivers, and she longed to be far away from this house, and from the time that she had spent here. Switching on the television, she navigated with the remote to a news channel, wondering if anything had emerged on the murder of a woman in Bayswater. There was nothing, but it didn't assuage her feelings of unease and, until she found the money, of helplessness. With less interest, she listened to a report on the death of a man near Blackwall in East London. Police were investigating the matter with respect to the killing being a possible hate crime. She couldn't disagree with the sentiment. The death of a man in a road traffic accident on the eastbound carriageway of the East India Dock Road also got a mention. Another passenger had been seriously injured, and the driver of the vehicle had not been accounted for. A little mystery for the police to solve, she thought.

In a cupboard, she found a can of baked beans with sausages. She opened the can and emptied the contents into a bowl. One and a half minutes in the microwave and the tomato sauce in the mixture bubbled and spattered. She stirred the contents with her spoon and returned to the sofa, relishing her first meal for more than a day. While she ate, she tried to think logically of a place where Alex might have hidden the details to her bank accounts. As each idea popped into her mind she committed it to memory, intending to examine it when the dawn came. She prayed that Alex had not been overly diligent in what she'd done.

She must have dozed off once again, for when she awoke she immediately noticed the dank greyness of the sky over the hill tops. She peered from the window into a wet morning; it seemed to have poured down all night.

After a visit to the toilet and quickly freshening up at the wash basin, she wasted no further time in rummaging through the remainder of the cottage. In minutes, she had exhausted every notion she'd had of where Alex might have hidden the information she desperately wanted. Her searching became frantic: drawers were pulled from their housing, mattresses in both bedrooms were dragged to the floor and wardrobes were ransacked to find nothing. There was little within the cottage to indicate that Alex Chase or Sheena Bateman had ever spent time there.

She was fearful now that Alex had lied to her. That she had intended for her secret to die with her. Had she sent her former lover on a fool's errand? Sheena cried with frustration. Still her eyes circled each room, searching each corner and every piece of furniture for the merest clue.

An hour later, the rooms of the cottage were in disarray, and she lay on the sofa crying in self-pity. What more could she do? She had gone outside and paced around the patch of garden at the rear of the house. There were no signs of any disturbance, that a hole had been dug. She looked into the coal bunker. It contained a half-full bag of coal and a few logs. She rummaged through the wheelie bin, but there was nothing but a few empty milk cartons and plastic trays of ready meals, probably from the time of Alex's last visit, although Sheena had no idea exactly when that would have been. Cold and wet, she traipsed back inside and dropped onto the sofa once again where she remained for what seemed like hours. She felt as though she could die there. And why not? The lives of Alex and Ella and that fiendish taxi driver, Joe, had been destroyed. So much tragedy because of what Alex Chase had tried to do to a sex-mad Russian. One morning, a year ago, in this cottage, everything had changed. Lives had been changed, lives had ended. Why not hers?

Her throat was sore and dry. She rose from the sofa and picked her way through the mess she had created to reach the sink. She filled a glass with cold water and took a long drink. Refilling the glass, she wandered back towards the sofa. She felt a crack beneath her foot. Looking down, she saw that she had stepped on one of the DVD boxes that she had tossed from the drawer of the TV unit. It was the plastic cover for the *Shawshank Redemption*. She opened the box, but it was empty; she assumed that the disc had been left in the DVD player. She lifted another case from the floor, a copy of *The Holiday*, starring Cameron Diaz and Jude Law. This time she found the disc inside. As she moved on, she kicked yet another case and it slid across the carpet, coming to rest by the sofa. Absently, she picked it up—a copy of Series 1 of *Breaking Bad*. Again, she prised open the case and examined the disc within. Immediately, it was obvious that this was not a copy of *Breaking Bad*; it was a re-writable DVD. There was no label on it to indicate what it might be, but her mind leapt to only one optimistic conclusion. She could hardly wait for her laptop to start up before inserting the disc. She set the laptop on the breakfast bar and waited for the disc to run. She couldn't stifle her tears of joy when she saw the files listed within a single folder labelled 'money'.

Everything was there: account numbers, statements, bank names, sort codes, access codes, passwords and, of course, those beautiful numbers, the balance in each account. She was a rich woman. Everything was in the name of Sheena Bateman. Alex had intended to ditch her real identity permanently, had been prepared to allow her former lover to live as Alex Chase and to suffer at the hands of a Russian gangster. But now the tables had turned. The real Alex was no more. Fuck her. She deserved everything she got. She had brought it on herself, but she had never reckoned on her lover, Sheena Bateman, being her equal.

Hot water poured down her bruised and exhausted body. She would never be the person she was a year ago. Too much pain, too much sorrow and too much evil had run through her veins. But a fresh start hearkened. She washed the grime of a year's battle from her short hair. When she got back to London, she promised herself a fresh look, a new style. With money, lots of money, she could do as she pleased, go where she pleased, sleep with whoever she pleased and walk away without regret. Sheena Bateman, she told herself, was a fully independent woman for the first time in her life. When she stepped from the shower, she dried off and dressed in the best clothes she had brought with her—the only clothes she had with her—a blood-spattered T-shirt, blue jeans and a denim jacket. Again she smiled, knowing that once back in London she would wear only the very best. She phoned for a taxi to take her to the station.

She looked around at the disorder in the lounge. She didn't care. The mess belonged to Alex Chase, whoever she was. She heard the sound of a car horn. Quickly, she gathered her small bag with the laptop and the precious disc inside and slipped her boots on. Already, she felt a new woman. She would catch the evening train to London, check into a pleasant suite in a good hotel, and then she could make plans for the rest of her life.

The front door caught on the step once more, but she had renewed energy now, and with one hand she pulled it clear and stepped outside. With more force than was needed, she pulled the door closed, and it slammed into place. She hoped it was closure on a sordid past. Drawing a lungful of damp air in the driving rain, she hurried to the taxi and climbed into the back seat.

'Penrith Station, please,' she said.

She heard a noise, the sound of the locks clicking shut on the doors. Strange. The driver turned and smiled at her. It was the face of a man she had once known, albeit for a single night. A terrifying night. Her mouth dropped open. She felt tightness in her chest. Time stood still. It couldn't be. She had watched Joe as he was swept away in the icy waters of a swollen river.

His smile cut her deep inside. Then he spoke.

'Hello, Alex, nice to see you again.'